ALL THAT GLITTERS ISN'T OLD

Also by Gabby Allan

A Whit and Whiskers Mystery
Much Ado About Nauticaling
Something Fishy This Way Comes

A Tallie Graver Mystery (Written as Misty Simon)
Cremains of the Day
Grounds for Remorse
Deceased and Desist
Carpet Diem
Varnished Without a Trace

All That Glitters Isn't Old

Gabby Allan

Kensington Publishing Corp.
www.kensingtonbooks.com

To all the readers who are loving Goldy . . . me too! Thanks so much for making her and the rest of the group within these pages come alive!

This book is also dedicated to Shannon, who made this book shine!

Thank you for all your work and for helping me!

Chapter 1

Outside my small house on the hill above Avalon Bay, a glorious Saturday afternoon was just getting started. A light breeze rippled the floral curtains, bringing with it the smell of the sea, warmed pavement, and a hint of the bougainvillea in my window box.

Inside that small house, I should have been getting ready to go snorkeling with my boyfriend, Felix Ramirez, a scuba diver for the police. I should have been wondering what he was packing for the picnic he'd promised me. I should have been figuring out which bathing suit showed off my curvy figure without going overboard.

Instead, I was standing in front of my closet trying to choose an appropriate outfit to wear to a funeral of a woman I barely knew. On an island as small as Catalina, off the coast of California, there were few people I didn't know, but Therese Milner had been a recluse for years, since before I had even been born, almost thirty years ago. It wasn't unheard of to not know everyone, but in a town with about three thousand permanent residents, it wasn't exactly the norm.

And the Milner family was all about not being the norm, or at least that was what Goldy had told me. Goldy was my grandmother but she refused to be called Grandma, Grammy, Gran, MomMom, Gam, or any other variation. Ever. It was a personal preference, from what I'd been told, but it was also a rule etched in stone. No one crossed that line without risking great consequences.

She'd known the Milners for years and had actually dated one of their sons before she'd found my grandfather, Thomas Dagner. He, unlike Goldy, was very proud to be a grandfather and loved to be called Pops.

But because Goldy knew this family and had dated one of the sons, she was adamant we all go to the funeral to show our support. Of course, my brother, Nick, had backed out the morning of through text, and Pops had said no from the get-go. So it was only me and Goldy.

What could go wrong with that? I didn't even have the time to start a list that big. Just call me Whitney Dagner, dutiful granddaughter to a non-grandmother.

Other things had to take up my time, like finding something to wear. I was used to a normal, everyday look that featured mostly shorts and a T-shirt. The island was laid back, and I dressed accordingly. I very much welcomed this attitude after spending years on the mainland and having to jam myself into skirts, heels, and jackets for my job with the railroad and container-shipping company.

I did still have some formal/business wear, but was that the appropriate outfit for an island funeral? I had no idea. I hadn't been to a funeral here since I was a teenager. With so few residents, there weren't many to go to.

In the end, I went with my gut, which was about fifty percent right fifty percent of the time. I was positive that if I was dressed wrong, Goldy would let me know right away when I got to her house to pick her up.

Pulling a charcoal skirt from the closet, I sneered at it for being much smaller than I remembered and hoped it would still fit. I'd debated throwing away all my corporate clothes when I moved back to the island, but had held on to a few, just in case. And this was one of those just-in-cases. After pairing it with a gray boatneck blouse, I decided to skip nylons because I had to draw the line somewhere. While it wasn't hot on the island, even at the end of August, there was no weather or temperature where I liked pantyhose of any kind.

I threw the clothes on the bed behind me without looking and got scolded by my chonky kitty, Whiskers. She yowled so loudly, I was afraid she'd wake up my roommate, Maribel, who had come home about an hour ago from her overnight shift at the police station.

"Oh, baby. I'm so sorry. I didn't see you there."

The orange-striped cat clawed her way out from under the skirt and shirt and then sat on them to groom herself. Of course.

"No, no, no. Come on, get off my stuff." I went to pull the skirt out from under her but stopped when she hissed at me, unsheathing her claws. Thankfully she didn't dig them into the fabric, but if I wasn't mistaken, she was daring me to take one more step toward her, therefore giving her permission to gleefully dig in. Little brat.

At the sound of a laugh behind me, I closed my eyes.

"Sassy," Maribel Hernandez said from the doorway, leaning there as if she had nothing better to do than make fun of me.

"No doubt. Does she do this to you?"

"No, she's more into fighting me for my curling iron in the bathroom." Maribel fluffed her dark brown hair with its perfect curls to show me she had won that last round. "She's not into my clothes. Then again, I don't throw things on her, because I know better. You should too."

"Can you grab her so I can get dressed?" I kept my eye on Whiskers to see if she'd back down, but that paw was still hovering and those claws were still out.

"Nope, I think I want to watch and see how this plays out,

chica. If Felix were here, I guarantee we'd be placing bets on who's going to win."

"I'm sure you'd both be betting against me. Nice, Maribel."

"Anytime, Whit."

"I wish you'd come with me to this funeral." I didn't want to sound desperate, but there was still a slight whine to my words. And if she was up and looking fresh, then she could help me out now and sleep later.

"No, thanks. Hey, at least this isn't something you had anything to do with. You didn't have to catch a killer before the case could be wrapped up and the victim put in the ground or shipped back to the mainland."

She wasn't wrong, and I was eternally grateful for that. "True. And I have absolutely no plans for solving anything else. The last three months have been more than enough for anyone." I waved one hand near the window and got ready to grab my skirt out from under my problem-child cat. Distraction sometimes worked. Not this time, though. Whiskers again hovered her paw over the blouse, as if daring me to try to take it from her. Dammit.

"And now that Ray Pablano has been moved to station commander, I'm pretty sure he'd have some very strong words if you got yourself involved in anything new."

I blew out a breath and tried to come up with a new distraction for Whiskers. "He already told me that in no uncertain terms. It was unnecessary, but whatever. I'm perfectly happy for there to be no more murders on the island in the first place, and in the second place I'm happy to have nothing to do with them. That's almost your job now."

"Ha! Not if I can't pass this next class. I don't know if I'm going to. There's so much work." She rubbed the back of her neck and blew out a breath. Her pajamas had frolicking avocados on them, and I wished I were back in my own pjs instead of trying to figure out how to wrestle my clothes from a sassy cat.

"You're totally up for it. You're doing great." I meant this with my whole heart, though I couldn't ignore the fact that if she graduated as a criminal justice major, she probably would not want to remain a receptionist at the small police station we had on-island. I would worry about that later, though. Now I had to get my outfit and get out the door.

"Could you please try to take the chonkster off my bed?" I asked.

"Nope, she's your animal. You take care of it."

"Thanks so much for no help at all." I rolled my eyes.

"My pleasure." She turned away from the door, then turned back. "Catnip?" she said, and did Whiskers jump right off the bed and run after Maribel?

Of course she did.

"Thanks!" I yelled, and Maribel laughed. Whatever, as long as the cat was gone with her sharp claws and her cattitude.

Glancing at the clock, I realized I had about three minutes to get dressed and make it to my grandparents' house. Since they only lived a short distance away and I was quick with the clothes, I shouldn't be too late. After pulling on the skirt and blouse and shoving my feet into a pair of low heels, I hustled out to my golf cart waiting in front of the house and zoomed away. Or at least I zoomed as best as could be expected in a car that only went seventeen miles per hour downhill.

I screeched the tires to a halt when I reached the bungalow where I'd grown up, and texted Goldy to let her know I was waiting for her. Only two minutes late. I would probably be able to get away with that.

When the door didn't immediately open and Goldy didn't come steaming out at full speed to berate me, I beeped the horn I'd installed last week. Well, it didn't actually beep. I'd instead programmed it to play the yo-ho song from *Pirates of the Caribbean*. Not everyone loved it, but they didn't have to.

No sign of Goldy still, so I turned off the cart, stood, and straightened my skirt, which thankfully had no holes in it, then approached the door. As I made my way up the short sidewalk, I could hear raised voices. I quickened my pace.

Even though I couldn't make out the words, it sounded like Goldy was angry and Pops wasn't far behind her. I had a key to the door. I could let myself in. I completely chickened out at the last second and knocked instead.

No answer, so I knocked again. At this point, if no one opened the door, I was going to go home, call Felix, change into my bathing suit, and go snorkeling. I hadn't wanted to go to this funeral anyway, and I certainly didn't want to take an angry Goldy. It would be like putting one of the island's bisons on a leash and expecting it not to drag you up a hill.

Unfortunately I didn't leave the scene and get into my golf cart fast enough. Goldy whipped open the door, stomped out, and then slammed it shut behind her.

"Your grandfather is a pain."

This was the part where I just kept my mouth shut. Goldy was a force to be reckoned with in any circumstance, all five feet of her. Goldy on a rampage was a hurricane dancing with a tsunami.

"He is so stubborn. I told him to get ready to go to the funeral and he refused."

I could have said I thought he had already told her that but all it would get me would be a scowl and, more likely, yelled at to transfer her anger to me. No, thanks.

So I kept my mouth shut while turning the cart back on and then taking off, letting her continue to talk. I listened but didn't respond as I admired the flora and fauna along the way to Cemetery Road. People's flowers were flowing from their window boxes, brilliant white rocks took the place of grass along some of the sidewalks, and potted plants sat on small porches or hung from the latticework over the front door. I'd seen the same landscape a thousand times, but it was worth a thousand and first look if it kept me out of target range.

"I wanted him to come with me because I'm not a fan of Darren's family at all. It would have been better to be able to introduce my husband to Darren and to have someone to lean on if I need to. But does he listen?"

I could feel her staring at me, but I kept my eyes on the road. I wanted to be a good driver, of course, and on the way to a funeral was a very bad time to get into an accident. Besides, wasn't I enough of a person to lean on?

In my peripheral I watched her fix the cleavage on one of the fanciest black dresses I'd ever seen her wear. Had she bought it just for the funeral? Probably something else I shouldn't blurt out.

"No, he doesn't listen," she said, answering her own question and crossing her arms under her chest.

She sat back so I could no longer see her, and I released a slow and nearly silent sigh.

Still, she kept talking. "I told him how important this was to me, but he doesn't care."

I had no answer for that since I had never heard of Darren before this week, and I had no idea what the circumstances were from long ago or now. It was always better not to guess with Goldy.

"He thinks this is just some stupid excuse to see my old boyfriend, but it's so much more than that, and he should know."

I did the noncommittal "hmmm," because continued silence could be interpreted as my not agreeing with her. I kept driving, wishing Cemetery Road were just a little closer. At least I wasn't trying to traverse the 405 in Los Angeles, where it was almost guaranteed to take an hour to go three miles.

"Well, it doesn't matter now. He can just sit at home and mope all he wants. It was just an opportunity to see an old friend and support him during this difficult time. That's not a bad thing, is it?"

That one I had an answer for. "Of course not, Goldy."

"Are you mocking me?" She shot forward and the new highlights in her light brown hair glowed with the fire of the sun.

So maybe not the right answer, and I should have just continued to keep my mouth shut.

"Can this go any faster? We're going to be late."

I did not point out that I had been at her house on time and she was the one who was making us late. Good for me.

Fortunately, we rounded a corner, and the cemetery was in sight. I let the conversation go and peeked at her as she pouffed her hair and pulled out a compact mirror to check her lipstick and reapply.

Because we didn't have many funerals on the island, I wasn't surprised to see so many golf carts parked at the side of the road. This would no doubt be an event to be seen at in support of the family but also to rub elbows with whoever else was here and to show people you were a good community member. They could have it. I was only here until the service was done—no standing around to chat afterward. And then I'd be on the way to my wonderful picnic with Felix. The thought of the picnic and escape was enough to keep me in place in all my finery so as not to irritate Goldy and then have to endure a lecture instead of being able to leave right after Therese was put in the ground. And, yes, at almost thirty I was still very prone to receiving those lectures if I was doing something Goldy would prefer I didn't.

The funeral itself shouldn't last too long once it got started. I could hang on to that and the lovely feeling of being outside on this gorgeous day. I wasn't a huge fan of cemeteries, but this one was stunning with its lovely green shrubs and vividly colored flowers swaying gently in the breeze coming off the Pacific.

And if I kept my eyes on the shrubs, then I could ignore the fact that a lot of the funeral-goers were talking and laughing among themselves with their circles and turned away from the grave and Therese's remaining family. Only Goldy stood looking at the coffin on top of the contraption that would lower it into the ground.

The deceased's husband stood on the other side of the gathering with another man; both of them were dark-haired and dressed to the hilt in suits, and no one seemed to be paying attention to them. Or maybe no one was approaching because they seemed to be exchanging strong words. Their facial expressions were not happy or sad. They were angry. What was it with the anger today? I wouldn't have approached them, either, if Goldy hadn't grabbed my arm and dragged me along the path toward them.

"Now, when we get over there, don't say anything, just stand next to me and smile with some sadness in your expression."

"What is this, a casting call?"

She turned and scowled at me. "Behave."

"Yes, Goldy."

Of course, my grandmother nailed the sad smile as she horned her way in between the two arguing men and took the younger one's hands in hers. His face went from angry to shocked to a smile that probably could have outshone the sun. His tan set off his blue eyes perfectly, even with the sheen of tears.

"Oh, my gosh, hon, it is so good to see you!" He scooped her up into a hug, with her feet dangling about four inches off the ground. He was a tall man and looked a lot like his father, though the older one was a bit stooped in the shoulders. And since he had to be at least ninety, that, too, was to be expected. But this one was broad in the shoulders and filled out his customized suit like someone far younger than almost seventy.

Laughing, she cupped her hands around his jawline. After placing a kiss on each of his cheeks, she sighed softly and then kissed him on the nose.

When the guy set her down, she reached a hand behind her and pulled me forward. "Darren, this is my granddaughter, Whitney."

"You're a grandmother?" he asked, and I gulped. This could only go one way, as it usually did. They might want to start digging a second grave now.

But instead she laughed as if he'd just said the most complimentary thing in the world, and blushed. "I'm called Goldy. I'm not really old enough to be a grandmother."

Throwing an arm around her shoulders, he pulled her in to kiss her forehead. The band of his silver watch flashed in my eyes, momentarily blinding me. It was on my tongue to tell him to stop with the overtouching, but I kept that behind my teeth too. It was getting crowded in my mouth with all the things I wasn't saying.

"Whitney." He turned to me and had my hand in his before I even realized it. He brought it to his lips and kissed the back of my knuckles. "She's the spitting image of you, darling. How is it possible that God allowed two such beautiful creations to exist at the same time?"

Now it was my turn to blush, but I fought it down because he seemed very smarmy. I was not a fan of smarmy, even on a good day, and certainly not at a funeral.

"Oh, you." Goldy placed a hand on his lapel and rubbed off what looked like her setting powder. Must have been quite the hug.

"Oh, him," another man said as he joined us from the left and put his arm around Darren's waist, then snuggled in right where Goldy was on his other side. He had to be around a decade older than me but nowhere near Goldy's or Darren's age. To each his own, but this guy looked like he'd walked off a magazine advertisement for some dark and dangerous cologne. The suit had a light sheen that made it sparkle. His black hair was streaked with silver, giving him that salt-and-pepper look that made ladies swoon. And his bright green eyes were crinkled at the edges with his smile. Yowza.

"My partner, Jericho," Darren said as he let go of Goldy and put his arm around the other man's waist. "He's new to the island, and despite the sad reason for being here, I'm trying to get him to love our slice of heaven so he'll want to come back."

"I wish you would have stuck with the broad and kept on lying." The words were muffled under Darren's father's breath, but I was close enough to hear them.

"My father, Stu, has not always approved of my choices, but I think anyone would be lucky to have a Goldy in their lives."

Oh. And then it clicked. That was why this was special and different and why Goldy would have such a soft spot in her heart for a guy she'd dated but hadn't married. I got it now, and I appreciated her willingness to help hide something that would have not only gotten you shunned fifty years ago but definitely could have gotten you beat up, ostracized, and sometimes even killed. We were a small island, and while there were absolutely people who were open to a lot of different lifestyles, as they should be, I would bet my shop that that was not the case back in the day.

I smiled, this time for real, and put a hand on Goldy's shoulder. She covered my hand with hers, not saying anything. I did wonder why Pops thought Darren was a bad guy, given the circumstances, but that was a conversation for another time.

We all turned as the funeral director approached and greeted people. It looked like it was going to be an ordinary, run-of-the-mill funeral. Everyone turned to face the coffin as the service began. Some cried. Some whispered behind their hands. A swirl of wind proved that many of them had used the extra-hold hair spray this morning, as their hair didn't move an inch.

Therese's husband looked lost to the world in his suit from the 1970s, with his dark comb-over that he must have been keeping up at the salon with monthly dye jobs.

Everything seemed to be running right along, and I was calculating how long I had to wait before leaving. But then I heard the rough sound of a full-sized car zooming up. I turned, wondering who on earth would press the accelerator to the ground on such a quiet road, when the car headed toward the coffin and the crowd gathered on the other side of the final resting place. Tires screeched, brakes squealed, and then the car crashed into the tent where the body was stationed, ready for burial, and knocked the coffin to the ground.

Chapter 2

We all just stood and watched as the coffin tipped in slow motion and the lid popped off. No one moved for what seemed like forever. Then everyone went into hyperdrive as some went to the car to see what had happened and who was inside, while others went to the casket to find out what the damage was and how they could help. Me? I just remained frozen in place, with Goldy digging her nails into my arm.

"Shouldn't we go help or something?" I whispered.

"No, I think it's better if we stay right here." She even took a step back from the crowd and seemed to want to hide in those beautiful bushes I'd noticed earlier.

"What is the matter with you? The person driving might be in trouble. We should find out what caused the accident," I said, trying to remove her claws from my arm. I'd survived Whiskers only to have to worry about my shirt again with my grandmother.

"I highly doubt that was an accident. And she's not supposed to be here," Goldy said cryptically.

"Who?" I looked around for anyone I might not have known because I highly doubted she'd say something like that about someone who'd been on the island for years. I saw no one who was out of place except for Darren and Jericho.

She dragged me back another step, and I was getting pretty tired of being manhandled by a woman who was several inches shorter and forty years older than me.

I stood my ground as she tried for another step back. "Stop it. You're being ridiculous."

"I'm being cautious."

"What does that even mean? Cautious about what? It was an accident. The coffin fell. I'm sure they'll help whoever was driving too fast and then fix the coffin and then we'll finish out the funeral."

"No, it's more than that." She pointed in the direction of the car, and I watched a woman emerge. "She's the girl Darren was supposed to marry, and then I took him from her to save him from a marriage he did not want. I wouldn't be surprised if she still hates me."

What alternate universe was I living in? I hadn't even wanted to come to this funeral and now I was trapped in some daytime soap opera. "Well, that's quite the story. Why was Darren supposed to marry her?"

"His grandmother set up a betrothal between their family and Elsie Jacobs's family."

"A freaking arranged betrothal? Are you kidding me?" I'd watched those historical romance movies on television, and I was also known to get completely lost in those kinds of books. But betrothals had gone out of style some time ago in America, and I was having a hard time believing that.

"It was a custom in their family, but when Darren realized he couldn't go through with it, he asked me to save him. So I did until he could get the money to go to the mainland and leave all this behind."

It wasn't like I couldn't see how that might affect someone in the moment or even a year later, but fifty years? And how did this woman get a car on-island?

"Should we hide?" I felt stupid for asking but didn't know what else to say.

"We Dagners do not hide."

That was quite the turnaround from how she had just been trying to sink into the bushes in her satin-trimmed dress, but I wasn't going to fight with her.

Well, that was the plan until she started dragging me again. This time toward the crashed car and the woman who had just gotten out from the driver's side. I didn't think that was really a better idea than when we were trying to hide. Apparently, though, at this point, I was in for a pound.

"Elsie, what are you doing here?" Darren was standing next to the car and almost caging the woman into the V between the door and the car frame. He didn't look like he was moving any-time soon, and he was a big guy.

"I came because we can get married now. I know all those years ago you had to leave because your mom didn't want us to be together, but now that she's gone, we can say our vows."

Goldy snarled next to me, a sound I never thought I would hear from her, and tried to launch herself at the couple—four-inch heels, shiny black dress, and all.

Not on my watch. I was quick enough to keep her in place, but I couldn't do anything about the noises she was making.

"Calm yourself down right now or I swear to the bottom of the sea I will take you home right this minute." I made sure to whisper the words to Goldy, but they still packed a punch, and she knew I wasn't kidding. Especially because it was exactly what she used to say to me and my brother, Nick, when we were younger and misbehaving.

"Sweetheart, darling, Elsie . . ." Darren cleared his throat and threw a look at Jericho before taking the well-dressed and perfectly coiffed woman's hands in his. The body language was so much different from when he had interacted with Goldy. Here he was stiff and seemed only to touch her fingertips, but it was enough for her to smile up at him with adoration and incredibly white teeth.

"Yes, my love. I've waited for almost fifty years for this. What do you want to tell me? I'm here for anything you need."

"Well, right now, I, ahem, need to bury my mother. Perhaps we could talk later about everything. After the funeral." He glanced over the woman's head at Goldy with a pleading look.

"Whitney." She turned on me and tried to pull her arm out of my grasp. Good luck with that. I might not be the strongest person in the area, but when it came to family, I held on for dear life.

I'd even gone after a killer to save my brother. Surely I could keep one Goldy from getting herself punched—or worse—by a woman who thought her long-lost love could now be hers.

Elsie reached her hands up and cupped the sides of Darren's face, much as Goldy had earlier, but this time he looked repulsed. He hid the expression quickly enough that Elsie didn't see it, especially because she was looking back over her shoulder and smirking at Goldy. The gold tips on her fingernails seemed to glint a warning for everyone to back off.

"Folks, if everyone could pay attention for just a minute?" The funeral director, who was patting down his blond hair and shaking out the cuff on his left arm at the same time, stood at the side of the righted coffin with the lid re-secured. He cleared his throat, then repeated himself, in a yell this time.

Finally, everyone turned and looked at him. He cleared his throat again and pulled at the tie knotted tightly around his reddened neck.

"We're going to have to postpone the funeral for the moment. We'll need some time to get things back to where they should be on this solemn occasion. I don't want to take up everyone's time when this won't be a quick fix, so we'll let you know when to return."

Wouldn't be a quick fix? That was an understatement. The station commander had just pulled up and was trying to grab hold of Elsie, who kept running around Darren and sliding along his body in an effort to escape Captain Ray Pablano. Darren looked miserable; Ray looked as if he'd had enough, even though it had been about a minute, and Elsie looked like a cat who had the bead on the canary. And each time she slid along Darren she smiled at Goldy.

Time to move things along.

But then Darren's father took the spot where the funeral director had stood. "Look, I know most of you are here out of respect but probably not a lot of true love for my wife. She could be standoffish and snubbed a lot of people, and I know she wasn't the easiest of people to deal with. Lord, do I know that. So let's just call the funeral done. Thanks for coming by and standing here, but I'm not going to ask you to do it again." He pulled a handkerchief out of his breast pocket and wiped his brow, then walked slowly toward his golf cart, his shoulders drooped, mumbling to himself.

I took that as our cue to leave and ushered Goldy along to the golf cart, sidestepping every once in a while to block her and threatening to strap her into the damn seat with bungee cords if I had to.

I should have never come to this funeral and I was incredibly glad it was over. I'd be very happy never to see any of the Milners again if I had my way.

Of course, I had probably just cursed myself to see them every time I turned a corner, but I couldn't take it back now. I could, however, take Goldy home and hopefully forget this whole thing once I dropped her off.

"You have never acted like this before," I said as I got into the cart. "It's like having a toddler running around with a sparkler firework. What is wrong with you?" It was a short drive, but as I pulled away from the curb, thirty feet felt like thirty miles.

"I told you the story." She didn't try to get out again when I took off or as we trundled along behind several other golf carts. Probably because she didn't want to embarrass herself by having to tuck and roll to not destroy her dress. Honestly, I'd take whatever I could get at this point. I only had three more blocks to drop her off and then she'd be Pops's issue and not mine.

"You did tell me the story, and it was very honorable of you, but come on, that was almost fifty years ago, a lifetime. He can mean something to you without you always having to save him."

"You don't know what it was like. I cared so much for him and knew his struggles. Then he left and went into the Navy. That had to be difficult for him too. I just wanted to see him happy. You will never understand." She clasped her hands around her elbows and looked out to the sea on our right. Waves hit the rocky coast and a fine mist shot up to sparkle in the air.

"I won't, and I'll never say I do, but this seems a little extreme. He looks healthy, appears to have a good relationship with Jericho, and he was dressed expensively. You are not required to save him from a situation he walked away from all those years ago. He's old enough to handle it now without you running interference."

Two blocks to go and it couldn't come soon enough.

She sniffed and I relented. Maybe I was being too harsh on her.

"I get it, and I know how caring you are for a lot of people. I'm sure at that young an age, something like that makes a real impression on you." And I would know, since that was around the age I was when I had last heard from my mother. My father had left even before that. But I still carried that message from my mother around with me no matter how many times I'd tried to put it down. It hadn't even been a call or a letter. It had been a postcard with the words *See you later* on it, and nothing else.

Finally we pulled up in front of my grandparents' house and I gave Goldy a hug before she got out. "You know I love you. I just don't want this trip down memory lane to be a stumble into a hell you didn't ask for."

"Oh, sweetheart, it'll be fine. You know how I am. And we'll be able to check in with Darren later this afternoon when we help set up the theater in the Casino for his movie premiere."

"What? No." I even shook my head so there would be no way she could misinterpret what I was saying.

"Oh, yes. I asked for your assistance tonight and you told me you were available after your dive with Felix. You can't back out now."

Oh, but I could.

"You just asked if I was available, not what it was for. I thought you needed help, maybe around the house before you fed me dinner, so I said yes."

"And I do need help, so the yes stays."

"I don't want . . ." But I trailed off because she shot me a narrow-eyed look. After everything she had done for me, what was one evening fixing up a theater so that an old friend could have a movie premiere? Goldy had been my rock through the turmoil of my whole life and had often taken the place of my parents when they decided life was just a little too much for them and jetted off without a single thought to how that would affect their kids.

Damn! Even though I did not want to, it appeared I was going to the Casino, one of the biggest buildings on the island. It had opened in 1929 and had never actually had any gambling. It was a gathering place that you couldn't miss as you sailed into Avalon, and apparently I was going to be there tonight, fixing up the theater inside for Darren. Just great.

"Okay, fine. But I am not dealing with anything having to do with this Elsie woman, and neither are you. Got it?"

"Fine." She smiled and had the audacity to wink at me. "It'll be a blast!"

That was almost what I was afraid of.

Being in the ocean was one of my favorite things and only one of the reasons I had chosen to move back to Avalon. There were other reasons, of course, to completely uproot my life on the mainland and quit my job at the railroad. I could easily have gone in the ocean on the mainland, a short distance from my apartment in Bellflower, but something had been calling me back to where I'd grown up, and here I was.

I'd enjoyed my time with Felix in the water. We'd snorkeled and explored a cave around the south side of the island. I'd found some debris in the cave I intended to come back and clean up. A lot of the debris was made up of a bunch of broken crates with a weird logo, and I wanted to know who was responsible and which manager to complain to. I hated when things washed up onshore. And since this was a pretty private cove, I figured no one else would see it, but I'd know. The whole time, I had shut out the events of this morning and the small knot of dread about this evening. I had allowed myself to simply exist, even as a curious octopus had tried to make friends with me, and it had been just what I needed. And now I was back home and ready to tackle whatever came next.

After petting Whiskers, I turned on the shower before heading to the closet. This time picking something to wear would be easier. Since Goldy had called and asked me to bring her sneakers to the theater, I assumed not everyone was going to be dressed to the nines. I pulled out a T-shirt and some shorts and then made quick work of washing off the salt water. Calling myself done once I felt clean, I got dressed and laced up my own sneakers. Twenty-two minutes from the beach to dressed. Not bad. If it wasn't good enough for Goldy, she could just tell me and I'd leave. No sweat off my nose.

As I was running around, Whiskers decided that it was time to play. She pounced on my shoelaces and refused to let go.

"Whiskers." I removed her from the laces by lifting her up. She simply rolled over in my hands and attacked again. "Whiskers!" I said it a little louder, knowing full well she could hear me. She was only a couple of years old and was in no way hard of hearing, as evidenced by the fact that no matter where she was when I opened the cupboard with the catnip, she was sure to be already climbing up my leg.

And I might have to do that this time too. She was not giving up her imaginary war with my poor bows that I'd double-knotted just as I'd been taught to when I was a little girl. Specifically by Goldy, who was going to have a fit if I ever finally got to the theater with her shoes.

As if to save the day, my doorbell rang and I shuffled across the floor, trailing the orange cat from hell who was still growling at my laces but refusing to let go.

"Seriously, Whiskers, you're going to get hurt and then meow like the world is on fire. Let go!" I reached the door without actually hurting her, but it was a close thing.

And when I opened the door, Felix looked down and then back up at me with a half smile. "Rough twenty minutes since I last saw you?"

"Well, it hasn't been my best, but I've had worse."

He held out the shoes he'd retrieved for Goldy from Pops, and after I took them, he bent down to get my cat. Of course Whiskers, the little traitor, went right into his arms and then turned over so he could pet her belly. Brat.

"We should probably leave while she's calm," I whispered as she purred and purred.

Felix placed her on the back of the couch and pulled a blanket up to her neck. She kept purring as I closed the door quietly behind the both of us.

"Thanks." Listening for just a moment, I didn't hear any running around or meowing, so I figured she was settled, at least for the next little while.

Felix put his arm around my shoulders and pulled me in for a quick kiss. "All part of the service, ma'am."

"Ma'am? Really? Who says that?" And why did his dimpled smile always make my heart flutter?

"My grandfather does."

"Yeah, well, so does mine, I guess." I let myself snuggle into Felix for just a second and then kissed him on the cheek.

"I'd help at the theater but I have a diving lesson later tonight."

"Please don't even worry. I wish I was going with you. Goldy is being very strange today about this whole situation. Honestly, I'd give almost anything to not have to be there."

"I'm sure everything will be fine, Whit. Let me know if you need anything."

"You know you'll be the first to get a call."

"Just don't let it be about another dead body. I think we've hit our quota for the summer."

Truer words were never spoken.

Chapter 3

Scooting along in my little golf cart, I made my way down the road from the hills to the main street of this tiny town I called home. Because of the funeral earlier and the swim with Felix, I'd kept my trinket shop, Dame of the Sea, closed for the day. Tomorrow was soon enough, but I cringed a little at the thought of all those tourists wandering around and spending all that money everywhere but at my business.

For the most part, people stayed on the sidewalk, so I had no trouble zipping along the roads around and through Avalon. The breeze, smelling like a subtle mix of the sea and burgers and grilled shrimp, lifted my bangs and kept me cool on this relatively warm afternoon. It wasn't evening yet, when the temperature would drop a little more.

I drove around several parked carts and found myself a spot near the theater without being in the main parking lot since it was already full. I had no idea what this Darren thought he was going to do for parking or if he just assumed everyone would walk, since few things in Avalon weren't within walking distance.

As I strode up the sidewalk toward the Casino, I was minding my own business until I was distracted by someone yelling about a banner and then heard a crash.

Looking up, I saw a ladder wobbling and waving arms before it toppled. And then I watched in awe as my brother started going sideways into the bushes but then did a tuck and roll onto the grass at the bottom of the ladder. He even avoided having it crash on him.

"Bravo! You should consider joining the circus as an acrobat." I stood in the circular driveway of the theater, slow clapping for his idiocy.

"Did you get it on video? That was pretty smooth, if I do say so myself."

"Very smooth, like a hand-churned kale shake, and, no, I didn't get it on camera. What? Do you want to be on one of those social media channels of best fails for the week? I'm sure you have much more to offer than a tumble off a ladder."

"Ha, ha, ha, you're hysterical." Nick stood and brushed off the back of his shorts. Apparently I had been right that dressing low-key casual was an option here, and I was glad I'd taken it.

"What are you doing up there, anyway?" I didn't see a sign he was hanging, or lights, or anything in his hands, though I supposed he could have dropped them from his perch before I arrived. It would have been typical Nick.

"I'm supposed to be checking out the measurements for a marquee, and I have no idea why Goldy thought this was a good job for me. Or why we'd be doing it on the night before the show."

I knew. . . . It would keep him out of the way. If he didn't know, I wasn't going to tell him.

"Good luck with that." I eyed the area he was supposed to be measuring and wondered how they thought they could get a sign up there, much less a marquee. The rotund building had stood on this piece of land for years and years. It had been built as a place that all eyes would be drawn to as people approached the island in a boat. It was beautiful, but it had only smooth walls, and nowhere in the town would anyone be allowed to nail anything or would there be any places to hang something from.

Fortunately, that was not my problem, and the longer it took Nick to come to his own assessment that it wasn't going to work, the longer he'd stay outside.

"What's it like in there? Should I be ready to enter a battleground?" After the debacle of the funeral, and the way that Elsie had come slamming into the somber occasion, I wondered if it would be chaos and gossip, or if Elsie had been told in no uncertain terms that things were not going to go her way, making her leave the same way she'd come in.

I hadn't heard anything at all, but then I'd been snorkeling with Felix and stalked by an octopus, so there had been no one else to talk to. I made a mental note to go back to the cave and clean up the few broken crates we'd seen. It was something to look forward to anyway. And that was sad, if that was what I had to look forward to.

"It's fine, I think, but I've been out here for the last two hours, so I can't say for certain. Plus you're the one everyone seems to want to talk around, not me, so your experience might be totally different."

I was more like a wallflower, the kind few noticed when I was there. But that had worked in my favor in the past, and I wasn't in a place to want to change the advantage now. Although there was nothing for me to figure out with the Elsie thing, so it didn't matter anyway.

"Okay, then, I'm heading in." I waved to Nick as he ascended the ladder again. Hopefully he wouldn't fall a second time.

Walking into the theater, I took a moment to let my eyes adjust to the dimness after the bright sun outside. The lobby was a sight to behold. With art deco as the main theme and plenty of gold leaf and silver accents, it was lush and retro, and I loved it.

The structure stood at the equivalent of almost twelve stories and had a movie theater on the main floor as well as a ballroom on the topmost floor. Since I wasn't going to do any dancing in my sneakers and Goldy was probably pacing impatiently, waiting for me to bring in *her* sneakers, I hightailed it into the theater.

It had been renovated a few years ago and it was magnificent. Tons of people bustled around the seats that had been recovered and admired the paintings that had been restored. Like the lobby, it was art deco through and through and had once served as a musical stage as well as a movie theater. With the rise of streaming services, the theater had stopped showing first runs of films, but it could still be used for screenings, which was exactly what we were setting up for.

I had barely made it through the side door when Goldy came running at me, snatching the shoes, and sitting down on the seat closest to her. "Thank you, thank you, thank you. My feet are killing me!"

I watched with a smirk on my face as she put her high heels aside but said nothing. Seriously, my mouth was going to be so filled with the words I wouldn't let slip out that I might choke on them.

"You ready to work?" she asked as she laced up the second shoe and tied it in a double knot.

"It's why I'm here." The lights dimmed further and there was a flicker on the one enormous screen the building housed. Images started cascading over the big white rectangle on the painted wall, and I caught sight of two people talking on the screen, even though there was no sound.

A room came into view stacked with crates with a variety of shipping labels on them. It reminded me of the crate we'd found earlier in the cave and made me wonder again why it had been there and how it had gotten there. The logo had been distinctive and I kept trying to remind myself to look it up. The fish-and-hook design kept crawling through my mind but I couldn't place it. I knew I had seen it somewhere and I hoped I could remember, because if the debris contained more than one crate, I might have to see about contacting the company to take them down a notch for littering on my island.

The camera panned over wall after wall of ceiling-to-floor crates and now I was really curious as to the subject matter of the film.

"What is this thing about anyway?" I asked as Goldy stood from her seat and shook out her capris.

"I have no idea, but I'm sure it's going to be brilliant." She glanced over her shoulder at the screen and then turned back to me. "Can you help with the bows? Darren wants to put them on the end of each aisle."

"Sure, I guess. I saw you put Nick outside."

"He's better kept out of trouble there."

"And I'm better kept out of trouble by being the bow processor?"

"Something like that . . ." She kissed me on the cheek and walked away, sassy thing that she was.

I followed her to the stage to pick up my bag of bows, listening to the conversations of about fifty people on our way up front.

As we approached the stage, I could make out raised voices high above us in the rafters, where the rigging and curtains were stored. Maybe the lighting wasn't right, or perhaps there should have been sound.

I walked up the stairs to the left of the stage and found a box of bows. I looked around for a dolly or something to cart it off, because it was big, when someone shouted, *"Look out!"*

Since I didn't know where "out" was, I stared into the theater, where the audience would sit. But I should have looked *up*, not out.

Something hit the box with the force of an anchor being

dropped from the sky, sending every bow flying in every possible direction. Stunned into immobility, I looked down at the poor dead guy who hadn't been saved by landing on a bunch of tied-up ribbon.

Jericho.

What on earth had happened to Darren's partner for him to fall out of the rafters, dead?

And then I stumbled back. Although calling it stumbling was not a fair way of putting it, as it was far more dramatic than that. I stumbled, yes, but then I also tried windmilling my arms to balance myself and ended up hitting someone in the shoulder or arm. It couldn't have been Goldy, since she was calling out from somewhere in the theater for Darren, probably trying to make sure he was okay when her granddaughter was about to take a real honest-to-goodness stage dive. Not that she appeared to notice.

I was still trying to save myself from a complete fall from grace—or the stage, as the case may be—when I hit the curtain behind me and went down not only in a blaze of glory but in a tight cocoon of velvet fabric, kicking legs, and some sort of rope that bound it all up like a Christmas present. The kind you definitely did not want under your tree.

Everyone was yelling now and I could hear it just barely as I was cut off from most of the noise, due to the volume of the fabric wrapped around me. I heard a clank and wondered if it was the rod or the bar that had held the curtain up and was thankful it hadn't come down on my head.

Now to get myself out of this predicament. I didn't feel anyone trying to pull the curtain off me and I was pretty certain I had been forgotten in the melee. After all, there was a dead body in the Casino and yet another death on the island. This one might have been an accident if he had just fallen, but I had a feeling that would not be the case. Again.

This time I was not getting involved, no matter who was getting the finger pointed at them. And if anyone needed a defender against the police going after the wrong person, I was most certainly not their girl. But even as I told myself that, my brain had been going through all the reasons someone would have wanted to end Jericho's life.

I lay still for a moment because I'd started sweating and told my brain to shut the hell up.

If I was going to get out of this mess—and I would, no doubt—I had to be smart about it. I must have had about forty feet or more of fabric wrapped around me. Because I'd backed into the curtain when I'd fallen, it had been jerked down and swirled around my whole body before I hit the stage, where it draped the rest of its heavy weight and volume on yours truly.

So it would make sense to start sifting my way through the layers and try to unravel myself instead of clawing at the material to get it away from my body. There had been a fund-raiser last year to redo the Casino and especially the theater inside it. In my current state, I still remembered that one of the most prized purchases had been this particular set of deep red curtains, which had been handmade for the theater. So ruining them was out of the question.

But it was getting very hot in here, and no matter how much I let my mind go around and around, I couldn't ignore the fact that I was sweaty not only because it was hot but also because panic was setting in that I might die in here from lack of air and no one would ever know. Who would work to figure out I'd accidentally done this to myself?

So I started inching my way through one layer after another. Except my feet seemed to be tied up on some kind of cord or fastening, so I imagined myself as an onion being revealed to the core.

At first it worked, and I could start making out the things that were being said around me, even as no one realized I was still there.

"Everyone out into the lobby, but don't leave. We're going to have some questions for all of you, and I don't want anyone wandering off." That was Ray putting on his official voice. It was far different from the resigned one he used with me whenever I brought something to him, such as a death of an islander or even an old woman who was lost.

Of course, I did have to give him credit, because the woman hadn't really been lost two weeks ago. She had been trying to enjoy the sun and was ignoring me as I asked her if she was all right. It escaped my notice at the time that she had her earbuds in and was enjoying the sunshine. I was the one who had made it into a thing when I saw Ray walking by on his way to the Daily Scoop, our island ice cream shop, and stopped him from getting his treat to make sure the woman was okay.

She hadn't taken kindly to him scaring her by touching her arm. In fact, she had thrown her flip-flop at him, along with a bottle of sunscreen, a bottle of water, and a hardcover book, which he had taken right in the face. Needless to say, he hadn't been pleased with me.

So he was now corralling everyone out into the lobby. It would make sense if he was bringing in some officers, if they weren't already here. Then they would do some kind of investigation and talk among themselves. Which meant if I lay really still and didn't move, I could get the deets of what they thought had happened. At least I had moved enough fabric around to feel air flowing around me, so I wasn't scared of suffocating anymore. And they wouldn't know I was here, which meant they would probably talk about things I wouldn't normally have access to, unless I could get Maribel to break her protocol and tell me what she was hearing around the office. She didn't often do that—with good reason. She valued her job and was dedicated to doing it well, but every once in a while I could get her to talk. I always liked to know what was happening on the not-so-mean streets of Avalon.

"Is everybody out?" It was Ray speaking again.

I rested back into my nest of velvet, ignoring the fact that I was still sweating. Although it wasn't so bad now that I had stopped panicking and was settling in for the reveal of what was known and what they still needed to figure out. Which I assumed was everything. I had to admit that I was interested in learning more about the death and very possibly doing something with the information I had gleaned. Damn my nosiness!

"Yes, Captain, everyone's out. I have Deputy Jeffrey out in the lobby with them, and he'll start taking statements. You want me to get some more guys down here? It doesn't look like it's only an accident, if you know what I mean."

Ray grunted, and inside my cocoon I groaned. Me thinking it might not be an accident and promising myself I wouldn't get involved was one thing. Ray's grunt meant that there was a very real possibility I was lying to myself.

I wouldn't be able to ignore the fact that Goldy was all up in Darren's business. And if I knew Goldy, which I definitely did, that meant she was going to ask me to look into stuff, as she had when Nick had been a suspect and again when things had blown up between two long-standing families on the island.

And I also knew without a shadow of a doubt that I was almost completely incapable of saying no to her, especially when I was overly curious myself.

I thumped my head back on the floor and all chatter stopped. Had I just given myself away? Damn!

I stopped all movement, even my breathing, desperately hoping they would continue talking and no one would try to come to save me from my cocoon of death.

It wasn't to be, though. I heard the heavy tread of Ray's boots striking the wood floor of the stage and started coming up with excuses as to why I hadn't made myself known when they had sent everyone else out of the theater. I hadn't come up with anything yet when I felt a tug on the fabric and started to unroll like a pig in a blanket.

"I should have known you would be in here," he said as I hit the wood with one shoulder and tried to stop myself from falling off the edge of the stage.

"Whatever do you mean?" I asked, but then jumped right back in to talking so he wouldn't have a chance to chastise me for my sneakiness. "I think I might have passed out in there. Thank you so much for finding me and saving me, Ray. What on earth would I ever do without you?"

Okay, so I was aware that I was probably laying it on a little thick, especially when a couple of the deputies laughed into their hands. One cutting look from Ray had them all covering their mouths collectively and coughing to cover the misstep.

"Whitney Dagner. Always where you're not supposed to be, doing what you're not supposed to be doing. Is that luck or is that a special form of being a thorn in my side?"

"I prefer to think of it as coincidence." I patted myself down to make sure nothing was broken and no clothing was out of place, then smiled up at him.

He just sighed and then groaned and then sighed again.

"You're not going to keep out of this, are you?"

"Of course I am. I have no stake in this and I'm very confident that you are more than capable of doing your job. Jobs, I mean, since you have this possible murder and you also have the thing with that Elsie woman and the accident with her hitting the coffin. You'll do fine. With all of it."

That got me a slow blink from Ray and yet one more sigh. He was going to run out of breath if he didn't stop exhaling so heavily.

"And if I ask you to go out into the lobby with everyone else so that we can do our jobs?"

"Sure thing. No problem. Though I do want to just let you know that if Jericho was alive when he fell from twenty feet above, he didn't make a single sound. Not even when he hit the ground. So that might be something to take into consideration when you're doing your job." I just barely kept myself from making the air quotes. I was no longer dealing with the other captain who'd been in charge of the previous two cases. I'd had to watch him like a hawk because he often swept things under the rug just so he didn't have to do the very job Ray and I were discussing. But Warrington was gone now, and that was no longer my business. Hell, it hadn't been my business in the first place. Though I knew for certain the people who had been the wrongfully suspected were eternally grateful that I'd helped to make sure they weren't thrown in jail while the real culprit was out and about living their best life.

"Deputy Franklin, can you escort dear Miss Whitney out with all the other people?" He turned to me and gave me what I could only call the stink-eye. "I'd like you to keep your observations to yourself until I have more information, if you could possibly do that."

I was very aware I wouldn't be able to do that, especially if Goldy tried to talk to me, or Maribel asked what I had seen or heard, so I merely smiled at him and led the way out of the theater with Ryan Franklin trailing behind me and softly chuckling.

Of course as soon as I exited to the lobby, the noise level increased tenfold, and everyone and their mother—along with my grandmother, who had finally torn herself away from Darren—had questions and wanted to know what I knew.

With Ryan standing off to the side, I just shrugged and said nothing. There would be plenty of time later for dishing to those whom I felt should know.

Felix was there and was quick to put his arm around my shoulders. "Are you okay? I couldn't find you out here, and since this has nothing to do with water or diving, they weren't going to let me back in to see if you had been left behind."

He was sweet, and I loved that about him. But I was also

very capable of taking care of myself. "I'm fine. Had a little scuffle with the new curtain. I think I might have won, though it was a close call there for a second or two." More like several minutes when it felt like I was buried alive, but I didn't want to exaggerate and stop him from telling me anything he might know. "And aren't you supposed to be at a diving lesson? I thought that was why you couldn't help here tonight."

"The client canceled at the last minute, so I headed over here to see if I could help, then I heard about the body on the police scanner and made the cart go a little faster."

I eyed him up and down to see if he was going to give me grief about another dead body, ready to defend myself vigorously.

However, I didn't get a chance to get into that conversation because Goldy pushed her way to my side, her knee-length sheer jacket trailing behind her in the breeze from her stride, with Darren close on her heels. Then again he couldn't have been anywhere else because she had a death grip on his wrist and wasn't letting go.

"You will be trying to find out what actually happened, correct, Whit? We both know they're going to look at Darren as a suspect and we have to give them someone else or something else to concentrate on because I'm not going to have one of my favorite people hung out to dry."

So Darren couldn't be hung out to dry, but let's let Whit take on the police to save one of Goldy's favorite people. Why wasn't I surprised?

Chapter 4

I hadn't taken more than two breaths before Darren started talking about how horrible this was and how he had no idea what had happened.

That was understandable, but as I looked at him more closely and watched the way his eyes shifted all over the foyer, I couldn't get rid of the feeling that he was looking for another culprit. In fact, I wouldn't find it hard to say that he was looking for an escape route. Now, why would that be?

I held off on asking because Goldy had started pacing, dragging Darren along behind her every step. I'd experienced her death grip before and knew that even though she looked small, she could haul a person around with more force than a bulldozer moving earth.

And while Darren appeared to be straining against her, he wasn't pulling that hard for a man of his size. His dark brown hair stuck straight up as if he'd been tugging on it, but his face appeared unlined as he rolled his eyes. So was he not sad that his boyfriend had just died either by accident or due to being murdered? Where were the tears? The sorrow?

His gaze flashed to mine, and a second later a tear leaked out of the corner of his eye. Goldy caught it with her fingertip and kissed him on the cheek.

"It's going to be okay, Darren. I'm so sorry Jericho is gone."

For his part, Darren gulped and nodded solemnly, then cut his gaze to mine again.

I was about to tell him that he had better up his acting game when his dad, Stu, came streaming into the lobby from the front doors.

"Hello there! Hello! What's everyone doing in here? I thought we were getting the interior ready for this wonderful movie that my amazing son has created?"

Everyone stopped talking and looked right at Stu. He didn't seem to get the message and laughed jovially like a big old Santa. "Did I miss it? Has Darren been complaining that I never seem to be on time? I'm sorry, son, that wasn't my intention. I had some things to sort out at the house before I could get here." He slapped Darren on the back, which forced Goldy to let go of his wrist with the forward movement.

Still no one really said anything, though I did hear a few whispers in the background.

"Where's that boyfriend of yours? He leave you in the lurch? Doesn't surprise me. I told you that you should've just stuck with what had been set up for you." He grumbled something else under his breath, but I was standing too far away to catch it.

"Dad, Jericho is . . ."

Elsie burst through the front doors like she had a tidal wave at her back. "I just heard Jericho is dead! Oh, Darren, I told you it was our time to shine. Now we have no more barriers! Nothing to keep us apart."

And that was when I saw Darren reach for Goldy's hand and pull her to his side.

Why did I suddenly feel like we were in some kind of wild movie that no one had the script for?

Elsie made a beeline for Darren and kissed him on the cheek while breaking his contact with Goldy. The woman then brought his hand up to her chest, over her heart, and leaned her forehead against his shoulder. "Meant to be." She sighed out the words with a happy little hiccup at the end.

What in the hell was going on?

Yet again I was cut off from asking when Ray and his team came out of the theater to join my babysitter, Ryan.

"Everybody, if I could have your attention. We're going to be conducting interviews, so if you all could form a line around the perimeter, we'll do our best to get whatever information you have and then send you on your way." He didn't smile but he didn't sigh either. Maybe they had found something that would help them know what had happened.

As much as I wanted to ask, I didn't, especially when Felix tugged on my hand and said, "Let it go for the moment."

So I did, and I was happy to do it, but avoiding Goldy was going to be a tough thing to pull off when she sidled up next to me and started babbling about Elsie.

Then everything went quiet when Ray yelled for Darren's dad to stay right where he was.

"Where are you going, Stu?" Ray asked. "I just told everyone to stay put."

Stu looked sheepish but then straightened his shoulders and puffed out his chest. "I wasn't here when whatever happened happened. I just walked in and had no clue until Elsie said the man had died." He held one hand out in front of him with the palm turned up. "Honestly."

"I'd still like you to stay if for nothing else than to support your son in his time of grief." Ray waited until Stu removed his other hand from the door handle to turn away.

For Darren's part, he looked far from grieving. He was trying to shake Elsie off without hurting her as he kept twitching and moving to put some space between them. But she wasn't having any of that and seemed to have grown four additional arms.

"Darren, I know this must be a painful time, but really it might just be for the best that he fell from that height. Imagine if he'd only tripped and just broken his nose or something. Then you'd have to take care of him and we both know you like to be taken care of, not having to do the caretaking."

That was news to me. Then again, nearly anything would be news to me, since I knew almost nothing about this guy at all. And the more I watched him, the more I wondered how he and Jericho had gotten together and for how long. If something happened to Felix, I'd be wailing like a guitar. There was no way would I be as stoic and silent as Darren was being. Then again, that was just me.

Perhaps he was overwhelmed. Although from his look and from the way Elsie was clinging to him, I was not willing to give him the benefit of the doubt at the moment. I'd reserve judgment. And once I came to a decision, I had a feeling I'd be keeping it to myself, too.

"All right, everyone," Ray said. "We need to make room. I know there are a lot of you here and we're going to want to talk to all of you, but I can't have this clustering going on. Please get into the line like I'd asked you already and we'll get things moving."

I went to stand at the back of the line and took Goldy with me.

"You're going to be looking into this, Whit, so don't even think about saying no."

I barely stopped myself from rolling my eyes. I had known that was coming, and irritating her would not help my case, it would only hinder it.

"Ray already told me I can't be involved." I didn't really think that was going to stop her from asking me again—or demanding as the case may be—and I already knew I wasn't going to be able to keep myself out of the fray, but it was worth a try.

"You mean like every other time you weren't supposed to be in the middle of things? And yet, you always manage to not only solve the case, but also get the right person and why they did it out of them before they're officially arrested?"

She did have a point, but I was not conceding just yet. She would have to work a little harder than that to get me to go against Ray, even if I already wanted to. The other station commander had been a dumbass, but I respected Ray and really didn't want to get on his bad side. I glanced around the lobby and found a few people whispering while staring at us. I tried to give them reassuring smiles, but it didn't quite quell their hushed conversations.

Then I looked at Darren and his dad and Elsie.

Why was Darren so distant? Why hadn't Jericho screamed on his way down or at least grunted when he hit the floor? Who had been up on the catwalk with him? Had they fought? Did things get rough, and had he been pushed over the railing? Was it not an accident at all?

See? All these questions and while I wanted to know, I also wasn't sure I'd be able to promise Goldy that I'd be saving Darren. I had a feeling in my gut that he could have done it. I kept it in my gut, though, and added it to the other words I was locking behind my teeth.

"I'm pretty sure I will not be a party to this and I'm not going to get into trouble with Ray again. He'd laugh at me now, but later on he'd probably throw me in jail for obstructing justice or some other thing." I didn't truly believe that, but it was a way to string her out a little bit more. After the way she'd been snippy with me earlier, I wasn't against making her wait a bit until I was ready to say yes.

"Don't be ridiculous. He's not going to throw you in jail and he should be thankful for any help he can get. I know the police department is getting smarter each time one of these things happens, but they could always use another set of eyes and ears."

"But . . ."

"No buts, and if they aren't happy with what you're doing, then they can do it themselves and we'll see who comes out on top. It'll be a race to solve the puzzle."

Ray was certainly not going to consider this a mere "puzzle" to solve. I did roll my eyes this time but turned away fast enough so Goldy couldn't see. That of course put me face-to-face with Darren, who was staring at me as if I held the keys to the universe.

"Your grandmother says you have helped with other issues before." He spoke the words softly so that only he and I could hear. Elsie was trying her damnedest to get as close to him as possible without crawling inside his shirt, but he hunched forward to keep her away.

"Goldy is wrong, and I would really think about not calling her a grandmother. She hates the term and has never let any of us call her that. I don't know why it's okay for you, though."

"We go back a long way."

"I don't doubt it, but I don't have to like it." And I wasn't kidding about that. Goldy was preoccupied by watching Elsie, so I dived back in.

"I don't know what you think you're doing here, or how it's all going to work out, but if you did push Jericho over the edge, then I am certainly going to let the cops know."

He leaned in further and I felt like we were exchanging air—not a pleasant experience. "I didn't. I swear to you. I was downstairs and any number of people can vouch for me. I loved him. Why would I want to kill him? We made this movie together and it was everything to the both of us."

I saw tears gathering in his glassy eyes, and I wondered if it was all bullshit. But then he sniffled and straightened his spine. He pressed his lips into a firm line, and I was reminded of my father. I hadn't seen him in almost twenty years, but I very much remembered how he'd react when my mom decided to leave for the mainland and not tell him when she was coming back. His heart would be broken, but he would never show us. It was only late at night when I could hear him sobbing that I realized she really did hurt him every time she walked away.

Was I giving this guy too much leniency because he reminded me of a father I hadn't seen in forever and would have done anything to have back? I patted my pocket where I sometimes carried my postcard and decided that was not a question that needed to be answered right now, if ever. While the postcard was from my mother, I'd never received anything from my father, not even a goodbye. And since he was Goldy's son, and had left without a word, we didn't talk about that.

"Darling, please tell me you'll help." Goldy turned back to me with pleading in her blue eyes. Apparently, I had kept my voice low enough that she hadn't heard a word I'd said to her former friend and fake boyfriend. But I was immediately reminded of all the things she'd done for us, the way she'd put her life on hold, and had taken us in whenever my father had left and my mother decided she needed a week away. Goldy might be a pain sometimes, but ultimately she was the one who had taken care of me and saved me on many occasions. Telling her no was probably something I couldn't actually do. Damn!

"Look, I can't make any promises, and I didn't make any to Ray, but I also can't know for sure that I can help in any way. I might just be stepping on toes. This really could have just been an accident, but we're so trained right now to think every dead body is a mystery that needs to be solved. They aren't all murders, and I can only do so much."

"Of course, my darling." Goldy stroked the side of my face. "I'm not asking you to put yourself in any danger or even in harm's way. Just help out a little here and there. And keep me updated."

Yeah, that was never how things worked, with or without a dead body.

Ray came over at that point and put an end to my having to come up with an excuse or make that promise I wasn't sure I'd be able to keep, no matter how curious I was. I'd thank him later.

"Okay, so we're going to have to shut this whole thing down, Mr. Milner. We have to treat this as a crime scene until we can determine what exactly happened. So no movie tomorrow night."

"No movie? But this is my life's work." For once, Darren truly looked devastated, and it set me back. How could he want the show to go on when his beloved had just plunged to his death? Part of me was trying to believe that he just wanted as much to stay normal as possible so that he wouldn't have to face the loss, but the other part of me was very suspicious.

"It'll have to wait. No movie until I can find out exactly what happened. If you'd like to tell me how the victim fell from that distance and didn't even yell, then I'm ready to listen to it." Ray had his hand braced loosely on his holster with a grim expression on his face.

"I don't know," Darren responded. "I was down talking with Goldy when it happened. I didn't see anything but a burst of ribbons and bows when he hit the floor."

Hadn't Goldy been looking for him? Not standing right next to him? I'd clarify that with her later, since I didn't want to start my own interrogation in front of Ray.

"Well, we're going to need you to come to the station to make a more formal statement than the other people here. If you could come with me, I'd appreciate it." Ray gestured toward the lobby, but Darren didn't move.

"I really don't think that's a good idea, Captain Ray. I think it might be better if we take him to our house and give him a little time to get himself together." Goldy placed her hand on Darren's forearm, her cool stare daring Ray to contradict her.

"You mean the time to get his story straight." I thought I had said that under my breath, but apparently I did not make it soft enough and those words escaped the big old bundle of things behind my teeth. Oops.

Ray, Goldy, and Darren looked at me as one, all with different expressions on their faces. There was disgust from Goldy, which I was very much not used to seeing, resignation from Darren, which made me feel bad, and a cocked eyebrow from Ray, which could have really meant anything.

"Sorry. I don't really mean that. I'm sure Darren had nothing to do with it and that it was just an accidental fall." But try as I might to backpedal, no one was taking me seriously, and to use a phrase from those historical novels I liked so much—I was given the cut direct.

Chapter 5

Felix came to my rescue and pulled me away from the extremely awkward exchange where no one was reacting to either my words or my apologies. I hadn't really thought they would forgive me for my gaffe, but I hadn't expected Goldy to turn her back on me either. She held Darren's hand while murmuring that everything was going to be okay.

I caught Elsie's eye on the way out of the door and she smirked. I wasn't sure what that was for, but I wasn't sticking around to find out. And if Ray wasn't going to stop me from leaving, then I was going to take that as permission and hightail it out into the early-evening breeze, which was far better than the tension and the irritation of the lobby.

"Thanks," I said, giving Felix's hand a squeeze as we went out to the street and found my golf cart. If I had been on the mainland, I probably would have jumped into a car, turned the music up on high, and only stopped driving when I ran out of gas. As I was here in Avalon, I could maybe do a couple of miles and then I'd end up exactly where I currently was and no amount of music would take away the crater in my gut.

"I'm not going to say it was my pleasure to save you since I hate that you had to be saved at all, but what's going on? Goldy looked pissed."

"So you weren't the only one to notice that." I shrugged and wished I could go back to this afternoon, when Felix and I were snorkeling and my biggest worry was a broken crate in the cave and an octopus that seemed a little too familiar with people.

"I think everyone was paying avid attention to anyone standing around with the guy who might be the number one suspect. Not to mention they were also trying to keep an eye on the captain as well as Goldy and that Elsie woman. Sorry I didn't get to you sooner. I was being interviewed."

I didn't stick around to be interviewed by Ray, but then again I hadn't seen anything that I hadn't already told him about.

"Don't apologize. I'm the one who stuck my foot in my mouth. Although I really do not understand what Goldy's obsession with this guy is. She hasn't seen him in decades and then he comes in like a golden eagle and she just can't seem to stay away from him." I sighed. "And she wanted me to look into how he could possibly not be the suspect, but I'm not so sure she's going to ask me to do anything with that at this point. Which might be better for me in the long run with the police anyway." I dropped my chin to my chest and took another long breath. I knew that at some point I would stop feeling that I'd let Goldy down, especially since I hadn't, but right now wasn't that moment.

"I heard that Jazzy Do Dah is playing over at the country club if you want me to sneak you in. Maybe a darkened bar with no one you really interact with there might be just the thing for you."

That sounded like heaven. But at this point I didn't know if I could handle any more lying, and getting caught at a country club I didn't belong to was not something to mess with.

"I don't want to get into trouble."

"Since when?"

That surprised a little laugh out of me and made me feel much better. It was something Felix was very good at, and I was very lucky to have him.

"Come on. We can get you a Shirley Temple. They make them for real over there. I'll make sure it's okay that you're there just in case. That way they won't throw you out and you don't have to worry about being caught."

Again, it sounded divine, but what if Goldy wanted to talk to me? And shouldn't I be waiting for Maribel to call or let Pops know that something had happened?

But all the people I felt beholden to were also adults and they could deal on their own this time.

"Fine. Let's go, and maybe I can clear my head." No, it wasn't a car with the music turned up high, where I could sing at the top of my lungs, but being with Felix and getting lost in a dark room with music might have just been the thing I needed.

The interior of the club was not nearly as dark as I would have wanted it to be. Felix cleared us at the door. He did some diving instruction for the people who stayed here, so technically he was an employee. That made me feel a little better. The last thing I wanted to do was see Ray again, and for something I had actually done wrong, instead of accidentally being at the wrong place at the wrong time, as per my usual.

I sat and massaged my head for a moment. When I looked up, Felix was on his way from the bar with a Shirley Temple. It was a drink my grandmother used to make me when I was younger so I'd feel like a grown-up while everyone else drank wine. It remained one of my favorites to this day.

Felix placed the drink on a napkin on the table in front of me and then sat down with his soda. The band on the stage was just warming up, which meant there was still time to talk for a few minutes before I could really get lost.

I turned the drink around in front of me on the napkin a few times, then picked it up and made a bunch of wet circles on the napkin.

"Is it really that bad?" Felix tipped my chin up with the palm of his hand and looked into my eyes with a furrowed brow.

"I don't know. I'm used to Goldy and me butting heads over things, especially when it comes to Dame of the Sea. She has to be brought back down to reality every once in a while and we've had disagreements about stock before or how badly Nick is behaving, but this is the first time I feel an absolute divide. Why is she so sure Darren is innocent? She hasn't seen or talked to him in decades. Plus, Pops is not a fan, and I can see why."

Or was I being too harsh on him because I felt he somehow threatened my relationship with Goldy? That seemed weird, but it did ring a little bell in my head. I would have to think about that some more later. But the band was starting with their intro, and I didn't want to be rude.

I sat back with my straw up to my lips and let the music take me away. It was a mix of old-school jazz with an island feel, and it was beautiful. So full and round with pieces of staccato in there and a beat that had my toes tapping, even though the rest of me felt like crap. I closed my eyes and Felix kissed me on the forehead.

I spent a few minutes processing what had happened: the way I'd been caught in the curtain and certain I wouldn't be able to get out, the way that yet again someone had died on the island under mysterious circumstances, and the way Goldy was treating me.

I let that last one go, because it made my insides tighten and my teeth clench.

The trio moved into another song and Felix reached for my hand and gave it a squeeze. I opened my eyes to smile at him and thank him and found myself seated with the very man I had just been thinking might be guilty. Why was Darren holding my hand, and where was Felix?

"He went to the bar for something for Goldy. Sorry for scaring you. You just looked so troubled, and it's natural for me to want to reach out and help."

I didn't exactly snatch my hand back, but it was a close thing. He let go when I tugged briefly against his hold, and I was thankful for that.

"Is there a reason you don't like me, or is it just that your grandmother does?"

"I don't not like you." My college English teacher would have fallen off her chair at that double negative, but there was nothing more I could say.

"If you're afraid I'm going to take her from you or something, then please know I would never do that. And I have the utmost respect for your grandfather. I knew him when he was younger. If anyone was good enough for Goldy, it was him."

I was not going to tell him what my grandfather's opinion of him was.

"I know you and Goldy were close."

He sat back in his chair with his hands steepled under his chin. "Close doesn't begin to cover it. Your grandmother saved my life and my sanity until I could get off the island and away from my family. I have barely talked to my parents in all the years I've been gone, and I'm only here for the funeral because I wanted to make sure my father didn't need to go into a home with my mother gone. It's hard to tell that kind of thing over the phone, and the man has no idea how to use any kind of face-to-face computer or phone program, so I didn't have much choice. And, in not having much choice, I also decided it would be a positive move to bring the premiere with me to shift from sadness to hopeful, bringing joy with me during this difficult time."

"Pops isn't much on the computer either." I circled my

drink again and kept my eyes on the swirls of grenadine and the clinking ice cubes.

"So I've heard. And while Goldy might be a bigger user of tech than he is, she's still not going to start calling me every day or checking in with me. She and I only talk when we're near each other. It was as if no time had passed when I saw her. I appreciate that, after what I've lived through over the last several decades, and I assume it will be like that every time I see her. Is there something inherently wrong with that?"

Not quite the segue I'd been looking for to move into why he looked like the death of his lover wasn't bothering him at all, but I was going to take it anyway. I'd seen cold people before, and even stoic ones, but this was a whole other level of suppressing. "I don't think there's anything wrong with that, but I'm surprised that with how you seem to feel so deeply for Goldy, you don't seem to feel anything about losing Jericho. Had you and Jericho just started dating?"

His sigh lasted for several seconds and ended with a groan. "Actually, yes, and I can tell you think I'm not being emotional enough. That's why I asked your grandmother if she'd bring me over to talk to you and occupy Felix while we did." He put his hand over his eyes and then pinched the bridge of his nose. "Jericho and I were together for the last several weeks. We'd gone on our first date and were together as much as possible after that. I thought maybe things were going well, but relationships haven't worked out for me over the years, so I'm always overly cautious. I'm sure you're too young to completely understand how devastating life can be when you're the one left behind." He laughed derisively, and I laughed too but topped it with a big handful of sarcasm.

"You must not have talked to Goldy much about anything other than your old days together, then, because, believe me, I know all about being left behind. And Goldy was my rock. Pops too. So when I think someone might be coming in to make waves in that relationship, I can absolutely guarantee you I'm going to protect my territory like a dragon with a hoard of coins."

"Fair enough," he said after a moment in which he just looked at me. "Here's the thing. Jericho was someone I was really hoping to get to know better and have a relationship with, but we hadn't yet had a chance to get particularly close. He traveled for business often, and we were only dating. I'm sad he's gone. I really hope it was just an accident so he wouldn't have realized what was happening before he was gone. It breaks my heart that a human life has been snuffed out, especially one I liked so much, but I learned a long time ago that grief has a different path for everyone. So just because I'm not crying into my handkerchief doesn't mean I'm not devastated."

"Fair enough," I parroted back to him. "So did you talk to Ray?"

"The captain? Yes, he, of course, thinks I did it. First, because no one else knows Jericho on the island, so why would it be anyone else? And second, because someone in the theater realized they hadn't heard Jericho scream on his way down from the drop. They're waiting for confirmation that he was either already dead before he fell or if maybe he was so surprised that he froze and couldn't call out. I don't know, and I won't know until the captain decides to share that with me. But in the meantime, I have to stay here until they figure out what actually happened. Are you going to be okay with me being near your grandmother?"

Was he asking for permission? What if I said no? Would he just jump ship and not see her ever again? And how would I explain to Goldy that it was my fault he was giving her the cold shoulder?

"Look, I don't have a problem with you specifically, but you seem to bring some serious trouble with you, and I just don't want her to get hurt."

"I promise you I won't hurt her. But I really do need a friend right now, and she's the closest thing I've had to a friend in too many years."

I smiled at him, and of course that was right when Goldy walked up.

"Oh, good, I'm so glad you two are getting along now. Whit, Darren is going to need our help and by 'our,' I mean you and your crew's help. I cornered the bartender because you know how he seems to know things he shouldn't, and he said they're looking into Jericho's death as a murder, after all, and since no one on-island knew him, they're going to keep a very close eye on Darren. So we need to come up with a plan ahead of time on how you're going to prove it definitely wasn't him. I'll help, but only from behind the scenes, because I don't want anyone to think I'm interfering."

"But it's okay for me to interfere?" It was pointless to sigh so I didn't.

"It always is, my darling, that's why we're counting on you."

Chapter 6

Great, so now I had to defend someone who I wasn't entirely sure hadn't done the deed, *and* I had to come up with an actual plan for how to do it. I never came up with plans. My two previous forays into being an amateur sleuth had been an on-the-fly kind of thing. Something where I had happened to hear some information and was able to put it together in my mind in a way that made sense, which then ultimately caught the culprit. But there had been no plan, not really, besides surviving the turmoil, and even that had been sketchy.

But Goldy looked so hopeful and determined that I had a feeling I wasn't going to get out of this no matter how I tried or what I said. So, a plan. I would totally need my crew, as Goldy put it, on this. And it wasn't going to be easy, especially when I didn't know if I believed Darren was innocent.

"A plan? Any ideas? I guess I'll need to know more about Jericho, like where did he come from? Did he have any enemies? What did he do for a living?"

People started coming into the bar in trickles and then in droves. It was mainly people who lived on the island, and they clustered in groups around us. No one talked directly to us but you could tell they were talking about us, since they were whispering and kept shooting our table little covert glances.

I was tired already.

"I think we might want to move this somewhere else," Goldy said, rising from the table and grabbing her sheer cardigan. She caught the bartender's eye, and he went to the register to ring up our bill. I wasn't sure who was going to pay for this, but she looked at Darren as she walked out of the bar in her four-inch heels. When had she put those back on? Last I remembered, she was wearing the sneakers I'd brought to her. Then again, Goldy would rarely go out in public without being dressed and shoed to the nines, so I wasn't sure why I was surprised that she could have changed her footwear before going into the bar.

Darren and I watched her exit. I locked eyes with him as he patted the sides of his jacket, then reached into his back pocket and pulled nothing out. He gave me a sheepish smile before walking out behind her. I could have sworn that look over Goldy's shoulder had been a signal for him to pay the bill, but apparently not. No, instead I guessed I was waiting for the bill myself.

I took out my small stash of bills and a credit card I kept for emergencies and handed it over to Todd, the bartender. I couldn't be the last person to walk out of the bar without paying, as there was no one else who was going to pick up the tab. Nice, and I was no more enamored with Darren than I had been when I'd first met him.

After I got my credit card back, I walked out into the dark night. I took a second right outside the door to close my eyes while taking in a deep breath and releasing it. I did not want to tangle with Captain Ray, nor did I want to drag Maribel into it, as she was trying to finish up her degree. And Felix was trying to build his scuba-diving business and pull in customers. Although maybe he would get more customers who were curious about the murder. And then he could learn something as they were asking questions about the investigation. It had happened to me before at my shop, the Dame of the Sea, so it could happen for him.

Blowing out a breath, I walked around the corner, hoping they had at least waited for me outside the bar so I knew where we were going to talk about all these things I needed to know.

I didn't have a notebook with me. And I was pretty sure I wasn't going to remember everything Darren had told me about his former partner, so I grabbed my phone out of my back pocket, took the little stylus out, and got ready to make some electronic notes as best I could.

At first, I didn't see them. I walked around the whole front of the bar and then peeked into the alleyway, but they were nowhere to be found.

My phone dinged in my hand, and sure enough it was a message from Goldy. *Meet at the Sea Bounder.* I really hoped Nick wasn't running a tour, though we needed them if I was going to continue to get stuck with the bills.

I decided to walk instead of taking the golf cart. While I enjoyed driving that thing, a little too much sometimes, it would be better to give myself some time to think about what I was doing and whether I really thought I could do it.

Yes, I'd solved a few murders before, and I'd done that with hard work and some luck. But both times I'd had an investment in what was going on and, more important, a true belief that the person the police were looking at was the wrong one. I liked justice. I felt better knowing the right person was behind bars and no longer out and about, able to cause chaos and wreak havoc on those around them for their own petty needs.

But this was different. This was a guy I wasn't sure I even liked, much less one I wanted to trust. This would take time away from my business, my friends, and my relationship, while I trolled all over the island looking for clues, inserting myself into conversations, and doing the due diligence it sometimes took to sort through all the information and come to the right conclusion.

Plus, before I hadn't trusted the last station commander, and rightly so. But Ray knew what he was doing, and as this was not someone from the island, and therefore not someone he knew, I wasn't concerned the investigation would be stalled just so he could save a friend or family member from gross mistakes.

With all this swirling in my poor head, I started off in the direction of the dock where our boat was kept. I let myself drift for a moment in the breeze coming off the water, listening to the call of the birds in the palm trees above me. I was in my favorite place and had been for almost a year now. And in that year a lot of things had changed, but for the most part they were good changes and I appreciated them.

I had Maribel, who was the best roommate ever most of the time. I had a boyfriend who got me and gave me my space when I needed it, just like I did for him. . . .

Crap, I just remembered I had left him in the bar. My first thought was to text him, but that felt wrong. I turned around and headed back to the bar, hoping he was there and hadn't noticed I'd totally forgotten about him in the midst of all this chaos.

I brought my forefinger to my mouth and went to bite my nail before I stopped myself. He wasn't going to be mad, and I had to get over myself. Marching back into the bar, I found him standing at our table, looking around.

"You forget me?" he said as I approached.

I could lie, but I wasn't going to do that to him. "Yep."

"I figured as much." He laughed and pulled me in for a hug.

"Don't look so sad, Whit. It's not a big deal, and I know you have a lot going on."

Resting my head against his chest, I listened to his heartbeat for a few seconds. "But I don't want to always have something more going on. I'm tired, Felix, and I want my life to be normal. Why is it always me?"

"I think partially because you're willing and able. And it will get back to normal. For Maribel and me, this *is* normal. Being a part of the police department on the island isn't always about murder, obviously, but there are issues and death pretty consistently. Maybe you're just getting a better glimpse into what we do so when you're not doing it, you can be the one we bitch to and you'll understand."

I snickered. "I'll look forward to that."

"I'm sure you will." He kissed my forehead and squeezed my hand. "Now, where to next? Since you left in a hurry and totally forgot I was here, I'm assuming we're off to some place for information?"

"Goldy and Darren are on the *Sea Bounder* as we speak. Hopefully Goldy isn't helping him make up some story to tell the cops."

"You really don't like him."

"It's less about like and more about trust. I don't trust him. Some things are just too convenient, and Pops is not a fan, which is always going to sway me."

"Then let's go dig up the truth." He kept my hand in his as he walked out of the bar. "I heard you paid for the tab. Thanks."

"Yeah, not of my own free will, but maybe we can address that on the boat too."

Stepping outside with Felix next to me, I glanced up ahead and found a trio of people in an intense conversation that looked like it was not going to have a good outcome. The dog with them appeared to be fine, but the three adults standing on the side of the walk absolutely radiated tension with hand gestures and raised voices.

Normally, if it were a set of vacationers, I would have assumed it had to do with not being able to decide where to eat, or what to do next, or maybe that some of them were done for the day and the others wanted to party long into the night.

But since it was Pops facing off against Darren and Goldy, I had a little more stake in it than just being able to tell them that the bar was open and the wings were hot tonight.

I quickened my pace, pulling Felix along behind me, not wanting to appear to be running but also not dragging my feet. Whatever was being said dropped back into hushed tones, but the frown on Pops's face and the fact that he was almost toe to toe with Goldy and Darren, who were standing next to each other and holding hands, put a little more urgency in my step.

"Can we not do this out here?" I asked as we approached.

Scuppers, the beagle Goldy had gotten for Pops last week, saw me first and started barking and jumping with just his front legs rising off the ground. He looked like one of the low-rider cars in Long Beach that used hydraulics to perform stunts. Although, this one looked more like a yappy dog than any kind of mechanical feat.

"Scuppers, quiet," I said, and he looked up at me. I crouched down to pet him and then took a moment to look up at the three stormy faces. Or two stormy faces and one that was entirely placid, as it had been nearly every other time I'd interacted with him. Was Darren one of those people who hid his emotions or did he just not have any?

Either way, I had to come to terms with the fact that I had been asked to prove someone else was guilty. I'd better get on board with that fast or I was in for a miserable time over the next few days.

"Whit, tell your grandmother this is not something you're going to do. I will not have you put yourself in danger for a man who is not at all what he seems." Pops held Scuppers's leash, and it was wrapped so tightly around his fist, his fingers were turning white.

Goldy harrumphed, yet it sounded a little like a muffled scream. "Do not call me grandmother. And you don't know what you're talking about. Darren would never hurt anyone, much less kill someone, old man. This is not the time for jealousy. I'm yours, have been for years, but Darren needs help and we can help him."

Well, this was worse than I had originally thought. I had always been very careful not to choose a favorite grandparent because I loved them both and did not want to seem like one was more important than the other. But this could be a deal breaker on that. Because I was totally on Pops's side, but I knew Goldy would be devastated if I backed out.

"How would you even know if he was a bad guy, husband of mine? You don't even know him, and you haven't seen him in almost as many years as me."

Pops stared right at her. "I have the internet, Goldy, and no rose-colored glasses. If you'd looked him up at all, you'd know he hasn't exactly been idle or even good for the last little while." Pops eyed Darren. "Isn't that true, Darren?"

For Darren's part, he readjusted his collar and then made a point of shaking out the leg of his pants. He went to pet Scuppers, and the little dog growled at him. I was a big believer in trusting dogs to tell you who was good and who was bad. Whiskers not so much, since she could be bribed by a good rub to the belly and completely won over with catnip, but dogs knew their stuff.

"You have an answer?" I asked.

Goldy jumped right in, patting Darren's arm while he stood

back up next to her. "He doesn't have to answer anything. I'm sure whatever you've found is completely taken out of context. You know how people like to do that just to gain clout."

"Clout? Really?" I said. What did this guy have on her that she refused to even think beyond what he'd been as a teenager? "You don't even know what people are saying and you're going to hang it out on the clout cloud?" I knew she had liked him back in the day and that they had had a special bond. With what he'd gone through, hiding in his own skin until he could get out into the world and be himself, Goldy was totally the kind of person who would have held a special place in her heart for him. But trying to blame it on attention seekers? That was taking it a little too far.

"I'm sure of it." She turned toward the object of her blind affection and patted his arm again. "I'm right, Darren. Aren't I? There are things people have said about you that aren't true, and they're only saying them to make themselves look better?"

That wasn't exactly clout in my definition, but I didn't correct her because I was waiting for his answer. . . .

We *all* stood there and waited for his answer. Which didn't come.

He sighed dramatically, checked his silver watch, then walked away and kept walking. Goldy called after him to come back, to no avail. And then she ran after him in those killer heels, and Pops didn't even move to make sure she wouldn't fall.

I stayed with my grandfather and Felix as we watched her leave and then I turned to Pops. "What did he do?"

"He's been in some trouble with the law over burglaries and misplacing funds that weren't his to begin with. He always gets off somehow, but there has to be some reason they keep looking at him. It can't all be false, even if some of it is that they're just looking for a reason to nail him to the floor."

"True," Felix said.

"We should probably call her and find out if she made it to the boat." I didn't want to do it, but I also didn't want to leave her out there when I needed the information Darren might be able to give me as long as he didn't lie.

"You should call her," Pops said, twisting the leash around his hand until his fingers turned whiter. He was going to lose one if he didn't stop that. "I don't think she's going to answer me for a while."

"Why did you keep tabs on him?" Felix asked, beating me to the punch.

I tugged the leash, and Pops let go. Scuppers kept his head down, sniffing at the ground, unaware of the change in leadership.

Then Pops shrugged. "I guess just in case he ever decided to come back and try to make a bid for my wife. Or maybe because anytime she talked about him I always felt like he could do no wrong. So I looked him up the first time after we had that handy-dandy thing called the internet—just out of curiosity—and saw he'd been arrested. I didn't tell her. I didn't think it would do anything but hurt her, and since he was out of our lives, there was no need. But then I'd search every few years just to keep to an eye on what he was doing and where he was doing it, and there always seemed to be some new case that he had just skated out on by the skin of his teeth. I kept those to myself too, but in the back of my mind I had a feeling someday he'd turn back up like a bad penny."

I gave him a hug and handed Scuppers's leash back to him. His fingers had returned to their normal color, so I thought it was safe. "We'll figure this out. I promise. Maybe not for Darren, and probably not for what Goldy is hoping for, but I'll figure it out just to make sure the right person gets caught and justice is served." I laughed derisively. "Maybe instead of a gift shop, I should start up my own private investigation firm. I don't know if I'd need a license on the island or if I'd have enough work to make the bills, but I seem to keep getting pulled into these things for one reason or another. Maybe it's time to get paid for all my hard work."

Pops kissed me on the head as I dialed Goldy and waited, hoping she might at least answer her phone. Felix stood to the side, keeping an eye out for any trouble.

I wasn't holding out too much hope that she'd want to talk to me, but then again, she would have to answer if she expected me to help.

Chapter 7

She didn't answer any of my three calls, but I was able to track her through her phone. We had put one of those tracking apps on all our phones just in case of some kind of emergency, like if we were hiking, or diving, or sailing, or flying, in Nick's case. While I had not necessarily wanted my grandmother to be able to find me at any given moment on a whim, I was thankful for it now. And it looked like I had been right—her little beacon showed they'd gone to the *Sea Bounder* after all.

Turning to Felix, I drew him aside, out of Pops's earshot. "Look, this might get a little dicey. I'm thinking that it might be less dicey if we have less people talking."

"I'm usually pretty quiet," he said, his eyebrow raised.

I huffed out a breath. "I know that, but I just think it might be easier if we're two on two when we arrive at the boat." I tried to make my eyes plead with him to get him to listen but I'd never really been good at that.

Fortunately, Felix knew me well enough to take the half-hearted plea and run with it, or at least promise to walk away.

"You'll call me when you have any new information and you won't go running off to solve this all by yourself without backup."

It wasn't a question but I answered anyway. "Yes, I promise. No running off into the hills by myself."

"Fine. Keep your wits about you, Whit."

That had me rolling my eyes, but I did stop long enough to appreciate the back view of him as he strolled up the street and disappeared around the corner. Now to tackle the issue of Pops.

"Felix is going to let us handle this with just us so it will be less awkward." I reached down to pet Scuppers, since Pops hadn't even raised his gaze. He was avoiding me and I understood that, but it couldn't go on forever. We had to get to the bottom of all this.

"Whitney, while I love you and your optimism most times, there is no way this isn't going to be awkward and irritating, and quite possibly maddening. But you did pick a good one who knows when to fold and leave the table. I wish I could do the same."

Oh, I knew that feeling all too well.

But Pops did reluctantly come with me. It pained me to see him and Goldy in a disagreement. And, depending on how long this whole thing could take, I did not want it to go on forever or have consequences that I could have helped mitigate.

Goldy might not be happy to see him at the moment, but they did live together in a house that wasn't that big. And I had no room for one of them to have a snit at my house and sleep on the couch. Nick didn't either. So it was make-up-and-find-common-ground time.

The *Sea Bounder* was exactly where we'd left it for the day, tied up to the dock with a thick rope and gently moving with the waves from the other boats that were out cruising as the sun set. I loved the fact that this boat was here and had been here in some form for years and years, according to my family history. Back in the day, we'd been some of the first people to realize that just catching fish might not be enough to keep a roof over our heads. My ancestors had noted how much people enjoyed the thought of seeing what lived in the depths of the bay and had decided to modify their boats to put glass in the bottom for tours.

It had taken off for the most part in the beginning. There were some harrowing stories about glitches in the original boats, but after all that we'd been able to bring more commerce to the island and could stay where our hearts were happiest.

Out of everyone in my family, I was the only one who had really left and then come back when I realized that mainland life was not exactly what I had hoped for. Nick had never left, and neither had Goldy or Pops. And while both of my parents had left, they'd never come back, so they didn't really count.

Now was not the time to be thinking about the two people who had walked out of my life without a backward glance. I had other things to worry about. They didn't deserve space in my head while I tried to figure out if Darren had done the dirty deed of throwing Jericho over the railing, if it had truly been an accident, or if there was someone else out there who thought they'd gotten away with it.

"Permission to come aboard?" I called out, hoping Goldy would laugh like she did whenever she asked and I told her absolutely.

But there was dead silence, and it felt heavy in the salty air. Pops gripped my shoulder and gave it a squeeze.

"If you don't want to come in, you don't have to," I said to him, dreading that he might take me up on my offer.

"I think it might help to be in the boat to keep things on an even keel."

I smiled at Pops's nautical terminology and figured that was probably going to be my last smile in the near future.

We looked at each other and shrugged, a whole conversation communicated in that one gesture. I was the first to step foot onto the back deck of the forty-eight-foot boat, and I didn't wait for an invitation to open the sliding glass door or make my way inside the cabin. Pops was close behind. Scuppers pulled up the rear.

I found Goldy pacing back and forth, grumbling under her breath. Darren sat on one of the cushioned benches with his feet sprawled out and his legs spread wide with his head tipped back against the top of the cushion. His eyes were closed and his mouth was set in a very angry frown. No one appeared to be happy. That might be the first thing I had to wade through, but it certainly wouldn't be the last.

"Welcome aboard the *Sea Bounder*, Darren," I said to get their attention. "I'm not sure if we'll catch sight of anything through the glass, but since that's not what we're here for, then I think we can just get down to business."

He kept his head back but he did open his eyes and roll his head to the right to be able to see me.

"I don't know what business you want from me, but as I told your grand . . . Goldy, I am not going to cause a rift in the relationship with her husband, or the local businesses, or with you. So you're off the hook. I'll just stay in my father's house until they come to drag me down to the station. I can't handle much more at this point."

His face crumpled and tears leaked out of his eyes. Grabbing a tissue from the box next to him, he pressed it to his nose and mouth before staring back at the ceiling. He blew out a breath and then closed his eyes again.

My gaze darted to Goldy, and her expression was the one she used to get if someone was hurting and she was about to go after the person who'd thrown the first punch. I was never bullied when I went to school simply because they were too scared of what might happen if Goldy found out and came after them. For a small and thin woman, her presence certainly packed a wallop. You did not mess with her when her mind was set on something. Which was why I was totally not surprised when the next words came out of her mouth.

"Darren, I do not give a scurvy-filled rat's ass what you think is going to happen, but I'll be damned to Davy Jones's locker before I let a friend of mine fight something like this all on his own. If you say you didn't do it, then you didn't do it, no matter what's in your past." She cut her eyes to Pops, then looked away with her lips pressed together. "I don't care what has happened up to this point. If you need help, and if we need to find out what happened to Jericho so you are not wrongly accused, then I'm here for it, even if no one else is."

Oh, man, so she offered a challenge, another challenge, a shaming, a withering look, and a promise all in a few sentences. Didn't I say the lady was a force to be reckoned with? She could have been one of those witches standing at the cauldron in *Macbeth*, daring anyone to come up against her.

Instead, she was one very determined woman who was not going to rest until she saw justice done.

Apparently I had come by it honestly and hadn't rolled too far from the tree.

"We get it, Goldy, and I'm sure Pops and Felix will help too if there is anything I need them to do. And I appreciate your utter faith in your friend. But I do have some questions, and I do need some answers. He's the only one who can tell me certain things. I usually don't mind looking stuff up in the archives or the library, but this is someone who I don't know and who has never lived on the island. I'm going to be stumbling around in the dark and Darren might just have the flashlight I need. Do you understand?"

She harrumphed, but Darren raised his head from the back of the bench, straightened his shirt, ran a shaking hand through his hair, and nodded. "That's more than I can ask from anyone. I'd appreciate anything you could do. Thomas, I will try my hardest to not make too much trouble for your family, and then I promise to get out of your hair for good. It's the least I can do for the way you've taken care of a very special woman all her life in a way I never could have."

That little speech was all fine and well, but now came the hard part. When I'd asked Darren questions before, he'd not only been reluctant to answer, he walked away. So would this time be the same, or was he really going to try to be forthcoming with some actual information?

I certainly hoped so.

"Okay, so if you can give me anything you might know about enemies or any ties Jericho might have to the island. Did he say he knew this area? Had he been here before?"

Darren looked weary. The poor guy had been through a lot today. I reeled at the fact that just this morning I was complaining about wearing pantyhose as I got ready to go to his mother's funeral and only hours later we had another death, a possible arrest coming, and a villain on the island.

Or did we? I wasn't completely giving up on the idea that this could have been an accident, but I couldn't get the fact out of my head that the man hadn't screamed at all on his way down.

I made a mental note to see what Maribel knew. Since she worked the front desk at the station, she usually had at least the local gossip from the deputies. I wouldn't ask her to put her job in jeopardy by giving me confidential information, but even if she had something to add to the mix, I'd be grateful. Same went for Felix, though he was less privy to insider information unless it had to do with diving. But he was here and we could talk later about any sources he could tap.

Since we were on the boat, I knew I had a pad of paper in here along with one of my favorite pens . . . as long as Nick hadn't stolen it. Again.

I found both things in the port-side drawer up front and took a seat next to Darren for when he started talking.

Which he still wasn't doing. But I wasn't leaving until he did, and he wasn't going anywhere with Goldy blocking his only exit by standing with her arms crossed and a scowl on her face. I couldn't tell if it was for me or Darren or Pops, and I certainly wasn't going to ask.

"I haven't known Jericho very long." Darren paused and shook his head. "I haven't known him long at all, a little over a month, actually. When we met through a dating app, I was cautious and a little skeptical that this man, who was so perfect for me, had just been hanging out waiting for me to come along and swipe right."

I wrote *dating app* on my notepad, confirmed in my head that his words fit with what he'd told me earlier about their dating history, and then continued to wait for anything more.

He wasn't forthcoming, again. I highly doubted that was all he had to offer, so I asked, "And did you look him up on the internet after you swiped right and were connected?" I wasn't a huge fan of any kind of app for dating due to horror stories that weren't hard to find even if they were hard to fathom. I still preferred face-to-face meetings or being set up by friends. Not that I needed that at the moment, with Felix around. But I had friends who were heart-deep in this dating scene, so I knew at least some of the normal things people did when they connected online without seeing each other in person first.

He shook his head. "I didn't, despite knowing better. I think there was a part of me that didn't want anything about him to be wrong, so I was willing to risk going in unknown and letting whatever I found out unfold from him."

I made another note to check in on Jericho through the internet and then grappled with the fact that on one hand it would be good to find out he was not a good person. If he had a ton of enemies that could go on my list of possible suspects, that would be very helpful, versus wanting him to be a good guy for Darren, even if Darren seemed to always be the one getting in and out of trouble.

"So then we have the long-lost betrothal. Elsie is an obvious suspect, but I don't know if she'd have it in her to kill Jericho to get what she wants. She seems to just wait for it to happen, then take advantage of the situation."

He shook his head. "I agree with that. She seems a little off her stride but not to the point of killing. At least from what I can tell. But if it's her or me, I'd believe it was her first."

That made sense and I wrote that down, too. And then I dived into the elephant in the room.

"You're probably not going to like this question, but could someone have a vendetta against you and killed him to hurt you, or send you a message?" It was a pointed question and one that definitely had Goldy turning her head to stare and scowl directly at me.

But there was nothing I could do differently. And I had to have information if I was going to be at all effective in figuring out what happened. Goldy could be happy or nasty about that either way, but it didn't change the fact that I had to know.

"This wasn't my plan on how I'd reunite with my friend." Darren rose from his spot on the bench and headed toward the exit. Goldy remained where she was, blocking him, and after a moment, he seemed to get the hint because he turned the trying to walk out into a sharp turn and pacing in the small space left to him.

He took several trips back and forth between Goldy and the bow, but she wasn't moving, and he wasn't talking. He checked his watch as he always seemed to do when he didn't want to answer something.

"You should have one of those step trackers," I said cheekily. "You'd be at about ten thousand steps at this point."

As a tension breaker, it wasn't my best work, but he did stop for a moment and chuckled. "Actually that's exactly what it does. And with all the stress and walking and more stress, I should be about ten pounds lighter when I finally get away from here."

I didn't smile and no one said anything else while we waited for him to start answering our questions or offering us information. He got one icebreaker. I gave it to him, now he had to pony up and talk.

"Okay, look." He ran his hand through his hair again and it stood up on end this time. "I have secrets that have to do with the articles and issues you seem to have looked up at some point." He turned to Pops. They squinted at each other, then Darren looked away first.

Pops was not one to confirm or deny if it wasn't absolutely necessary, so it didn't surprise me that he'd wait Darren out.

Darren caved first. "I need help."

"Of course you do, but I want to make sure you're going to be honest with us. You need to help prove your innocence, and not snow the whole town and get away with murder."

Go, Pops!

"I—"

But he wasn't done. "I'm warning you now. If you do anything to hurt Goldy, or if your lies get her into any kind of trouble, I'd just like to remind you that I have quite the ability to find very hidden places that few know about on this little island, and absolutely no qualms about burying you out there."

Okay, then. Pops was not kidding, and I really hoped Darren was going to take him at his word.

"I remember your maps. I have one from a really long time ago. I'm perfectly aware you could probably even use this boat to take me out into the deeper waters, drop me, and make sure no one ever found me again. I understand, and I agree to your terms."

"You could cut the tension in this room with one of those daggers that we started stocking for swashbuckling children at the Dame of the Sea." Goldy slapped her hands on her hips and blew out what could have been a raspberry but was far more disgusted than funny or even cheeky. "Darren, did you kill Jericho?"

"No, I did not." He stated it emphatically and quickly but not too quickly, as if he were in denial or lying. He also kept eye contact the whole time and he sounded wearier than he did defensive or as if he were trying to deflect.

"Thomas, can you unbend enough to consider the fact that there is a possibility Darren did not do this, and it would be a lot easier if we could help him instead of constantly fighting him over a past that might or might not be true?"

Pops chewed on his lip and looked off to the side. Goldy for once was not steaming due to his taking too long. I took a second to glance at Darren. His brow was wrinkled and his arms were crossed tight over his chest.

There was something here. It was far more than a matter of how long ago these two had known each other and the fact that at one time Goldy had probably thought herself in love with and definitely found herself protective of Darren when he was on her island and in trouble.

The problem might be finding out if she could set it aside if the truth wasn't what she wanted it to be.

Chapter 8

I didn't look anyone in the eye as Pops's silence lengthened. While I had said that I was proud of Goldy for not giving in the first time to some kind of tantrum, I could see, from the way she shifted from foot to foot and would not look anywhere but at Pops, that his time was coming to an end. He would either have to acquiesce and help or he might be sleeping on my couch. My tiny couch that Whiskers had staked out as her own. My tiny couch where Maribel liked to take naps before going in for her second shift.

That tiny couch that I didn't want anyone who didn't live with me to sleep on.

Finally, he cleared his throat. "Fine. I can accept there's a possibility that what I found on the internet might be untrue, or some kind of bid for attention because of something you did long ago. Maybe something you shouldn't have to keep paying for when you might have been young and dumb."

Goldy exhaled and smiled at her husband.

Something silent passed between them again, and I was both encouraged that there seemed to be a small truce going on and yet terrified that a small misstep would be the first shot in a war no one would win.

"Okay, so now that we have that all sorted out, let's move on to facts. . . ."

"Maribel, I swear to you it was like the war to end all wars between two older men, and I just couldn't even figure out who to handle first, or even what to say to make it stop. I felt like I was in an oven and Goldy was turning the temperature up with every look." I shoved another handful of the best popcorn ever in my mouth and chewed. Maribel had the night off, which I hadn't realized, and I was grateful to have someone to talk to. I'd called Felix over right after leaving the older trio, but as soon as he had gotten here, he'd been called in for some boating accident involving someone dropping anchor out beyond the bay without permission or a permit. They were called "anchors out" and it was not only frowned upon, it was illegal. And now someone had had an accident, so Felix had left before we were done. I completely understood and was even a little envious that he could come and go out of this in a way I wouldn't be able to until it was solved.

Maribel wandered over to the couch and sank onto the cushions. I hadn't yet heard anything from Pops about needing to stay with me. I had hoped his bending to help Darren had been enough for Goldy.

"So, I'm not sure what I'm supposed to do here. I have very little information and almost no idea on who might have done this, why, or even if something had been done besides a misstep and fall from twenty feet."

Maribel laid her head back on the top of the couch, and it reminded me of the position Darren was lying in when he'd been on the *Sea Bounder*.

"Tired?" I asked, not wanting to keep her up if she was exhausted or in need of rest. This wasn't something I wanted to add to her plate, which was already stacked high like for someone who did not understand the beauty of spreading out the nacho chips for max toppings.

"No, just doing some thinking. One of my classes is all about pulling information and ways to lay it out to see where the connections are."

"Like a murder board?"

She raised her head and gave me a smile. "Exactly. And we could at least see about how any and all the things you do know fit on the board. I know you favor that little notebook of yours, and I like the computer, but this might be somewhere we can meet in between."

"I don't want you to risk your job."

"Meh, I'm not risking anything. If it goes right, it could even get me the job I really want."

My heart sank because I knew the job she was talking about probably wasn't here on this tiny island with approximately three thousand permanent residents. How could it be?

I left it alone. If she wanted to share, then I was willing to listen, but I wasn't going to willingly put myself into a position to hear that sooner rather than later she'd be moving out and moving on . . . without me.

"So where do we start? I'm not a huge fan of ordering a big whiteboard, considering we'd have to pay quite a bit to get it shipped here. Not to mention, it could take a lot longer than we have."

"We don't need to order anything. We can just use the wall next to the TV, and when we have an idea, we put it up and get them in order eventually."

I wasn't sure how I felt about having a constant reminder that I hadn't yet figured out who'd done it. But other than that wall, we had mostly windows. Another option would be to put it in one of our bedrooms. I was less into that than seeing it when I sat down on the couch.

"I could work with that."

"So what do you know?"

I took out that little piece of paper I'd used on the boat to write down some of the specifics and read it out like a list. "Darren and Jericho had been dating for several months. They met on a dating app. Darren doesn't believe in looking people up on the internet. He prefers to wait for someone to tell him something about themselves instead of knowing it already. He said that would make him feel like a stalker. And since he had a stalker who now happens to be on the island with him, he felt it was better not to make anyone feel like he'd felt."

"He has a stalker?" She sat up fully on the couch and tapped her finger on her chin. "Like a real 'if I can't have you, no one can' kind of stalker?"

"Not quite to that extent. At least I don't think so." I explained about the betrothal, and Maribel had the same reaction I'd had.

"They still do that? I thought that went out with whalebone corsets and dance cards."

"Apparently not. I guess it was a custom in the family, and there was some negotiating that Darren was not in line with. So he asked Goldy to be his girlfriend to save him until he could get off the island. Elsie didn't take it well and appears to have been waiting for the last few decades to make her triumphant return. She ran into Therese Milner's coffin in her haste to get to Darren at the funeral. Then she hightailed it to the scene of Jericho's death to say it was probably a good thing he fell and died so that she and Darren could be together without any issues." Spelling it out like that gave me pause. Why didn't I think she would go to any lengths to make her dreams come true?

"And we don't think it's possible this castaway betrothed killed Jericho to get her hands on Darren now that his mom is dead? This woman sounds unhinged. Running into a casket to grab the attention of some guy who left years ago without her and then sounding off about it right after someone died being good for her plans seems to be right in line with someone who would make that murder happen just to get what she wanted." Curled up on the couch with her popcorn bowl, she reminded me of the hoarding dragon I'd threatened Darren with at the bar.

"I don't know. I mean, that seems a little over the top, don't you think? To have to kill someone's boyfriend to get them to like you? Unless she truly is delusional and has just been waiting for his mom to die?" But that seemed bizarre too.

"Whit, I love you, but everything she's publicly done so far is the very definition of being over the top. I doubt murder would be too far-fetched for her to get what she thinks she deserved and never got."

"But all that time . . ." I trailed off because I wasn't sure how to say what I was thinking.

"It's been, what, like fifty years?" Maribel set aside her empty popcorn bowl and pulled Whiskers into her lap. She ran her hand over and over my cat's back. Whiskers rarely liked me to do that, but she was different with Maribel sometimes, or maybe it was the tension in the room and the uncertainty that made her want to be touched. Who knew?

"Fifty years, yes, but maybe we need to look more fully into her. Had she been alone these fifty years, or did something happen recently that made her think now was the time? How did she hear about Therese's death? And how did she get here so fast? She doesn't live here, so she must have taken a boat from the mainland or flown in recently. Does she believe in divine timing? I've been hearing a lot about that recently from the podcasts I listen to at the shop. If she had made peace with things years ago, but then something happened recently to make her think the divine timing was kicking in and she couldn't miss out on this chance, then there's every possibility she thinks she's being led to this. Maybe?"

It all felt so convoluted. I needed to remember the first thing was simply to find out who could have done it. Motive and reasoning and any other details could come in that search, but I had to start somewhere. Now I just needed to find out who had the most to gain or lose with Jericho dead and then go from there.

"This might be one of those things where you appear to work on it but not really do anything. Keep Goldy happy but let the police do their work. Things have been a lot better since Ray took over. He's not one to let something like this go, even if he could pin it on Darren and move on."

"I'm with you on that, but Goldy's not much for being lied to. I couldn't even sneak out when I was younger without always getting caught. It's like she has a nose for these things."

"Then why isn't she the one working on this? He's her friend, she has more at stake and more resources than you do, plus a better understanding of the history. It might come down to some detail you don't know enough to ask about."

I sank my forehead onto my hand and took a deep breath. "Believe me. I know and have thought of all these things. I've even said them to Goldy, but she thinks I'll have a better chance of getting involved. Supposedly, I won't lose my standing in the community like she thinks she would."

"That's awfully nice of her to leave you out there hanging on your own. I love your grandmother as if she were my own, but she is really expecting a lot from you."

"Yeah, you don't have to tell me twice. But I guess since I've proved myself before to get those crumbs of info from people without having to do much more than listen and piece it together, she's counting on me."

And since when had I gone from being a shopkeeper and boat runner to an amateur sleuth? Admittedly, it was fun in some aspects, as long as no one was trying to shove me down a ravine, but this one felt bigger for some reason.

"I guess they're shutting down the viewing of this movie until things are sorted out. Darren said he had really wanted to honor Jericho by showing it, but his lips kind of twisted when he said it. Almost as if he was choking the right words out instead of the ones he really wanted to say." And, boy, did I understand that, after holding most of my feelings and words back today.

"We'll have to ask if we can see the movie and find out if there are any pieces that make more sense with some background information." Whiskers jumped off Maribel's lap as my friend rose from the couch.

"That's a great idea. I'll start on that tonight and do some searches. I don't know if I'll come up with anything, but knowing the main players can't be a bad thing."

"Exactly. And now I'm heading to bed for the night. Let me know if there's anything I can do to help. I'll try my best to do what I can."

"I know you will, and maybe it will be something you can add to your résumé when you graduate." I gulped because I certainly had not meant to introduce that topic, yet avoiding it wasn't going to make it go away or have a different outcome. Why did it always seem that when things started going well, something happened or was on the brink of happening to change it all again?

Maribel just smiled at me as she took the few steps to her bedroom door.

"I'll let you know if I find anything worth mentioning." I took Whiskers off the floor and cuddled her close. My cat immediately jumped out of my arms and stalked into the kitchen with her tail held high and her mumble-squeak that she'd recently started doing when she wanted something from me.

"Let's plan to set up the board tomorrow then on the wall, that way we can see it all and discuss any connections." Maribel turned at the door and sized up the piece of wall. "We might need more room, but this is a good start."

"Why do I feel like I'm taking too much time with this when I should just be selling rocks and trinkets? Maybe even puttering around on my golf cart or in my boat to show people the wonders of under the sea?"

She leaned against the doorframe. "I don't think you're overdoing it at all. You can enjoy all those things and you can also want to see justice done. You can troll around in your boat and still feel like the person who actually did the bad deed should pay for it. And if you just happen to be able to get people to tell you things that others won't, then where's the harm in that?" She waved and went into her room without waiting for an answer.

And it was true. I wasn't going to seriously hang out a shingle as a private investigator, and I certainly didn't want to quit my day jobs to constantly immerse myself in murders. But if I could help, why wouldn't I?

Then again, it didn't escape my notice that if it hadn't been for Goldy pushing me on this one, there was no way I would have involved myself. I would have just merrily gone on my way feeling sorry for the loss of life but not determining that I had to have a hand in solving how it happened, why it happened, and who'd been the one to do it.

Maybe it was my complete fascination with murder podcasts that was pushing me along. I couldn't get enough of listening to them when I was doing busywork and even sometimes when I was in the shop and it was dead—no pun intended there.

But it was something to consider as I followed my cat into the kitchen to get her whatever she wanted. Because Maribel might be able to pet her and then go to bed without paying, but I knew for certain that Whiskers would be at my door caterwauling if I didn't give in to her demands.

As if to prove my point, she came back out of the kitchen, tail still high, and gave me a look that definitely said I wasn't moving fast enough and nothing should take precedence over her needs.

"Fine. I'm on my way, but it wouldn't hurt you to show me a little more affection even on the days you don't want to."

She squeaked at me and then growled. End of that discussion.

But as I got the cat food out of the cabinet, I was struck by the logo on the can. I'd been thinking about a logo for my shop, so I'd been paying more attention to them lately. I'd seen a logo on the crate in the cave and wondered what the brand was. It was bland and didn't say anything about the product, whereas this logo was definitely for cat food, with a chubby cat licking its paw.

I didn't often pay attention to logos, just grabbed the thing I wanted and continued about my business. They were designed mostly for that specific purpose: to tell a story in one image and catch your eye when you needed what they sold. There was at least some form of recognition and trust attached to brands. You would be at least partially aware they weren't going to disappoint and would deliver on the promise they implicitly made.

Maybe I should also look into what the crate was to see if I could find out how it had gotten onto the beach in the cove. I kept thinking about the litter and got angry that some company had just left the debris to clog up a beach with no thought for the environment or the sea creatures. Though that might have to wait due to the murder. I was not an artist in any sense of the word, so drawing it would not help me. And since I had no idea what kind of company it was, I couldn't exactly try to find images of it via an online search engine. So I had to go about this another way. Perhaps reverse image recognition. It was a thought for a different time, so I let it go. Maybe the crates would still be there when I got a chance to go back.

As I was opening the can of food for Whiskers, I called Goldy.

"Would it be possible to maybe see Darren's movie in the

privacy of his home? I know the theater is currently off-limits, but if he's got a copy, we could watch with him. I might have some questions."

"I'll ask him right away. Thanks for this, sweetie."

I still wasn't sure if she'd be thanking me at the end if I found out it really was Darren who had pushed his lover to his death, but I was willing to play the game to see where it went.

Chapter 9

Shortly after I'd fed Whiskers and she'd allowed me to throw her a few toys and rub her belly, I'd gone into bed. After curling up on my stomach, she promptly went to sleep, her breath wafting over me, lousy with fish. Fortunately I'd kept the window open throughout the day and the smell of the sea eventually filled the room, allowing me to finally fall asleep while my mind ran around and around with the possibilities of what had happened throughout the day.

I woke up refreshed and ready to take on whatever came my way. I didn't want the universe to take that as a challenge and ask the stars to hold their beer, so I got up, got ready for my day at the store, and fed my pretty kitty again so she'd be happy until I came home to do it all over again.

But first I had a hair appointment to keep my highlights fresh and get just a little trimmed off. I entered La Fluencia Day Spa and signed in. Flipping through the magazines sounded better than scrolling through my phone, but since I had some research to do on at least three people and a brand to find, I took the time to pull up my favorite search engine and plug in some words.

Darren had indeed been in trouble throughout much of his

life. No matter how he had tried to hide it or downplay it, there were quite a few items that needed to be looked at closer, preferably on my computer instead of the little screen in my hand.

Jericho seemed to have almost no internet history. I couldn't imagine how you'd manage that in today's world, and it wasn't like he was old. I would have placed him in his late forties at least, but when I put in his name, I came up with a few obituaries and an article on an auction house. None of the pictures looked like him either. I put that off to the side to look at on the big computer too.

And then there was Elsie Jacobs. She'd been a beauty queen on the mainland and was very into charities and hosting them. She'd made thousands of dollars for children and millions for shelter animals. So what kind of breakdown had led her to pursue an old love?

She had been married at one time, and details were scarce under her name. Yet when I put in her husband's name, it was as if my phone wanted to explode. Page after page of sites with Eli Jacobs's name very prominently displayed.

What in Neptune's name was going on here?

"Whit, we're ready for you." Marcella must have called me several times before breaking out that tone of voice, and I must not have heard her. Oops.

"Yep, on my way, sorry." I walked past several other ladies waiting in the lobby and tried to smile even as my thoughts were careening around inside my head.

She smiled and shook her head. "It's like you go into this other world. I've seen people get pulled into their phones enough, but you take the award for most single-minded, in my book."

I laughed, not only because it was true, but because it was both a blessing and curse.

"Sorry. I'm just trying to look up some . . . um . . . stats on some things."

She led me back to her chair and put the cape on. "Stats,

huh? I would think you'd be looking up the main players in this possible murder investigation and trying to work out who did it and why."

"Why would I, um, do that? I'm sure the police have it in hand." And just because I'd helped in the last two situations did not mean I was always going to be the person to figure things out when a death happened on the island. Therese Milner had died too, and I hadn't taken an interest in that except to be dragged to her funeral.

"Honestly, I'd rather people just stop dying, and then I wouldn't have to worry about anything."

She smiled softly at me through the mirror as she ran her hands through my hair, picking up layers and using her knowledge to start the process of evening things out and bringing it back to what it had been before.

"I mean, the last two times it was a very distinct pattern and involved people I knew either as victims or perpetrators. This time I've got nothing."

"Except that Goldy has already called just about everyone in town and told them that if we know anything of worth or anything that might help you, we're supposed to bring that information to you immediately and make sure you write it down and pay attention."

I wanted to drop my head into my hands but since she still had her fingers measuring the length of the pixie, there was no way I could do that without yanking some of said hair out.

So I rolled my eyes instead. "Everyone in town?"

"Well, most of the business owners. I know you've had some issues with the chamber of commerce, but you really should think about joining us. We're not all bad and you might want to be involved in some of the plans we're putting together for the upcoming year. It wouldn't hurt you to be aware of things before they become finalized."

I distinctly remembered thinking that moving back here would lead to a much easier pace and a slower, more laid-back lifestyle. I was completely off base. I was busier here than I'd ever been when I'd worked for the railroad. There I just clocked in on time and clocked out when I was done. I'd go to the gym sometimes—okay almost never but I did at least keep my membership—and then I'd go home and hang out with Maribel or maybe hit the beach. But none of this getting involved with the chamber of commerce or murder investigations.

"Think about it."

She motioned for me to move over to the sink so she could wash out my hair, and I followed her, biting my nails along the way. If I did want to see where this all went, and Goldy had already asked everyone to help me, then there would be no need to hide anything in the cloak of just being curious. However, it was also possible she'd alerted someone who had had a hand in all this, especially if the culprit was a resident. Which could be bad if they instead told me lies to keep me sniffing in the wrong direction. *Damn.*

I laid back with my neck on the bowl rest and let the flow of warm water calm me as I tried to empty my thoughts and just enjoy this salon visit for what it was. Me time. Not as a storeowner, not as a friend, not as a girlfriend, or as a dutiful granddaughter, not as a sister. Just me. Well, me and about twelve other women getting salon services, but I didn't have to interact with them if I didn't want to.

"You know, when I did that woman's makeup for the funeral, her husband very clearly told me he did not want anything flashy and that she could go in the ground just as they'd found her. That son was the one who agreed to pay more for the full makeup job."

There was a murmur of approval and a few hushed comments, which I tried to ignore. I didn't know who was speaking and I certainly didn't need to. I wasn't going to get involved in the conversation. That was crap, of course, but I wanted points for at least trying to be circumspect about my curiosity.

I opened my eyes and shifted my gaze to the left to find another woman in the chair next to me listening to her own hairdresser, a woman who'd started here about a month ago. She'd come into the Dame of the Sea a few times and we'd chatted. I was pretty sure her name was Narina, but I wouldn't stake my laughable fortune on that. I did know that my brother, Nick, had gone out with her a few times and that it hadn't worked out. But that was the norm for Nick.

I closed my eyes before either of them saw me looking and settled back into relaxation mode. Me time.

"I was surprised because Annaliese told me the husband has loved that woman to distraction for years and years. He did everything for her and always made sure she never had to lift a finger. So why wouldn't he have wanted her to look her best when everyone was going to see her in that coffin?"

But no one had seen her in the coffin until it had been pushed over and the lid had come off. It had been closed casket from the beginning, with no viewing beforehand, as far as I knew. Maybe I should make a note to check that with Goldy. After the me time.

"I'll tell you what, though, it's a good thing I did do the makeup because even though it was a closed casket, she had some very strange scarring on her face. I never did find out where it came from. I tried to be coy in asking the husband and the son, but they both just glossed right over it and went right on as if I hadn't said anything."

My ears perked up and I told them to just settle the hell down because . . . you guessed it, me time.

"Scars can be from a lot of things, though. I had acne scars for years and still do. I have to get this special cream to cover it up."

"Oh, what cream?"

Narina laughed. "I can't remember, but it has the weirdest logo. Of course no one is looking at the logo when it sits in my medicine cabinet, so there's that. They're just enjoying the coverage after I'm done putting it on."

I could either open my eyes now and find out why this was important or I could continue to ignore them, and they'd probably continue to talk until I couldn't stand the suspense anymore. Better to do it in my own time.

When Marcella shut off the water and gently pushed on my shoulder to let me know it was okay to get up, I pulled the towel tighter around my neck and looked at them both. The lady in the chair ignored me but one of the owners had come along at some point and smiled at me. Damn that Annaliese.

"Need something?" Annaliese asked. She had been instrumental in helping with the other murders I'd investigated and solved. She liked to rib me every time I saw her, often referencing any mystery that was happening around the island from missing lawn gnomes to golf cart accidents to deaths that were far from mysterious.

"I thought we were better friends than that."

All she did was laugh. "Oh, Whit, we are, but you have to understand that I've known Goldy far longer and have done a lot of things for her and with her. And if all she's asking is that I make sure to pass along some info, then I'm not going to tell her no."

"What is she, the matriarch of Avalon society?" I knew her and loved her and understood her, but recently I'd realized that more people took her more seriously than I had admitted. I always thought she was the good-time Goldy, but maybe she had a different fierceness that created a special kind of loyalty that extended beyond being a family member.

"Goldy has done a lot for me over the years. She's given me some very on-point business advice, as well as help in situations I couldn't see my way out of. There's a lot about her that makes me want to be her when I grow up . . . though I will never wear those heels, and my worst nightmare is to spend the majority of my days in a bathing suit. Who wants to shave all the way up that often?"

There was general laughter in the room as we probably all thought about the task of shaving from ankles to crotch.

"But why me?" It was a valid question and one I had just voiced to Felix yesterday. I'd thought it before. But normally, I'd kept it behind my teeth. I'd contemplated it but I don't think I'd ever asked anyone besides Felix.

Annaliese stopped washing her client's scalp and let the water run freely over the woman's hair in the sink. "Because you're good at what you do, from what I've heard, and somehow you always seem to figure it out." She winked. "Now, let Marcella do your hair and see what you come up with. If I hear anything at all, I'll let you know, and I'm sure you'll be able to use it somehow in that very wonderful brain of yours."

An hour later I was at my front counter at the Dame of the Sea. We carried all manner of awesome things, from souvenirs to rocks to blankets. I was delighted that we also offered a service by which I could get Pops to make up a map and bury a treasure chest for a spouse, or a date, or a child as a fun activity with a cool prize at the end. Sometimes that prize was provided by the purchaser, like an engagement ring or tickets to a lifetime goal of a cruise through the Adriatic Sea. And sometimes it was just a little bauble Pops had stocked in his garage for kids. You could get the map from the shop or have it wash up on the shore in a glass bottle. It could appear at your dinner plate or be buried in the sand next to your beach towel.

I'd thought about moving out to sea earlier and allowing people to find the treasure in one of the caves around the island, but I wasn't sure what the liability was on that, and as there were enough people who liked the assortment of choices we had, I didn't think I needed to change something that wasn't broken. But the caves got me thinking again about that logo. What was it for? What company did it represent? I was almost positive I had seen it before in my everyday life, but I couldn't for the life of me place it. It was driving me crazy. If I could find it again, I was going to take a picture of it and show it to everyone Goldy had called. Maybe someone else would remember what it was for. Definitely worth a try. I wasn't sure why I was focused on this, but I had a feeling it had to do with distracting myself from the fact that I had no facts when I came to this whole murder thing. That and the coincidence of seeing the crates on the same day as the murder. It was as if they were connected in my head as I combed through everything that had happened that day to see if I'd missed anything.

I wanted to solve this, and soon, so I didn't have to keep avoiding Goldy, who would want some answers.

And, speak of the devil, she came waltzing in with a filmy bathing-suit cover and a suit in fire-engine red. It looked ravishing on her, and I only wished I might look like she did when I grew up. She also had a sarong wrapped around her waist and those shoes that Annaliese had said she'd never want to wear.

"To what do I owe this pleasure?" I asked as she came around the corner, humming to herself. "I didn't think you were working this week, since your friend was in town."

"I wasn't going to, but Darren is not in the mood to go tramping around the island, seeing old haunts with all this turmoil going on. We tried to go to breakfast this morning, and not only were we followed by the police but we could barely get to our pancakes before they got cold, because everyone and their mother stopped by the table to see if he'd done it or if he knew who had. They all started nice enough, but when he didn't have answers, some of them got snotty, and then so did I."

"You? Snotty? I don't believe it."

She bumped me with her hip and eyed me up and down from head to toe and back again. "You know damn well I am very capable of being as snotty if not snottier than anyone else in the world."

I would neither confirm nor deny that because, either way, she could take offense.

"Goldy, I have a store to run and stock to inventory and a few maps to have Pops make. I already got into it at the salon. I hear that you've been telling everyone to help me in any way they can, plus I now feel pressured to join the chamber of commerce. I think maybe the store might be the best place for me at the moment."

"No, the best place for you is solving the case. Take a lunch, put the sign up in the window, and come see Darren's movie. I got us a viewing, and I think you're going to be blown away by the film and maybe you'll see something that neither of us has."

"And where's Pops?" I hated to ask but I had to.

"He's out bird-watching with Aaron. He told you he was fine with this, and he is fine with this. The faster you find out who killed Jericho, the faster we can get back to our regular life. If that's what's worrying you, then you should be raring to go."

It was so nice to be manipulated, guilted, and encouraged all at the same time. "You really are a piece of work."

"A piece of art, darling, not work. Now, let's go get cracking."

A customer chose to come in at that point and Goldy was all smiles, even as I could feel the impatience radiating off her.

"Are you the one who does those treasure maps?"

"Yes, we are. Are you interested in seeing the different sites we have available? We have everything from five minutes to an hour walk and can customize as needed."

Goldy brought out the book of maps and the woman flipped through each page carefully. I could feel Goldy growing more impatient—which I hadn't thought was possible—but she didn't want to rush the customer along. Instead, I nudged Goldy with my elbow, and she rolled her eyes.

The woman bit her bottom lip and tucked her red hair behind her ear. "Um, is it at all possible to get one that comes out near the pet cemetery?"

"We've never done one of those before but—" I started.

"No, darling, I'm so sorry. We don't do them out that way. It's against our policy and the policy of the island to have them out near any place that really shouldn't be dug up. Just in case, you understand."

I didn't say anything because I had never heard that before. I didn't remember sending anyone out near the cemetery or the pet cemetery, but with adult supervision I didn't understand why it wouldn't be okay.

"Oh, I was really hoping." She clasped her hands in front of her chest. "Our youngest just lost his cat right before we left for vacation, and I wanted to show him how lovely and peaceful the resting place for animals can be in hopes that maybe he'd feel better and let himself enjoy our vacation. He's really struggling. But I wanted to make it something fun, and have him open the chest to find a picture of his beloved cat as well as maybe a card for the local shelter back home."

I figured we could make an exception, especially for someone who was struggling. "I'm sure we could—" But I got interrupted again.

"I'm so sorry for your loss, but unfortunately, there's nothing we can do to change the rules. I'd be happy to have something put over by the deer farm or where he could see the bison, but we can't do the pet cemetery."

She hung her head and sighed. "Okay, let me think about it. Thanks for listening. I'll be back if we decide to do anything."

The bell dinged behind her as she left, and it almost sounded like the death knell played at old funerals. I turned to Goldy with my mouth open, but since she already knew what I was going to ask, I didn't even start before she jumped right in.

"We do not, under any circumstances, ever, make maps out near the pet cemetery."

"Is it really illegal? And don't lie to me."

"It's not illegal, but it could be considered in poor taste."

"That's not what you told that poor woman."

"And I'd say it all over again. There's only one person who's ever gotten a map to that area, and since I don't know if he ever used it, I can't let anyone else go out that way." She crossed her arms and her joviality from earlier completely disappeared.

"Darren, I take it. And what exactly did he hide out there? Why do you think he might have never gone to retrieve it?" I was tired of the twists that seemed to come up every time this man's name was mentioned.

"I don't know for certain, but I think it had to do with his brother's disappearance the day before he left and the angry, threatening words his family exchanged. From what I gather, they've never been able to find Jackson Milner, and I'm not going to be the one to bring that up to him."

Chapter 10

I stated my demands before I even entered the house at the top of Palmetto Drive completely. I had barely cleared the doorway when I called out, "Popcorn. Lots of butter, the more the better."

Goldy nudged me with her elbow, but I wasn't budging. Popcorn, or I was leaving.

"Coming right up," Darren said from where I assumed the kitchen was. I'd never been in this house and wasn't sure I wanted that status changed once I walked in.

From the outside the house was beautiful, one of the bigger ones on the island, almost as big as the Wrigley Mansion. The colors were both nautical and muted: a blue on the wall that had tones of navy in it to match the sea, off-white trim around the porch, and a front door of solid oak with lovely glass inserts.

"What did these people do again?" I asked softly. Although it was only Goldy and me in the room, I still wanted to keep my voice down so as not to anger anyone.

"I believe Darren's father retired from some kind of job where he traveled a lot, and I'm pretty sure Darren's mother was a stay-at-home mom. I don't remember Therese ever really having a job, though I could be wrong. It wasn't something I asked those few times I was here trying to convince his parents that we were in it for the long haul until he could get out and do his own thing."

"Makes sense. But these decorations are . . ."

"Odd, if you ask me," Darren said, coming into the living room from the left. He didn't have popcorn in his hands, but I really hoped that was because it was in the process of going from kernel to butter-slathered awesome.

"Popcorn is almost ready, and if you're anything like Goldy here, I'm sure I have enough pounds of butter to make it palatable."

Goldy laughed, and I hummed. I still wasn't sure about this guy. I wanted to be. I wanted to know that if I was going to work through how the death had happened and why, it would yield me something other than that he was a bald-faced liar and a murderer as the cherry on top. Not to mention that any loss in his family seemed not to bother him in the least. His mother was dead, his lover was killed, and his brother had gone missing the day before Darren had left all those years ago. How come he never seemed bothered by any of it?

Darren then interrupted my thoughts, so I put them on the back burner to see if Goldy had any insight.

"Seriously, I have no idea where my parents got half of these knickknacks, I just remember them always being around."

He gestured toward a mantel that held a series of small figurines. They were all animals and looked as if they had been made out of blown glass with gold glitter painted along certain lines. I was pretty sure I had seen them in a catalog from one of those discount places, but I shrugged.

"My dad always seemed to be bringing something back from wherever he was off to that month."

"Your dad was gone every month?" At least his had constantly returned, unlike mine, but that was a thought for another time and another place.

"Yes, he was in sales and his career took him all over the world. I can give you the tour if you want to see the Japanese teacups with the hidden woman's face at the bottom or the matchstick collection that takes up the inside of an entire nautical glass ball."

"No, that's okay. I'm really only here for my lunch break and then I have to get back to work. I serve a hard boss."

He looked puzzled, and then his brow cleared. "Oh, you're talking about yourself. Funny. Unless you meant that Goldy is a hard boss?" His eyes twinkled and for just a moment I could see why Goldy would have been willing to do almost anything for him.

I shook my head to clear it and gestured toward the television. "Is this where we're going to watch?"

Something dinged from the left and Darren looked over his shoulder. "Yep, in just a minute. I'm on butter detail and then I'll get it rolling."

Goldy followed close behind as I went to look more closely at the glass menagerie and then slid over to the desk at the back window. I didn't touch anything, but some turned-over papers had my fingers itching to see what was on them.

"Don't touch anything. Darren did not do this, and his father wasn't even at the theater. He came by once everyone was already out in the street."

"Yes, Goldy."

Fortunately Darren returned at that point and the smell coming from the vintage teak bowls was divine.

He had three in his hands, and I was quick to grab the one I thought had more popcorn than the other two.

"Thanks," I said as I seated myself on the couch and took my first handful. Gah, this was beyond wonderful. I even closed my eyes for a few seconds to just really savor the taste. And when I opened them again, I found myself being watched with small smiles from Goldy and Darren. They looked at each other as if sharing a secret. Since Goldy had been reluctant to talk about anything, I wasn't going to ask.

"So the movie? Can you tell me the context?"

I hadn't taken the time to watch much of it as I was walking around and then grabbing the box of bows before Jericho had almost fallen directly on me, but thought this was a nicer way of asking instead of just blurting that I had no idea what we were going to be looking at.

"I think it might be better if we view it from start to finish without any foreknowledge. The film speaks for itself. I had started it long ago, but with Jericho's encouragement, I finally finished the thing and I'm proud of it. Now it feels like it was me honoring Jericho since he was the one who'd inspired me to do it."

Okay, so cold read. There were worse things in life. At least I knew it wasn't going to be some steamy romp that I wasn't prepared to view with Goldy. I didn't even like to look at racy pictures near her, and when we'd gone to see a movie a few weeks ago I'd put my hand over her eyes during a few of the sexy parts. Of course, she smacked my hand out of the way.

At least this wouldn't need that kind of response.

Darren also set a glass of soda down on the end table next to me, then he dimmed the light and perched on the arm of the couch next to Goldy.

The opening credits rolled and the island slowly came into view through a haze. It zeroed in on a few of the more prominent features, such as the Wrigley Mansion, the Casino, and the Airport in the Sky, then it seemed to set down in the middle of Crescent Avenue, our main street, and a voice-over talked about the beauty of the place and how when you went deeper, it might not be all that it seemed.

"Darren, you'd better pause this movie right now," Goldy said in the low and intense voice that signaled some real trouble, and I had a feeling I knew exactly what she was going to say.

"Don't you want to watch it all the way through?" he asked, taking his own life into his hands. No one questioned Goldy when she was using that voice. He had to know that.

"No. Now."

He paused it, but with the lights lowered, I couldn't see his expression.

The glint of the television screen very clearly showed Goldy's face though and she was livid.

"When were you here to film this?" she asked. Her hands were clasped in her lap, a sign she was reining herself in as best she could.

"Well, just over a weekend a few months ago." Since I couldn't see his expression, I could only go by his voice, and that sounded baffled.

I hesitated to save him and Goldy dived in.

"And yet I don't seem to remember any call that you were in the area. No note on social media, no text, not a knock on my door, or a casual stop by the dock to say hello or let me know you were here. I find that very interesting."

Interesting was not a good word when used that way. I hoped he would at least pick up on that.

But, sadly he did not. "I wasn't here long enough to do more than film a few of the spots. I didn't want to bother you when I knew I wasn't going to be here for more than a short visit. It seemed like there would be too much to explain and I didn't have time."

She turned toward him and I could no longer see her expression, but I could feel her irritation radiating off her like a supernova.

"And yet you see no issue with interrupting my life now expecting us to help you put everything on hold to save your life, looking into the nefarious and horrible thing that happened to your lover. Is that because you figure you'll be here for a week or two this time before you head out? Again."

Ohhh, I wouldn't touch that with a ten-foot oar, but he was going to have to or risk getting tossed off the couch.

"Ah, I, uh, see how that could be hurtful and I'm going to take the cue to apologize profusely. I should have contacted you when I was here."

I sat in silence, waiting for the rest and so did Goldy.

"That's it?" she said. "I don't believe I heard an apology in there at all."

It had also occurred to me that he'd lied about not being on the island since he was young, with no mention of his visit to film. I wanted to ask about that little fudging of the truth, but now was not the time.

He cleared his throat. "I am so very sorry. I truly did want to see you when I was here and considered asking after you, but my mother told me that you were in the midst of helping your granddaughter get settled into her shop and turning over the boating business to her and her brother. I did see you one day and waved but you had your head down and were obviously deep in thought, and then your husband came up behind you and whisked you away to the beach. I didn't want to interrupt that and it was time for me to head out anyway. So it is with very deep regret and a most sincere request for your forgiveness of my mistake that I beg your pardon."

Not bad, especially when Goldy mock-smacked his biceps and giggled.

"That was way over the top and you know it," she said.

"I tried to give what you asked for! I didn't want to disappoint you."

Now she slipped an arm through the crook in his elbow. "You never could, darling. I'm just glad you're here now. And we'll figure this out for you. No one is less a potential killer than you." She briefly laid her head on his shoulder, then flicked her hand toward the television with a smile on her face.

Darren dutifully turned the movie back on and I settled back into the couch. I was not going to ask my question now. Upsetting the peace Goldy had just given would've only had her aim any lingering irritation my way, and it wasn't that important for the moment. I'd wait.

A few minutes later, I put my popcorn bowl on the end table and leaned forward. But then Darren as the voice-over went on to say it was even more beautiful than your mind could ever conjure up, and I leaned back. It ran like a commercial for tourism on the island. Going through the many pluses, like the campgrounds and the horse farm in the middle of the island, the caves and boating, and our resident bison, which had been left after a movie in the 1920s. It talked about the deer, and I wondered where he got all the footage, because I assumed he would have let Goldy know if he was coming over here as he had this time. Especially if he was going to hang around the island long enough to capture all this content.

There was nothing new here, so I went for my popcorn again when I caught the image of that logo out of the corner of my eye. "Can you rewind a bit and play that part again?"

Goldy looked puzzled, and Darren looked taken aback. But he did rewind and I watched it and flicked my eyes to him. He was stiff, sitting in his chair and not looking at me. Part of me wanted to ask whose house he'd filmed in. Because the logo was in someone's house, on a wall, like a brand seared into the wood of an entryway. Despite wanting that information, though, the other part of me knew in my gut it would be a bad idea to ask. I forced myself to shrug and let the movie continue to roll. I tried to trust my gut as often as possible.

I got lost a few times during the viewing. I couldn't tell if it was a documentary or an advertisement for the island, or if eventually there would be some kind of story over the scenery that we were treated to again and again. Things turned a little darker at the end, with pictures of the cemetery and the pet cemetery, and with mention of the recent deaths in the area as well as the history of everything on the island not always being so idyllic. But in the end, he turned it around to say there was something on the island for everyone and every taste, and to come visit, because he'd be more than willing to give a private tour.

My first question was how on earth did this honor Jericho? The second was about how he would be giving private tours. Would he be moving back here? I waited on the first until I could phrase it much nicer than what was rolling around in my head, and Goldy beat me to the second one.

"Oh, my, Darren, do you mean to say that you will be moving back? Are you opening a tour business? How fun!"

Or his company could be competition for our glass-bottom boats and semi-submersibles. And there was a very real possibility that Darren would be a longer-term irritant for Pops. I'd say "awesome," but I'd be lying.

"Oh, Goldy, you were always my staunchest supporter, and I so appreciate that. I was considering asking if we could partner up with your boat business to offer tours at specified times so that we aren't your competition but a complementary-type business."

The man had all the right answers at all the right times with just the right tone and a smile that made you feel like you were everything. I didn't like it. My gut wasn't speaking to me through the abundance of popcorn, though, and I couldn't properly make the call at this moment. Plus, I wouldn't, because if I said anything but hip, hip, hooray, Goldy would probably shoot me down with one of her side-eye looks.

"An interesting proposition. I'll definitely let Nick know you'd like to discuss business with him when you get started." Goldy said nothing and didn't frown in my general direction, so I went on. "Do you have a logo for your business? A name? How far into the plans are you? Is this something you were planning on running with Jericho? Is that his house in the film with the great decorations on the entryway?" I still wanted to know how he thought an hour-long commercial was in any way a tribute, and since I'd seen my chance to ask, I did. But Goldy thwarted me.

"Now, Whit, so many questions and so many directions that have nothing to do with what we're here for—to clear Darren's name. Let's keep our eye on the correct priority here and not get off track with questions that have nothing to do with Jericho's untimely death."

"Of course." I popped some more of the popcorn in my mouth and then was sad when I realized I was scraping the bottom of the bowl and didn't want to ask for more.

"So, Darren," Goldy asked before I could. "Was there anything in there that you think might have something to do with the death of your partner? It all seemed on the up-and-up and was pretty complimentary for the most part. Maybe a little dark when you discussed the deaths, but I don't think anyone on the island is unaware of that. You only mentioned it briefly and not with any details, plus, they were all solved cases, so no one should feel threatened."

That about covered it for my questions too, so I sat and waited for an answer. Darren paced the floor and tugged on his bottom lip over and over again. While he took his time answering, I tried to come up with some way to ask if I could take the video home to get a better look at that brand and figure out where it was and what it meant.

"This island only seems to bring disaster to me. Maybe I shouldn't try to start a business here."

Goldy stepped close to Darren and patted his shoulder. "It's not that bad. I know losing your brother all those years ago was rough on your family, and I'm sure being here without your mother might be difficult at first, but you'd be with family."

"How is it that you're out of the loop, Goldy? Surprise, surprise." Darren chuckled but, it was definitely not out of happiness. It had a dark edge that made me pause. "Oh, yes, it is that bad. My brother did disappear, and I've never heard from him myself in all these years. Apparently at some point, he contacted them but refuses to talk to me at all. He passes messages through my parents but won't communicate with me himself. And I don't even know why, since I can't talk to him. Then my mother dies, now my boyfriend is dead. I don't know what more I can take."

Part of me wanted to be sympathetic, because it did suck to have that many things happen in one place, but it was also life. Maybe not usually the disappearing part, although that was my life. I didn't even get messages through Goldy. My parents never contacted anyone. But it wouldn't have kept me from pursuing my dreams in coming back here. Even though since I came back here, I'd been involved in more chaos than I ever had been on the mainland. There it was traffic and sometimes sirens at all times of the night. Here it was murder, but I also had my best friend with me, spent more time with my grandparents than I had in years, hung out with my brother—and the icing on the cake was Felix.

Felix, whom I was going to have to ask if he could go back out with me to that cave. I really wanted to see if the crate was still there and try to find out what it meant. And how it seemed to be lurking in the background of so many things. Was it a tie? A through line? Who knew? But I was at least going to take some time to find out.

"And you never found out what happened to your brother?" I asked, because while that might have nothing to do with the death . . . well, now hold on a minute . . .

I started again. "I know this might be an insensitive question but I'm going to have to ask it anyway."

Goldy and Darren turned to me with skepticism on their faces. Yeah, I didn't want to ask either, but it might be worth a mention at least.

"Is it possible there are some provisions in the will your

brother might have come back for? You and Jericho are similar in height and build. Could your brother be back for the funeral like Elsie is? Maybe he wants something and Jericho got in his way?"

"That's reaching, Whit, even for you."

Nothing like having your grandmother totally not on your side when she was the one asking for your help in something you didn't even want to do.

"No, it's valid," Darren said. "Let me think about it, Whit, and I'll see if there's anything in the will. I believe any will would put everything in my father's hands, since he's still alive. I can't imagine my mother giving away anything of real value to either of her children when my dad was still around. I'll let you know what I find out."

"I can tell you right now there's nothing." Stu Milner stepped into the room.

I wondered how much he'd heard and what his take on this whole thing was. He was not the most supportive person when it came to his son's choices in partners, and he had seemed stoic and resigned about how the funeral had turned out—he didn't even seem that surprised. Almost as if he'd figured that, at any given moment, if there was something bad that could happen, it definitely would, and it would happen big.

But maybe I was reading too much into him, and I needed to just let him talk instead of making judgments with too little information.

"Jackson left right about the time Darren did, yes, but he's been in contact with us throughout the years. Currently, I think he said he was somewhere in the Cayman Islands. I told him it wasn't necessary to come here for his mother's funeral since she was already gone and I believe he can say goodbye to her wherever he is. The spirit is not locked in the body once death has occurred. It's free to roam as it wants."

He shook his head and ran a hand over his mouth.

"And the will?" I asked before he got off track into some wilderness of religious beliefs.

"The will leaves everything to me. If I wanted to give something to someone, then I could, but the full distribution won't come until I'm also gone. No need to go splitting things up now unless one of my boys needed something I have."

Darren scoffed but it was a low sound, as if he hadn't wanted anyone to hear. Goldy heard, though, and I did too. But Stu went on as if nothing had happened. I'd have to corner Darren later to see why he thought his dad's words were shit.

"I really do think it would be better to leave everything up to Ray at the station." Stu pressed his hands into the back on the couch and curled his fingers into the geometric-patterned afghan that contrasted loudly with the floral couch. "We don't need to be meddling in things, and you'll be gone soon enough, Darren, that there's no need for you to stick around. I'm sure you have many other things to do in your fast life around other parts of the country."

So dear old Dad had no idea that Darren was planning on being some kind of guide here on the island? Was Darren planning on living with his father, or had he already bought or rented some other place? I hadn't asked him that either, but I was going to have to start making a list if I wanted to keep everything straight in my head.

"All I know is, I'm selling the house and moving on." Stu patted his stomach and then hooked his thumbs into the pockets of his blue polyester pants. "I think I might take up the nomad life on my boat. Nothing like being out in the open and going from port to port to see what I've been missing here on this little slice of Catalina. I think it will be fun to do all those things your mother never let me do. And once you're gone too, I can get on with things the way I've wanted to even before this whole thing started. Elsie is very excited to move in and take over the place when I leave." He laughed derisively. "It's a good thing she already signed the papers before she hit your mother's coffin. I might have said no after that."

My whole brain stopped in shock. What the heck? But while Darren might have tried to hide his groan earlier, this noise sounded more like he was choking. My gaze zipped over to him and his face was pale, his throat working, and the veins straining under his skin, not in anger but in what looked like a whole lot of distress and dread. Why?

Chapter 11

"What do you mean you sold the house to Elsie? Why on earth would you do that without checking with me?"

Stu pulled his eyebrows down into a fierce scowl. "Why would I check with you at all? We haven't seen you in years. Your mother asked you again and again to come back for a visit, and you refused until you wanted to make your little movie. Then all of a sudden we were supposed to open up our house to you and your film crew while funding everything you needed. You didn't buy groceries, you didn't offer to help with the bills that quadrupled while you and your friends were here, and you certainly didn't say thank you to us for putting everything in our own lives on hold while you came in playing your part. Now, I don't know what other people expect from their children, but I know what I expected from mine. I also know how we raised you, and you've turned into nothing that we wanted or expected." He narrowed his eyes and grunted. "So I'm getting out of here. Especially if you think I'm going to foot the bill again for this ridiculous tour guide thing you think you're going to pull off. Do you even have the money to get it started with the equipment you'll need? Do you realize the scheduling that will need to be done? The basics you'd need to have on hand as you tour around an island with a bunch of people who don't understand the first thing about hiking?" He snorted in disgust. "And I can tell from the look on your face that you hadn't even thought about any of those things. You expect to float through life with the blessings of angels over and over again. Angels who are very much human that you never pay back and never see again once they've run out their use, unless you need them for a second time. Then, of course, you'll come back in with your smile, and your charm, and they'll be used again. I'm not having it."

I most certainly did not want to be here for this. Holy wow, Stu certainly had a lot of pent-up things to be said and they were bursting forth as if a dam had broken.

I snuck a glance over at Goldy. Her mouth was open and her eyes narrowed. I knew I had to get her out of here soon or she was going to blow like a volcano.

"We're just going to, um, leave you to your, um, thing here, and we'll see you later." I tugged on Goldy's arm, trying to get her to move. If she decided to stay, then I'd wait outside, where hopefully I couldn't hear any more words being slung like arrows.

"Darren, why don't you come with us?" Goldy asked. "We'll let your dad have some time to cool down. If you need a place to stay, I'm sure we can find something for you. Right, Whit?"

She'd better not ask me to have him stay at my place. She had more room than I did, not to mention there were hotels in the area.

"I'm going to stay." Darren squared off against his dad, puffing up his chest. "Obviously, there are things we need to discuss that have never come to light before. Now is as good a time as any to just drag it all out onto the floor and smash it with a hammer."

My heart sank for him. When Goldy reached out for him, I

gently pulled her arm back to her side. This was not our fight. And while I was not a huge fan of trying to figure out who had murdered his boyfriend, I had far more concrete and unmovable feelings when it came to getting into the middle of a family fight with two living men I didn't know.

I backed out of the living room and into the foyer, not completely sure why I felt I couldn't take my eyes off the two men. Mainly, it was because I didn't want to turn my back on that level of anger.

At first Goldy stood her ground, and for once I decided she could do whatever she wanted without me. This was something I wasn't going to be involved in. I'd wait outside until she was ready.

Stepping out onto the wide porch, I looked over the houses terraced down along the hill, which then turned into Crescent Avenue, which then led down to the beach. Small waves lapped at the golden sand, where people played in the surf or relaxed on brightly colored beach towels while reading books or eating lunch. How on earth was it only lunchtime? I felt like every second lately was absolutely packed with angst, confrontation, or sadness.

I'd be happy to get back to my normal life. I'd ask the universe for a reprieve, maybe just for a little while. Keep your murderers at home and let me just have the peace and tranquillity I'd been looking for when I'd moved back. Jeez.

I could hear voices raised inside the house but couldn't make out the words. I highly doubted anyone was going to say anything that would be important to the investigation. Even if it was, Goldy was still in there. She could just tell me. Or keep it to herself and solve this thing on her own . . .

I walked up and down the sidewalk in front of the house just to keep myself busy, then decided to call Maribel to pass some more time after I'd stepped over the cracks in the sidewalks twenty times. Not that I was worried about breaking my mother's back—more so my own, if I wore myself out before I even got to open the shop back up. Lunch hour had been over some time ago. At least I'd only put up the BE BACK SOON sign instead of actually saying when that might be.

I sighed as I waited for Maribel to answer. If I was ever going to get this shop truly up and running, then I had to stop closing it down every time something happened that someone else thought I should take care of.

While I waited, I wandered the small patch of front yard. There were a number of sundials and birdbaths. Most people had only the sidewalk out front and would keep a small window box if they liked flowers, but the Milners had actual grass. After briefly wondering about how they mowed just this little spot, I dismissed it because I heard the front door open behind me as I got dropped into Maribel's voice mail. Goldy did not look happy. Her fists clenched and the veins stood out on the side of her neck. I held up a finger to ask her to wait. She snarled at me, but it couldn't be helped.

"Hey, Maribel, just me. Let me know when you have some time. I need to run a few things by you. And, yes, I know I could just text it to you, but I'd feel better actually talking it out. 'Kay, thanks and bye." I ended the call, took another one of those deep breaths that I seemed to be using an endless supply of, and then turned to face the growler.

"Anything worth mentioning?" I asked, putting the phone back in my shorts pocket and leaving my hand around it.

"No, nothing." She pushed the hair back off her forehead, straightened her bathing suit cover-up, smoothed the waist of her sarong, and then stepped gingerly off the porch. Putting her arm through mine, she started strolling as if we were just out for an afternoon walk, but her mouth going three miles a minute.

"There is something there with the selling of the house, though. I don't believe he sold it to Elsie. And why are they fighting now when they've been cordial to each other for the last few days?"

"Maybe they finally got to the point where they couldn't bottle up the words anymore." I was almost there myself and could totally understand. If these feelings had been simmering for some time, it wasn't hard to believe that they could just erupt like one of those sleeping volcanoes.

"No, this is different. I'm not sure why but his dad seems to be trying to push Darren away when he's never done that before."

"Um, I think you might be rewriting some history there. It seemed to me that Dad was not too pleased with any of the life choices Darren had made and was perfectly fine to not have to deal with him on a more regular basis. And from what he said about Darren's time here recently, I don't know that they have a good relationship, no matter how you want to spin it."

"They never really did, but his dad was always far quieter about his displeasure."

"Maybe now that Mom is dead, he can finally find his own voice. Isn't she the one who usually did all the talking and had the reins on their life? Maybe he finally feels free, like he was talking about with the sailing, and he figures it's his time, and he's not taking guff from anyone."

"I'm not saying there might not be some truth in there."

"Double negative for the win."

She chuckled at me but then got right back down to business. "I just really don't know what Darren is going to do if he gets kicked out of the house. He seemed so happy to be returning to the island, and it's always nice to have old friends return."

"Is it, though?" I asked, thinking about Pops and how he might feel with Darren as a constant part of their semi-retirement life. I mean, Pops did a lot of his own stuff, like helping out with the boat tours, fishing, and bird-watching. He made those treasure boxes. But I highly doubted he wanted Goldy hanging out with her old boyfriend on a daily basis, even if her old boyfriend wouldn't be interested in anything more from her than company and perhaps a partnership with our tours.

I was pretty sure my answer to that last thought was going to be "I'd rather not." Perhaps when not in the middle of being considered a suspect, he might be nicer and not so flighty, but I wasn't going to take a chance on that.

My phone rang in my pocket, and I disentangled myself from Goldy's grip to answer. "Hey there!"

"Where are you?" Maribel asked in a near whisper.

"We're just walking away from Darren's parents' house."

"We need to keep walking, Whitney. Now." Goldy grabbed my arm again, but I brushed her off.

"I'd walk a little faster," Maribel said. "I'm hearing there's a lot of talk in the office, and my understanding is that they're on their way over there now to find out why Darren hasn't been entirely truthful with his whereabouts. They want to know why Jericho as Jericho doesn't exist, but he does as Sammy Smithson, a pretty notorious manipulator who's been wanted in several states for fraud. Maybe even internationally."

Holy wow. I didn't even know where to start with all that new information. Maribel had just thrown enough at me to keep me busy researching for days. And I didn't have days. "Uh, yeah, that's not good, and I believe that this just got a whole lot bigger than me looking into something for Goldy."

"And I'm going to agree with you." Ray stood next to my elbow with his hand out. I shot a look at Goldy, but she raised her shoulders and shrugged.

"You weren't paying attention to me," she said, shrugging again.

"I'll take that phone. I'd like to talk to Maribel if I could." Ray's hand was still extended. I didn't really know what other choice I had than to give him my phone. I winced as Maribel gasped.

"Do not hang up," the captain said. He kept his eyes on me and the phone to his ear. "I want to make this very clear. There is no excuse for you sharing private police information with Whit even if she is your best friend. I've heard the other captain let it pass before, and I watched what happened last time. While I appreciate Whit's help, I can't have you talking to her about what is being brought into our office."

There was silence on his side. I could only imagine how Maribel was trying to defend her position. I'd go along with whatever she said. And, honestly, she'd told me little I couldn't have seen for myself or found out in a day or two. And, really, she had just been warning me to get out so I could stay safe.

"I hear you. and I'm willing to believe you were just asking her to back off." He zeroed in on me again with that gaze that said we were no longer playing games.

"I need both of you, and, in fact, all of you, to stay out of this now because it's a whole lot bigger than you think it is. Even you, Maribel. I don't want to hear about anyone digging around, anyone looking around, anybody searching around. I don't even want to hear your names unless I'm calling you into my office to file something, Maribel. And I am most definitely not kidding. Don't do it if you want to keep your job."

I could hear her squawking as he pulled the phone away from his ear and hit the end call button. Holy hell.

He handed the phone back to me, but at this point, I almost didn't want to take it. With one conversation, he had turned things upside down and threatened my friend. Oh, yeah, I knew my way around that tone.

"Captain Pablano, thank you for my phone back. I'd like to take a minute of your time to school you on exactly what just happened and ask that you never—and I mean *ever*—threaten my friend again. I might appear nice most days but believe me when I say, 'More of your conversation would infect my brain.'" I knew that Shakespeare education would come in handy . . . I folded my arms and hugged my chest with my phone under my armpit. "She did nothing wrong. She was letting me know you were headed this way. And it might be better if we were not in your line of sight when you got here, since you don't always appreciate that this is a small island, and it's very possible we could coincidentally end up in the same area without any planning on my part."

"And is that what happened? Are we ending up at the same spot with there being no connection between why you are here and why I am here? Tell me, Whit, what is this coincidence?"

I would not be mocked, and I most certainly wasn't lying. Therefore I had nothing to hide.

"I was asked to come here by Darren. He wanted to show me the film he had made to see if I noticed anything that might have set someone off. I ate popcorn, watched the movie, but found nothing except a slightly darker-than-normal advertisement to bring the tourists in. Then I left when Darren and his dad started arguing. I called Maribel to take up some time until Goldy came out of the house. We were already leaving before you showed up."

"Of course."

"You don't believe me?"

"It's not that I don't believe you, it's just that you always seem to be in the way of me doing my job. While I have appreciated your time and information in the past, I need to cut that off unless I want to explain to my supervisor why I can't seem to solve anything without your help."

He motioned for me to follow him away from the other officers and Goldy. I wasn't sure I wanted to go or hear what he had to say, but I also didn't want to deny the top police person on a very small island either.

He turned his back to the gathering crowd on the sidewalk and then leaned in.

I moved back a small step because he was in my face this

time. "Do you use those breath mint strips? Because I am getting some serious mouthwash vibe off you right now."

"Is there ever a time where you're going to take this seriously?" He sighed and rubbed the back of his neck.

"You know what? I will continue to take it seriously because I took it seriously from the beginning. Someone is dead, and while you think I'm playing Velma from *Scooby-Doo* or Nancy of the Drew variety, I assure you I am not. I don't want the wrong guy to go to jail, though."

"And you don't trust me enough to be able to do my job! Can't you just run your store and your boat rides and leave this to the people who know how to do their jobs?"

"I've tried to do that and look how it ended up the two times before."

"This is my watch now. That kind of thing will never happen again."

"The murder or the way the police would never have found the murderer if it hadn't been for me?"

"I . . ." He trailed off and rubbed his chin for a moment before starting again. "Look, I know you've been instrumental in helping with previous murder cases, and believe me when I say we very much appreciated your help last time, but I don't want this to become a thing." He held up his hand when I opened my mouth. "I don't want it to become a thing because it's dangerous. I'm supposed to look after all our citizens, and that includes you."

I closed my mouth and thought my way through that. I could understand where he was coming from, but I also knew that sometimes things got lost in the shuffle. If I could help, then why shouldn't I? People liked to talk to me. And if they said anything that might make sense and lead to something bigger, I wasn't going to stop them, and say, "Oh hey, you might want to go to the police with that because no murder talk around me."

There had to be a middle ground here somewhere. We'd just have to find it.

"I'm willing to not actively look for things." I should have crossed my fingers behind my back because I already had plans to look into at least three different things. But none of them were dangerous, and it wouldn't be too much trouble to then just give the information over to the police before going on with my day. Then I would be satisfying Goldy's need for me to help her longtime friend but also not put myself in danger. Win-win as far as I was concerned.

Ray squinted at me for a moment and seemed to see that that was all I was going to give and the rest we'd leave up to fate, or islanders, as the case may be.

"I'd prefer not to find you at the next location I visit before I'm even aware it's somewhere I need to go."

"Again, I had no idea you'd be coming here. Darren invited us over to watch his movie. I had only caught glimpses of it when it was playing in the theater for sound and visual checks. I came for the popcorn and apparently to be asked if we might want to go into a partnership with Darren on a new venture he's setting up to do tour-guiding on the island."

"That's news to me." He took out a notepad and jotted something down.

"It was to me too. And it wasn't something I asked about. I had no say in this, Ray, just for your information. If you've ever dealt with Goldy, you will know exactly what I mean by that."

He sighed. "Yeah, I do. She's already called the station seven times asking what we've done to move things along."

"Seven is nothing. Wait until you get into the teens. Now I have to go back to work and reopen my shop. I'll be available if you need anything, though I'm sure you will do everything in your power to not need a single thing from me."

He chuckled and shook his head. "I can't disagree."

"Then let me agree and get on my way with that. I'm out, you're in. I'm sure you'll do a great job figuring out who did what to whom."

"Why do I get the feeling you just cursed me?"

Now it was my turn to chuckle and turn away.

"I have no idea, but good luck figuring that out too."

Chapter 12

I hadn't heard a single thing from Goldy or from Darren for the rest of the afternoon. And I was fine with that. I finished up my day with some wonderful sales and lined up a series of treasure hunts for Pops. I planned to tell him the next day because at that point, I was a little Goldy'd out.

After a quick dinner, I shut down for the night, putting my notes about the death of Jericho, who maybe wasn't Jericho, aside and watching a movie with my lovely cat, Whiskers. Maribel was still at work when I got home so I didn't have a chance to tell her yet that we were off the case. Though I figured she'd probably gotten that all on her own when Ray had told her she'd lose her job if she kept sharing anything with me.

So I was ground to a halt, but that, if anything, gave me time to work on some articles for the local newspaper. I'd taken on a thread of articles involving the buildings on the island. I covered what the buildings were now and what they'd been throughout the years, who had built them, and what their original purpose was. I was having a blast doing them.

I also got paid by our local paper, which was never a bad thing. So, essentially, I now had three part-time jobs—shopkeeper, boat-tour giver, and newspaper-article writer.

Each spoke to a part of me. I'd gone to college for business with a minor in Shakespeare. No, I wasn't writing comedies or tragedies that would still be acted out hundreds of years later, but I was making a stamp on the writing world that would stay in the archives in perpetuity, as far as I knew. Someday, they might be microfiche like the articles I'd looked up a little bit ago. But most likely they'd just get hung on some cloud out in the international information highway, and that was good too.

I had one due to Reese at the *Catalina Islander* at the end of the month, but I still had time to do more research and make sure that what I was writing was good instead of just done.

First, though, I needed to go back to the salon. I had tossed and turned last night debating with myself if I wanted to keep looking against Ray's wishes. In the end I decided that if I had valid reasons, even if they were made up, to look into things and go certain places Ray would not consider going, then I wasn't doing anything wrong. And if I got some information that he might find interesting, then perhaps I'd tell him. Or maybe I'd tell him after he figured out who'd killed Jericho and let him know that if he hadn't shut me down, he could have known and made an arrest that much sooner.

Either way, I was going back to the salon this morning. I'd drop off some of my business cards, since I had seen yesterday they were low when I was there getting my hair cut. It was the perfect way to see if anyone had found new information for me or if they knew someone who would know. Since the Milners were a pretty private family, and it seemed few people interacted with them, it might be hard to get any solid information. But the hairdresser was the ear to every client, and since we had only one salon, I was pretty certain they might have a few places I could start asking.

The bell dinged over my head as I entered the building and Becca looked up from her phone at the reception desk.

"Oh, God, Whit! You don't have anything in the books

today, do you? Merry and Annaliese are going to be so upset with me. I don't remember calling to confirm your appointment yesterday, only the day before." She flipped her phone over and slammed it down on the computer, then started typing furiously, probably trying to find where she'd missed me.

"Becca . . . Becca! I'm just here to drop off some stuff. I don't have another appointment for at least six weeks if I remember correctly, and even if I did, I would never tell on you."

The typing stopped and she gave me a sheepish smile. "But you tell on people all the time from what I hear."

"I don't tell on them, necessarily, and it's only when they've done something really bad."

"I suppose that's true. Sometimes, though, it was a good thing it was done, even if it wasn't done in a good way."

Little bloodthirsty on this fine morning, but I wouldn't argue with her. All I really wanted was more information on the way Therese Milner was fixed up for her funeral and whether it was an easy job. I remembered Narina at the salon talking about all the scars she'd had on her face when Narina did Therese's funeral makeup, but a lot of people had some from maybe falling off a jungle gym when they were younger, or perhaps a boating accident, or something. It didn't have to be nefarious. Not everything was, even though my mind usually went there first.

"Did you hear what happened at the funeral?" I asked, and then admitted very quickly to myself that I should have probably picked something else to start the conversation with.

She laughed. "Yes, remember I was here yesterday and sitting right near you when they told you about the makeup job from hell. You know they have to go over and do it again today? When she fell out of the coffin they must have used her face to try to push her back in. Narina said it was a mess when the funeral director sent her pictures asking her to come back over."

"I thought they weren't having another funeral. That's what Darren's dad said."

"They aren't, from what I've heard but they still have to bury her, and Stu unbent long enough to ask someone to make sure she didn't look so messy when she went into the ground eternally."

See, a little piece of information, and now I had something I could ask Darren about. If his mother's face was okay with new makeup. Which could lead to any number of other questions and conversations without it seeming that I was trying to solve this for Ray. Nicely done, if I did say so myself.

"Oh? Is she over there now?"

"Yep, she took all her supplies because this time they asked for the whole shebang to be done. *Shebang*, that's such a funny word. Elsie said it day before yesterday when she came in to get her nails done, and I think it's a kick."

"Elsie was in here getting her nails done?" I tried to sound nonchalant and smiled benignly when Becca peered at me over the desk.

"Tell me you're not going to pin anything on that dear sweet lady. She's had a rough time of it, you know. She thought she had a marriage all planned and then it was ripped out from under her by Goldy." She gasped in horror, realizing what she had said. "Not that I ever want to say anything mean about Goldy. She's the sweetest thing to ever walk through those doors. Not that you aren't sweet too. Damn." She looked like she was doing everything in her power to hold back the tears, so I let her off the hook.

"Goldy is a force to be reckoned with sometimes, and she is not always sweet. I've heard there were some extenuating circumstances that had to do with the wedding being called off, and Darren didn't want to go through with it anyway."

"Oh." She breathed out a sigh of relief.

"And I was just wondering about Elsie because she seemed very distraught on Tuesday, then she seemed to think things were back on when we went to the theater so I wasn't sure when she would have had time to get her nails done." And whether or not that time was before, after, or during the time that this Jericho person might have been killed. Yes, I was adding a little emotional thing in there that I couldn't prove. I hadn't seen Elsie distraught at all. But since this woman thought Elsie was a dear sweetie, it didn't hurt to play along.

I wished Maribel could tell me more about the victim, since that was yet one more barrier to knowing what the heck was going on, but she wouldn't tell me anything after Ray had threatened her job, and I totally understood. I'd done some research on the Sam name she'd let slip but I hadn't been able to find out much. Most of it appeared to be under lock and key, or too high-level for me and my trusty interwebs.

"So you said she's over doing the makeup now?" I asked, bringing us back to my point.

"Yeah, she should be back any time now."

I stood there for another minute wondering what else I might be able to ask that would get things rolling in the right direction. I didn't really have anything more to say, but it felt as if I'd gained at least some info and I wanted more. Without more tidbits I would have nothing to offer Ray and no valid reason to be here. Other than my cards.

"Well, I brought these with me because I noticed the other day that they were running low."

"We appreciate it. It's always good to have some on hand. People like to pick them up to see what's around the island, and the owners always recommend you highly."

That might have partially to do with the fact that I'd helped them out on an occasion or two, and I appreciated it. "I recommend you all too."

"Great." Her smile was still in place as we stared at each other.

"Great," I said back, letting my mind race over anything else that could keep me here and not make me feel like an idiot for stopping by. I put my cards into the rack, squared them up, then moved them slightly to the left. I moved them back to the right, squared them up again, then moved the card in the back to the front because there was a slight bend in that first card.

I had nothing. No matter how hard I tried, I couldn't come up with any reason to stay, and no pretext to keep the conversation rolling.

When Becca glanced over at my card maneuvers, she smiled again, but this time it was a little strained. Okay, time to move on.

"Becca!" Merry yelled, streaming through the back door with her hand fisted around something and a scowl on her face.

"Yeah, boss? What on earth happened?"

"Narina just left me a text that she's out of here and taking off for parts unknown. Right after that, I got a call that Mrs. Milner's necklace is missing when they went to close the casket."

Well, well, well. Maybe I'd stay for just another minute or two.

My phone buzzed in my back pocket, and I tugged it out to see who could possibly need me in the middle of what should be a very telling moment. Darren. Darren was calling me. Did it have something to do with the missing necklace?

I thought about not answering but didn't want him to not leave me a voice mail and then get caught in a game of phone tag. So I stepped away from the counter and tried to keep one ear to the conversation that was going on at the counter and the other ear open for whatever Darren had to say.

"Hello?"

"Whit, we need you. My mother's necklace has gone missing and there's no way it got lost at the cemetery. I saw it before they closed the coffin again. It was right there. But then my dad wanted it opened at the gravesite to say one more goodbye and it was gone. That thing is priceless. I told him we should have kept it in a safe, but it was apparently in the will that she had to be buried in it. And now it's gone. My dad is about to have a heart attack. I don't need to lose another family member right now."

"Of course, of course." I tried to catch Merry's eye and mouthed *wait*. At first she was too tangled up in her anger to pay attention to me. But Becca noticed and she put a hand on Merry's arm, then signaled for her to look at me.

Wait, I mouthed again.

Into the phone I answered Darren. "I'm not sure what you want me to do about that. Do you need to call the police?"

"I'm not calling the police over this. They have enough to worry about with Jericho and the possibility he was not the person he said he was. Plus, they still need to figure out who killed him. So, no, I'm not calling the police. But I am going over to that salon that did her makeup because I want to talk to the woman who did the job. I want her to tell me *to my face* that she didn't just walk away with a very expensive piece of jewelry. And, if she did, I want it back."

"You might—" But he hung up on me, and I was left with the phone in my hand and racing thoughts that were actually taking some rational form.

"Okay, look, that was Darren and he's on his way over here right now. He thinks your employee took the necklace and sounds hell-bent on making her cough it up. I don't know where he was, but tops you have ten minutes to either find her or come up with some kind of solution about how we're going to get that thing back."

"Well, she couldn't have gotten far. She was just at the funeral home. The airport is at least ten minutes from there, and as far as I know there's no ship out for at least another hour." Merry twisted the rings on her fingers until I thought something might pop off.

"Which one do you think she'd take? And wouldn't she need to pack some things before she left?" I asked.

"Who knows? All right, we need a list of people who could be bribed or talked into making a quick trip to the mainland with no questions asked and a possible promise of money. I know she doesn't have a lot on hand, she just borrowed fifty from me the other day to pay her electricity, and we were talking about additional duties she could do to make ends meet."

"I'll start with the airport," I said, since my brother, Nick, knew just about everyone up there and might be able to chase down a lead before I could even get to the tarmac. Plus, I didn't want to leave right before Darren got here. I wanted to hear what he had to say. Although Darren was probably not going to be happy to see me at the place where he didn't know he was supposed to be until someone told him. That person wasn't going to be me.

My phone buzzed in my hand this time, and it was Goldy.

"Where are you?" No hello, no pause. "I need to know where you are right now because Darren is on a tear and ready to make a ruckus. That necklace that he wants so bad isn't real, and he knows it. If someone tries to look for the gradient on the rubies or find out where it came from, he's going to be found out. He used the real one to leave the island all those years ago and replaced it with a paste one. This could get ugly."

Ugly was not one of the things I wanted to be involved in. "I'm already at the salon. Should I hide in that closet again and wait to see what happens? Hurry, I think I hear a golf cart coming."

"You don't have to hide, but do not under any circumstances tell him you know the thing is fake, or don't tell anyone else either. Just listen to what he has to say. I'll be there in a few minutes." She too hung up on me without a goodbye, but this one I was fine with, since that meant she'd be here sooner and help with whatever damage control I might need.

"Let him come in and rant if he needs to," I said to Merry, who was standing at the ready. "I'm going to check in with Nick because I think they dated once and she might have gone to him. It didn't end badly so there's a real possibility she'd go to him first."

I turned away to make the call because I was not a fan of people watching me when I was talking on the phone.

Fortunately, Nick picked up on the first ring.

"I'm getting ready to take off, Whit. What do you need?"

"Do you have Narina with you?"

He paused and drew in a breath. "I do." The words were spoken very cheerfully, as if we were having a different conversation.

"I need you to keep her with you. She has something that doesn't belong to her and whatever she promised you, she's not going to be able to pay."

"Sounds good. I'll let you know as soon as I get things in order and have an idea of when I'll be back." His voice sounded overly chipper to me, but I hoped Narina didn't know him well enough to pick up on it. "If you don't mind taking this run on the tour boat I would very much appreciate it."

"You're laying it on a little thick," I told him, and he chuckled. "Do you want me to call the cops and have them come pick her up, or do you want to handle this yourself?"

"I've got it. Just wait until I'm back, and we'll get right on it."

"You'd better know what you're doing, brother mine, or I'm going to hurt you. I might just be the first in a long line if you fly her off the island and then we can't get her back."

"I would never leave you out. We'll talk soon."

And he too hung up. I only hoped that he wasn't going to leave me hanging.

Chapter 13

When Darren slammed through the front door of the salon, I stepped in his way immediately. He'd have to get through me before he could berate the people who had nothing to do with his loss or any of the bad things that had been happening to him lately. "Slow down. Take a breath. Think this through before you make a big mess. *Bigger mess* I guess is a more accurate phrase."

"I don't need your cutesiness or your shenanigans right now. I need you to step aside. I want that girl, and I want what's mine."

"And you'll get it. I have it under control. Do not go yell at Merry or I'll make it harder than even you can imagine to get the property you want. I just talked to Goldy so I've been brought up to date. Don't make this worse than it has to be."

He was nearly vibrating with rage when I put my hand on his arm, but he seemed to collect himself. He straightened his tie, smoothed down his hair, and then nodded. All the tension and steam didn't necessarily go out of the air, but it definitely moved from DEFCON one to more like a four.

"Now, we're going to be very nice to Merry and explain that your property is important to you and you'd appreciate any help she can give you to get it returned. In the meantime, I believe I have the woman in hand. She'll be here soon if Nick can be convincing enough and crafty enough."

At that he scoffed. And, look, it was one thing for me to make fun of my brother, that was part of the sibling code, but no one else was allowed to think he was anything but wonderful.

"I wouldn't be such a shit if I were you. I could have let her leave and done nothing to help. There's a bunch of stuff going on here and nearly everything is tied to you in some way. I'm trying to give you the benefit of the doubt, but your credit is about to be overdrawn."

His shoulders drooped. I'd hit a nerve, but I didn't care as long as he played nice and knew he was hanging by a thread.

"Merry, you said Narina took off from the funeral parlor?" I asked.

"Yes." Short, precise, but not happy. Then again, who was right now?

"And when did she go over there?"

The receptionist took that one. "About an hour ago."

"And when did you find the necklace missing?" I asked Darren.

"About six minutes ago, give or take a few seconds."

"Okay, let's sit tight for a second. Goldy will be here soon, and I'm hoping so will your culprit."

Since there was nothing really to do but wait, I wandered around. I picked up a magazine here and a magazine there, flipping through and then putting them back, making sure they were aesthetically pleasing in the way they were laid out.

I had run out of magazines and had moved to making sure the labels on all the product on the shelves faced front by the time Goldy finally came through the door. There had been times when I had been happier to see her, like when she picked us up from our parents or if she'd been gone for a vacation that she was just returning from, but this ran a close third.

"Okay, give me the sitrep." She stalked in like she owned the place and had decided to bulldoze it with people still inside.

"Sitrep? Really?"

"Let's not play with words. You know what I'm talking about. You watch enough of those cop shows, and I know for a fact you used to love to play those wartime video games. So give me what has happened and let's move on."

I gave her the sanitized version since I didn't know who was doing what and who was allowed to know what. It was all a jumble in my head. I was not used to that.

"We have a missing necklace, we have a hairdresser on the run, and Nick is trying to bring her down off the Airport in the Sky."

"And have you heard from him since?"

"No."

"Go ahead and do a check-in. Merry, what do you know about your employee? I don't think I've ever had her do my hair. She's newer, isn't she?"

"Newish but not newer. She's been here for a little while."

"Anything happen with her recently that would make her think it was a good idea to steal a necklace off a corpse and make a run for it? How would she even know what the thing was worth?"

As far as Goldy had said, it wouldn't actually be worth anything since it was fake.

"I have no idea. I thought she was a good person. She's been a model employee, so I'm not sure what changed."

"What's her name?"

"Narina Churman."

Darren groaned and then tried to hide it. But I'd heard it, and so had everyone else.

"Do we need to take this into another room?" Goldy asked.

"Just don't use the laundry room between the waxing and the massage because you can hear everything in there." I knew from previous experience.

"Fine, then, we'll take it outside."

She dragged Darren with her out the door. What was it with her being so handsy lately? Most people were very capable of following along where led without having to be treated like a grocery cart.

As soon as they cleared the doorway, I texted Nick really quick for an update and then ran to join them. Looking back over my shoulder, I saw everyone standing at the windows staring at us. I felt sorry for anyone whose timer had gone off to alert them their perm or hair color was done processing. It didn't look like anyone was about to be washed out.

"Why did you groan? And don't try to lie to me, or I'll escort you to the police myself with not a single regret." Goldy was not taking this lightly.

Darren covered his face with his hands, then shook his head.

"That name is all too familiar, but it's strange that she'd be here. And now of all times."

"Why is it familiar?"

"She's Jericho's cousin—or whoever my partner actually was since, I've now found out, he's not actually Jericho. When did this get so damn complicated? I just wanted to come home and be a tour guide and share adventures with my partner and tourists. Make friends, relax into the island life, and enjoy myself again. Yet here I am in the middle of something that I can't even wrap my head around."

While I felt sorry for him a smidge, I was not going to give in to that because we needed some more history. and now was the time to get it, before this Narina came back and caused Darren to clam up.

"So she's your partner's cousin? Or, at the very least, they definitely knew each other?"

"Yes. She was having a bit of trouble in California and thought it would be a wonderful place to start over, and since her cousin was going to be coming out here too, she thought they could make it a family affair. But she wasn't due to arrive until at least next month, once Jericho and I had some idea of when we would be opening."

"Okay, so then why would she have taken off with the necklace now? Did you talk to her at all?"

"No, I hadn't yet, with everything that was going on. I didn't even think she was here, much less doing my mother's makeup for the coffin. Really? My dad handled all that, but Jericho—or whatever his real name was—offered to follow up. God, this is such a mess."

He was not alone in thinking that.

My phone buzzed in my hand. Nick's text came through that he was not doing so well. Narina had run off as soon as he'd tried to coax her into the golf cart. I wasn't even going to ask if anything else could go wrong since I didn't want to provoke the universe into that scenario.

Find her, I texted back.

Okay, so we had a dead guy who was not who he said he was. A woman that was supposedly his cousin who had run off with Darren's mother's necklace. A necklace she apparently thought she could possibly hock but would have been in for a rude surprise if she'd shown up at a pawn shop or a jeweler. And Nick had lost our suspect. Excellent.

"I think we're going to have to talk to your dad and find out if anyone has contacted him about all this with the necklace. Were you the only one to find out, and does he know that it was fake?" I asked.

Darren's face went sheet white as he turned to Goldy. "You told her?"

"I had to or we'd never be able to get things done. Now, answer the question."

"My dad doesn't know that it was fake, and I can't face telling him. I'd have to admit to using the real one to leave them all those years ago, and I just can't. He has insurance on that thing, and we were supposed to remove it for safekeeping before Mom went into the ground. If the cops get a hold of it and then take it into custody, I won't be able to keep them from valuing it."

Darren's phone was the next to ring. He looked at the notification and closed his eyes and pinched the bridge of his nose. "My dad."

I had a flash of an idea and decided that, instead of chasing Narina all over the island, it might be better to lure her to where we needed her to be.

"Tell him we're on our way over. Tell him that if he wants the necklace back, we think we have a way to get it."

Darren did not look like he was onboard with my insta-plan, and I didn't want his skepticism to radiate when he answered the phone.

"Just trust me. This will work out, I promise."

"Dad, hey, I think Whit found the necklace. Can we swing by your house to see if we can get it looked at and make sure it's the right one?"

He paused to listen.

"Okay, give me a few minutes and I'll be right out." He tucked the phone in his pocket and nodded at us. It was go time.

Of course it took more than a few minutes, but I cut it before it hit three. I jumped into my golf cart, and so did Goldy, to follow Darren to his dad's house. I was assuming that whatever the fight from the other day was had petered out a little. I hadn't been asked to lend him my couch, and no one had said anything about his having to move out or leave. Let's hope I wasn't wrong and that we weren't moving directly into hostile waters without a boat, much less a paddle.

The journey to Stu Milner's house might as well have been to the other side of the moon. For some reason there was a ton of traffic out on the streets, and maneuvering our carts around the tourists was no easy feat. I sat more than once in my cart asking politely for people to move out of the middle of the street and onto the sidewalk. I got several very nasty stares from a few of the groups and one guy swore at me.

Well, then.

But I kept on going, glancing at the clock on my phone every few seconds to see how long we were taking. Maybe I should have just told Darren to have his father call the cops. What did I really think I was going to be able to do? Sure, I could ask this woman, Jericho/Sammy's cousin, what she thought she was doing. Or I could dig for more information. Maybe she was the one who had killed him, knowing she was going to take the necklace. Perhaps he hadn't wanted to play along with this scheme because he'd truly been in love with Darren. But then why had he lied about who he was and what he did?

I couldn't ask him that because he was dead.

I beeped my ridiculous horn at a set of men crossing the main thoroughfare and taking their sweet time to look around and talk. The sound of the yo-ho song from *Pirates of the Caribbean* made them glance my way, and one of them raised his dark, bushy eyebrows before turning back to his friend and gesturing toward me.

Whatever, just get out of my way.

Eventually they did, and we had about two minutes to make it up Palmetto Drive before Darren's dad exploded.

Finally we made the right turn onto the street and were able to climb along the road and up to the house. No one was parked in the street so we took the two front spots and then hit the steps running. Or at least Darren did. Goldy had on those killer heels, so she wasn't going anywhere fast.

And while I wasn't against running, I also wasn't exactly fiending to get into a house where a man was about to possibly find out that the necklace he thought was priceless was a fake.

How did I get myself into these things? Oh, right. The reason was right in front of me, coming up the stairs like she was entering the Met Gala and there were people waiting to take her picture on the red carpet.

"If you could speed it up a little, that would be great," I said drily, and then waited for the side-eye.

It didn't come, but she did wince.

"What happened?"

"I think I might have sprained my ankle. These shoes." She looked down at her feet and winced again. "I might be getting too old to be prancing around in these things."

Normally I would joke with her that of course she wasn't too old and those shoes were going to go with her to the grave, but something made me keep my smart-ass remarks to myself and instead helped her up the rest of the stairs.

"No witty comeback?" she asked as she gingerly stepped onto the porch and lifted her left foot to rotate her ankle.

"No, no witty comeback, and I'm calling Pops to come get you. I can handle this if you don't want him to come in and get involved even more."

She closed her eyes for a second and seemed to be taking a moment that I didn't want to interrupt. However, I heard yelling inside the house and a crash. I was going to have to get in there fast to stop whatever was going on.

Or I could call Pops and then Ray and tell him that I was just being a good citizen and keeping my nose out of things and letting him take care of this himself.

Those thoughts came and went in a flash as Goldy straightened up, shook out her ankle, and marched up to the house like a queen coming to sort out the peasants.

I followed along behind like her lady-in-waiting and then stopped short because of the scene before me. Furniture was turned over, papers scattered all over the room. Stu and Darren were both lying on the floor next to the mess. What in Davy Jones's locker had just happened?

Chapter 14

"What the . . . ?" I said, standing in the front entryway and surveying the damage. "Holy crap! What happened? Are they breathing? Goldy, we have to check! Who did this?"

But Goldy was already bent over Stu. "He's breathing." She moved to Darren while I stood there, feeling useless. "So is Darren."

"Okay. Okay. We need to find out who did this." My brain was whirling with all the things that had happened recently and I was trying hard not to trip myself over the edge of being completely overwhelmed.

"Whit, I don't know if that's a good idea. How on earth did someone manage to knock out two men and get out of here? I know they aren't exactly spry at their ages, but Darren is not exactly small or weak. I don't think that's someone you want to mess with, sweetheart. We need to call nine-one-one."

"You do that and I'll call Ray on my way out. I can't let the person get away."

Heading out the back, I placed the call to Ray. I couldn't exactly run and talk, so I made do with a quick stride, not caring if Ray heard me huffing and puffing.

"What is it now?" he asked when he picked up.

"Hello to you too. We have a situation over at Stu Milner's house. He and Darren are lying on the floor, knocked out. I left Goldy there with them while I try to find the person who did this."

"Whit, do not pursue. I'm serious. Whoever this is knocked out two full-grown men. I know they're older but they're not invalids. This is exactly the kind of situation you should leave to the police."

"You're breaking up." Oldest excuse in the cell phone user guide, but I had no other choice. I hit the end call button, tucked the phone in my pocket, and upped my game to a jog. Where on the island could this person have gone? And why would they want to harm two old men?

My jog didn't get me any information because, despite this being a relatively small island, it was still quite big when you were on foot. Stopping to bend over and get my breath back, I wished for my golf cart. Not that it could do rough terrain, but at least I wouldn't sound like a set of bellows.

My phone rang. I ignored it. It rang some more and I realized it could be Goldy. With the sun high overhead and my breathing still not steady, I didn't look at the display before answering. My bad.

"Whit, stop right now." Ray again. And this time I listened. Being that character in any movie or book who was labeled too stupid to live had never been a life goal.

"I have. I'm currently trying to get my breath back."

"Thank you." He blew out a breath that would have rattled the leaves if he'd been here in person. "Now, I need you to go back to the house and check on everyone, then try to talk them into pressing charges."

"What?"

"I have an officer there and neither of the Milners wants us to even look into what happened. They are adamant that this is a personal matter and want nothing to do with us. I need you to change their minds."

"I don't really know if I can do that. I'm not the one who knows them, that would be Goldy, and you know how she can be sometimes."

"Yes, believe me I do, but I'm going to ask you to try."

"I—"

"And before you say anything else, let me just make it clear that this will be your only part in the investigation. I know I told you to stay out of it, and I'm going to simply hope you have been and you were going to Stu's for some innocent, unrelated reason. I'm going to ignore the Nick flying thing and the rest of it, and just ask for your help on this one small thing. Then I want you to step out of the investigation altogether. I wouldn't even ask for this, but we're running on empty and I keep feeling like this is all connected somehow."

I sat down on a rock and stretched my legs out to rest my heels. Why? Why should I help when he'd made such an effort to make me feel like I was some kind of interloper? When I'd only ever tried to help and then handed it over to the police department when I figured it out? He'd specifically told me to butt out altogether. Making sure to tell me I was trouble. And then he'd threatened Maribel's job for trying to give me a warning. So why should I do his bidding now just because that was what he wanted?

"Are you still there?" he asked, sounding tense. Let him be tense.

"I'm here but I think you're going to need to take care of all of this by yourself. You've made it very clear several times that you think I'm nosy and get myself into trouble. Not to mention, you think I'm trying to steal your thunder or something. So roll across the sky like angels bowling, Captain Pablano. I don't know anything, and I don't have any sway. I would think you might be the one to get the lowly civilians to cooperate with you, not with another lowly civilian." And I hung up on him. I might pay for that later, but that would be on me.

I took my time going back to the Milner house because, honestly, I did not want to interact with any police officers and certainly not Ray if he happened to decide to come find me after I'd hung up on him. I was going to go through the back door, grab Goldy, and take her home. And then I was going to forget I'd ever gotten involved with this. Maybe I'd go to bed, even though it was still pretty early in the day. At this point, I didn't care. I could let the breeze blow through the windows, hopefully taking with it the irritation and the loose threads I couldn't do anything about except hope someone else could get them all tied into a nice little bow.

But not me. It wasn't going to be me, and I didn't care who asked or demanded.

The back door was unlocked, so I let myself in and went on a hunt for the people I assumed would be in the house. I heard Goldy saying goodbye and then the front door closed.

I was going to call out and say my own goodbyes and wish them the best of luck, but I stopped myself when Stu Milner started to talk to Darren.

"You have got to be hell-bent on bloody killing me. You already are killing me. I told you to sell that thing and get the hell out of here. Why on earth did you bring it back? Now we're both going to get into trouble, and I don't think there's anything I can do to save you this time."

"Dad . . ."

"Don't 'dad' me. You have to stop lying to Goldy, son. I was fine with holding up my end of the bargain for a bit, but you can't be serious about moving here and expecting me to continue to live your lie with you. It was one thing when you weren't a constant reminder of all I lost, but I can't do this every day." Stu Milner sounded defeated and done.

"And there's no way I'm letting you off the hook, old man.

Remember, you owe me. There's nothing that will completely pay off that debt. So no matter what I ask you, you'll do it with a smile or a frown, depending on what emotion I tell you to display. You were fine fighting with me earlier, and I know you managed to convince quite a few people of your innocence throughout your time on this earth despite the very opposite. Don't lose steam now. We're almost at the end of the game and then you can rest . . . forever."

I was stuck, and I knew I was stuck. I heard footsteps thud on the wood floors and knew if I did not get out of here, like right this instant, I might not be able to talk my way out of this one.

The footsteps drew closer. I panicked as I looked back and forth between the direction of the sounds and the back door behind me. Should I hide? Should I try to leave? Should I open and close the door loudly as if I had just come back and was looking for Goldy?

With fear clenching my gut, I had no idea which made the most sense.

The doorbell rang and I heard Goldy's voice in the front room. The footsteps receded, and Darren greeted her with a smile in his voice. I slunk out the back door, closing it as quietly as I could. Looking up at the last second, I found Stu Milner staring at me through the window in the kitchen. He smiled, put his finger to his lips as if this were our secret, and then winked at me.

Holy crap.

"All hands on deck, and don't you dare tell me no. I'm making dinner and everyone is going to be here tonight. Do not under any circumstances bring anyone but the people I invite. We need to have a family and friends meet up and get some stuff clear, and I can't do that if you bring a plus one." I dictated the text into my phone as I walked along the beach trying to catch my breath. What had that wink been? What about the smile and the shushing motion? Was Stu making us coconspirators? Did he think I was on his side? Did he feel I was in his debt for not telling on me? Would he keep my presence to himself?

All these questions were ringing through my head and drowning out the swish of the ocean on the nearly deserted beach. I had hoped that here I would be able to shut out the rest of the world and give myself time to come back down from the height of my terror. Instead, I just had more thoughts and questions, and few, if any, answers.

"I brought you a cone."

I couldn't adequately express how much I wanted that to be Felix's voice. I could eat my peanut butter chocolate ice cream and lean on his shoulder. Maybe quiet those voices as I sat and stared out to sea next to the person I had yet to totally admit I wouldn't mind spending the rest of my life with.

Instead, it was Ray Pablano. The third person on my list of people whom I did not want to see, interact with, or be near.

"What could you possibly want from me? We've already been through the whole you pretty much yelling at me for trying to help. You've threatened my friend's job, you have made it entirely clear you want me to stay completely out of things, and even when I do try to help, somehow I still do it wrong. Ice cream is not going to make that suddenly better." But, oh, did my mouth water at the thought of all that creamy peanut butter and the icy taste of milk chocolate. I turned my head to look out over my right shoulder and rolled my eyes at myself. I was not going to be swayed by ice cream. I wasn't. End of story.

"Can you at least take this before it starts melting on my hand? I even brought you napkins so you can clean off your hand after you eat the thing."

I did not take the cone and I did not look back over at him.

He sighed, and I knew that, yet again, I had done the wrong thing. But at this point, I cared about as much as I cared if Whiskers loved Maribel more than me.

And, yes, that was irony right there for you, in case you were wondering.

"Look, Whit, I know I've been harsh with you, and, quite frankly, I've also had to endure some serious shit because of it. I don't know if you're aware of how many friends you have on this island and how fiercely protective they are of you, but I got my ass handed to me by not only Maribel but Felix and then Deputy Mannon and Deputy Franklin, as well as your grand-father and Goldy. It's not easy to be talked to like I'm some kind of moron. And especially hard when I feel like a four-year-old who didn't get his way. But I listened, even as I cringed, and I'd like to make a deal with you."

My shoulders tensed because I could feel my brain telling me to look at him, but I didn't want to do it.

"Can you please take this cone? Please? I don't want to be sticky. I have a ton of paperwork to do today, and it wasn't a very good day to start with, nor is it any better now. If I can avoid having chocolate drip down my hand and probably onto my pants—because why not—then I'd really appreciate it."

I let my brain take over and looked at him as I took the cone. It was a triple threat, with so many sprinkles that it was almost too hard to tell what kind of ice cream was under them all. "Garry Templeton did this? What did you do, pay him four times the price of the cone?" The ice cream parlor owner was no-torious for keeping the sprinkles to a minimum and sighing heavily when I continuously asked him for more.

"Five times. And I had to hear from him too how I was a jerk. He peppered that with letting me know if I really wanted to be a part of this community, and not be seen as an outsider for the whole time I was here, then I should definitely give some ad-ditional thought to who I was serving and who was only trying to help me."

Wow, even Garry had defended me. Not that I didn't think he liked me, but I hadn't realized he liked me enough to stand up to the captain on my behalf. Certainly not enough to berate said captain while he charged him an exorbitant amount for the pleasure of bringing me a cone with five times the sprinkles normally allowed.

Taking my first lick of the cone, I closed my eyes, wondering why I hadn't known this was exactly what I needed to re-center myself and get grounded.

He waited a beat for me to open my eyes again and then jumped in. "I am aware I have not been the nicest of people about your involvement."

I snorted and almost got sprinkles up my nose. I would not do that again.

"Okay, we don't need to go all the way into me groveling, do we?" Pinching the bridge of his nose, he blew out a breath. "You know what, it doesn't matter. If you want me to grovel, then I suppose it's not the worst thing I had to do today."

"And what would that worst thing be?"

He chuckled derisively. "Talking to your grandmother."

"No doubt." I took another bite of the ice cream. This was not my talk, and I wasn't going to be the one to lead it anywhere. I wasn't trying to be a brat, but I honestly didn't know what to say or how to get through whatever Ray needed to get through, so I would follow his lead instead of trying to take the wheel and adjust the sails on my own.

"I'm not going to ask you to understand how difficult this job can be sometimes or how very hard it can be to do it in such a small bubble. I'm used to San Diego, where you're one of many and often are just in a dog pile. I did my job well, but hardly anyone was looking at me unless I did something horrendously wrong, and even then it was more reporters than it was my higher-ups. Not that I ever did anything horrendously wrong, but I watched it happen to other people. It was brutal."

I took another bite of the cone and just kept going. I had an idea of where this conversation might be heading, but I was not the one who had initiated it. I was not going to assume something and then be made to feel like an idiot if I was wrong.

"Usually you're more talky than this." He braced his hand on his knee and stared at me.

I held up the cone, toasted him with it, and then took another bite.

"Fine. I am trying to find my way around all of this, and I will admit that you have had some good information."

I hid my smug smile and he continued.

"I'm not a huge fan of having outside help that is anything more than something called into the tip line or a report made at the station of something you saw without going to search for it."

He paused like maybe he was waiting for me to say something or agree with him. I gave him neither, much preferring to enjoy my ice cream and let him talk himself into whatever he was trying to say.

"Whit, come on, help me out here."

I raised an eyebrow and got to the wonderfully sugary part of the cone that made everything right in the world.

"I'm not begging."

I shrugged.

"Fine, I'll beg."

By that point, though, I was done with the treat and ready to talk. Plus, we didn't need the tourists seeing the captain beg in the middle of the beachfront while they were trying to pick out a restaurant for dinner. It would not be a good look for any of us on Catalina.

"I don't need you to beg. In fact, let's be real honest here and admit I am not a huge fan of putting myself in harm's way to help. Yes, I've looked into things before outside of the cops, because they weren't looking in the right place and weren't getting the information they needed. I gave that to them because I wanted to make sure the right person was held responsible for their heinous crimes. I don't butt in to make you look bad. I don't butt in to make you look foolish or like you can't do your job. But if I hear something, I'm also not going to make you chase every single lead down when I am perfectly capable of trying to make sure it's not a lie. I'm like the human version of Snopes, if you will."

He stared at me and then just laughed and laughed. He even snort-laughed with an extra little guffaw. I was not amused.

I stood to throw away my trash in the bin next to me and huffed out a breath of frustration.

"No, no." He gasped. "No, please don't go. I am not laughing at you."

"That's what everyone says, and it's always a lie."

"No, seriously I'm not. The visual you put in my head with the Snopes thing was just too much, and it overtook me. If there is another better image than that, I can't even start to conjure it up." He wiped his eyes. "You're right. That's totally true, and I need you to be my Snopes this time too. I'm not asking you to put yourself in harm's way, but you do seem to have a knack for getting people to tell you stuff. I would encourage you to be a private investigator if I thought it wouldn't pit us against each other sometimes." He sighed and rested back against the bench with his legs sprawled and his hands clasped over his utility belt. "Look, here's what it comes down to. There are a lot of people on this island, and between the car wreck with Elsie and the death of Jericho, and now the stolen necklace, I am just not able to get a bead on any one thing. And each time I think I have it, it escapes me or becomes something totally different."

I sat back down because I didn't want to tower over him.

"So, let's make a deal. If you come across anything, or if something pops out at you as being something I might need to be aware of, then let me know."

"And how will you respond? Will you roll your eyes at me? Tell me I'm being ridiculous? Or maybe you'll yell at me for getting into trouble."

"I won't, but if you do something illegal to get any information, I can't save you."

"I've never . . ." I probably wanted to think that over before I said anything else, and then I let it sit there because I didn't want to have that discussion.

"Do we have a deal?"

"I didn't hear anything about a deal. I heard you asking me to tell you if I find things, but that seems to favor your house much more than mine."

"What? Do you want compensation?"

And now it was my turn to laugh. "I certainly do not need a fourth part-time job, so no. All I really want is to not be made to feel like I'm the criminal for trying to help or giving you information that might seem contrary to what you had wanted to see."

"I cannot promise I'll never yell. I'll try, but sometimes you bring stuff in that just makes me wonder how on earth you do it, and it rocks things. So I'm not yelling at you, I'm yelling about the situation."

"That doesn't work for me. You're a grown adult, and there is no way you can't control that."

"Fine, I will make sure there is no yelling. Not that I've ever truly yelled at you before, but apparently you don't remember that."

I scoffed at him to cover up the fact that he wasn't wrong. Then I continued on, as if I still had the upper hand in this. "And I don't want to be made to feel like I've done something wrong by having more information than you do."

"I actually have never tried to do that. I'm not in control of your feelings, and sometimes the things you've come up with seem so very out of the ordinary, even if they end up being true. I can't help that."

I gave that some thought. Running the scenarios in my head, I came to the realization that even if he did yell, I didn't have to stand around and take it. I could just walk away and let him do his thing. Or I could call it into the station and leave a message with Maribel, and then he wouldn't have a chance to yell at all.

But that brought up another point. "You need to apologize to Maribel."

He groaned and shook his head.

"You need to apologize to Maribel," I reiterated, and then shut my mouth. This was not negotiable.

"She needs to watch herself, though. She can't be out telling everyone police business. I can't have a leak in the department."

And I waited for more words.

"Fine. I will apologize to her, but I do expect her to take her job seriously, and I'm sure whoever she goes to work for after she finishes her degree will expect her not to share classified details with civilians."

I felt as if my gut had been punched when he put it that way, and almost wished I hadn't eaten all that ice cream. "You don't think she'll stay? You don't have room on the force for her?"

"I don't know that she'll want to stay. And I don't want her to feel like she has to. It'll be her choice when it's time, but for now let's worry about this new piece of the puzzle. What more do you know about this necklace and about this Narina woman? I can't find her, but there's something there that just isn't making any sense."

Time to come clean or time to back off and see if I could prove what I'd been told before sharing it with him? I wanted him to know what I had heard but didn't want to get in trouble for giving false information.

"Let me verify a few things before I tell you anything in particular. There's so much information going around inside my brain. I don't want to lead you the wrong way."

"While I appreciate that to some extent, if there's anything I need to know now, then I'd much rather have you tell me than wait until after."

I'd give him one thing and I'd keep the rest to myself until I knew more. "Jericho and Narina were cousins. Darren was under the impression she was coming over in a month or so, but she came over here ahead of time, maybe to see if she could set up some contacts, perhaps for this touring business Darren says they were setting up. I don't know that for certain, but it's been floated around. And I don't know why she took the necklace, unless she thought she had to go once Jericho was dead, and so she no longer had the means to get those contacts."

Massaging his forehead, he leaned forward. "Nothing can be cut and dried, can it?"

"I'm assuming murder almost never is. There's usually something going on in the background, and once you find that one missing piece, the whole jigsaw puzzle comes into focus. But I think getting her to talk to you is probably a step in the right direction. Why was she here? For what kind of business? Why did Jericho act as if he'd never even heard of this place, much less have someone he was related to right on the island? Or did she double-cross him, and that's why he's dead? I mean, it could be anything. And it's not easy when no one else on this island seems to know him. So was it an accident? Did someone get mad at him and push him, even though he'd only been here for a day or two before he dropped onto my box of bows? Or did he jump and not make any noises because he knew his cousin was going to do something that he wasn't going to be able to overcome?" I sat back and dabbed my chin with my napkins just in case I'd dripped.

"That's a lot of unknowns."

"They'll also help get some answers if you start piecing them together. Not that I want to tell you how to do your job, of course . . ."

"Of course." The radio on his belt squawked and he took it off to check it. "What's up?"

"Boss, Narina Churman just walked in the door all on her own."

"I'll be right there."

"Enjoy your afternoon, Captain." My brain was afire with curiosity about what Narina wanted and what she'd say, but I kept that to myself.

"Yeah, thanks."

I watched him walk away and waited until he rounded a corner to jump up from the bench and hightail it over to my house. Maribel should be home by now, and I texted everyone else to let them know the meeting was still on, with a slightly different slant. How committed was Goldy to Darren and, by extension, Darren's family? I didn't know, but I might just be about to find out.

Chapter 15

Leave it to Maribel to decide that no meeting should be without her chips and homemade guacamole. I'd been to restaurants where they made it at the table, but no one had ever been able to top Maribel's. Ever.

There was nowhere in our tiny house that we could all sit together, so we split ourselves between the minuscule table in the eat-in kitchen and the living room. It was close enough. I looked around the area and was happy to have everyone here, with no extras.

Pops and Goldy were sitting next to each other but seemed to be leaning away from touching. I didn't have time to deal with their apparent distance from each other right now. It was going to have to wait, and really it was none of my business.

Felix had Whiskers on his lap and was ignoring her as he went in for more dip and chips. He smiled at me before bringing the chip to his mouth. Maribel bustled back and forth between the two spots to make sure everyone had something to eat. And Nick had chosen to hang out on the sofa. I stood kind of in the middle of everyone so that I could see them all and the murder board that Maribel had put up at the same time.

We had some information on sticky notes, other info on

index cards that I'd taped to the board, and Maribel had hand-
written some notes on the paper she'd taped to the wall. She had
called it a murder board, though it really wasn't a board at all. I
didn't know if she thought we were going to keep it as a souvenir
at some point, but my answer to that would be no. If she wanted
to take a picture for her phone gallery, that was just fine with me,
but once this was all done, I wanted the board to be done too.

"I'm not going to call us to order, but I would like to see
how everyone is doing, and if anyone has anything to add to our
smorgasbord of crime up here."

Nick lifted his head from the arm of the couch just enough
to glance at the board, then shook his head and put it back down.
Goldy rose from her chair and glided over to the board as Pops
remained sitting. They hadn't even been holding hands when
they were sitting at the table, and I didn't know what to think of
that without getting into a panic. All bets were off on helping
with this if their relationship was going to take a hit. Nothing
was worth that.

Maribel brought out another bowl, this time filled with fresh-
chopped salsa. "Dig in, there's more where that came from," she
said cheerily, but there was an edge there. Maybe that's where I
should start.

"So as we gather here today to solve this thing called murder,
because I'm about ninety-five percent sure it wasn't an accident,
I want to begin by letting you know that Captain Pablano bought
me ice cream today." I ran through the conversation and how I
thought he didn't want to ask but he had to because I wasn't
doing anything wrong in trying to help. I didn't say much about
how Goldy had sicced everyone on him because I didn't think it
was worth mentioning and I didn't want to irritate her. But I had
to stay in the not-doing-anything-wrong category if I didn't
want him to try to nail me to the floor for stepping over the line.
I finally came to the part where I'd demanded that he apologize
to Maribel, and the breath left her body in a whoosh.

"Oh, my God, thank you for that. Even though you really shouldn't have had to do it, I appreciate it. I don't want to lose my job."

For the moment, I thought, but then I shifted that to the back burner. One of these days we'd actually talk about her plans going forward, but that day was probably not going to be today.

"So expect an apology. Anyway, somehow, we're supposed to get this cousin to talk. She went to the police but isn't really saying anything. Nick, are you up for that at all? She did ask you to take her on the plane." I paused. "How did she ask you to take her on the plane? Did she bribe you? Or was it a sob story?"

Nick winced and I rolled my eyes.

"Both?" I asked, really not wanting it to be the first one, but knowing my brother.

"I gave the fifty dollars to the police. I told them she'd left it in the plane and I thought she might have forgotten it in the cockpit." He shrugged when I growled at him.

"And the sob story?" I figured I should know all the things he knew before we went further.

"Typical 'have to leave quick' thing 'because of pressure'. She said something about a death in the family but didn't specify, and I didn't ask. I've taken many people to the mainland with far less than that, and we dated once. It didn't work out, but not because she's a bad person."

"So then you should be able to talk to her again."

"Yeah, right, dear sister of mine, and then I made her get out and tried to take her to the police. I'm pretty sure that's not going to be a chance she gives me a second time."

I was the one wincing now because he wasn't wrong. "Anyone else want to take a stab at it?" Perhaps that was the wrong choice of words, but Goldy looked over at Pops, who was snickering, and smiled gently at him. As soon as he caught her, he clammed back up but just for that moment it had been nice.

"Well, then, I guess I'll see if she tries to get her job back at the salon. Although that's probably not going to work either. Maribel, do we at least know where she is?"

"Still at the station, but not for long. Apparently, there's a song and dance she's doing to make them not suspect her, saying she had heard they were looking for her and wanted to make sure she was available before she heads out so there are no lingering questions. And they have nothing to hold her on without the Milners admitting what happened and who did it. They don't want to involve the police because the necklace thing is shady, so there's nothing there. I assume they'll have to let her go if they have no crime to charge her with, and then she'll go back to the room she's renting from someone. Then again, she could be out on her own."

"There's nothing we can really do with her at the station. Unless anyone has any other ideas?"

I got a series of shrugs, and that totally did not help at all. So I moved on to other things. "Does anyone have any new information about this Jericho-who-also-goes-by-Sammy thing?"

Felix raised his hand, and we all snickered.

"I don't think you have to raise your hand here, babe. Just go ahead and jump in."

He scratched Whiskers between her ears and kicked up just one side of his mouth in a smile. "I wasn't sure what the rules were since I feel more like I'm in a war room than getting ready to eat some enchiladas with my favorite people on the island."

"Noted." I circled my hand in the air to get him to move it along.

"I was out diving this morning and decided to go back to that cave to see if I could find anything new in there with the logo, since I had the morning off and not much else to do. And the whole thing has been wiped clean. Like the sand is raked and the whole enclosure smelled of cleaning products. That's not going to be good for the environment, but it seems like someone was very careful to make sure that if anyone came in, there would be no trace of them."

While I would have liked to have gone with him for the cave exploration, I totally understood I had been all over the island over the last twenty-four hours, and not everyone could wait to see if I had free time to help them out.

"Totally wiped clean?" I asked as I made a note for the board. "I don't remember there being anything in there except that broken crate, unless something happened after we were there, and they were trying to clean it up." I stuck my note to the board randomly, wondering how on earth we were going to be able to get any kind of organization on this.

Maribel approached after she'd set down the chips and started moving things around into clumps. Hopefully, she'd explain to us what she was doing once she finished, because it still made no sense to me.

I took out my trusty notebook, though, to see if there was anything I'd missed or any way to connect things to each other.

"I just don't see how this all comes together, and what does the necklace have to do with the death other than everything centering on the Milner family?"

Pops snorted and Goldy shot him her famous side-eye. But she was going to have to get over herself if we were to have any hope of truly making this murderer pay for what had been done to Darren's partner.

"Is there anything you'd like to tell us, Goldy? Anything at all that could help us figure out who would want to hurt Jericho or Sammy or whoever he is?"

"No." Short, succinct, almost staccato, and she looked as if not even dynamite would make her budge.

"The time for secrets is over, dear. You can't protect him if you won't help Whit out, and, frankly, you had no right to ask her to put herself in danger if you're not going to give her everything you know." Pops hadn't moved from his spot at the table and neither had Goldy, but it seemed as if the entirety of the Pacific Ocean were between them as their gazes locked across my small dining room table.

She crossed her arms over her chest and then so did he. She tapped her foot on the wood floor in a rhythm that sped up the more he just stared at her and waited for her to answer.

Was it getting increasingly hot with angst in here or was it just me waiting for the volcanic explosion that I was pretty sure wasn't too far off with the battle of wills going on right before our eyes?

"I have nothing to offer." She uncrossed her arms, patted her hair, folded her hands in her lap, and crossed her ankles under the table.

"Nothing at all?" Pops put his hand flat on the table and leaned in.

"Absolutely nothing. I know he didn't do this, and anything from the past has nothing to do with anything in the present. So let's move on. We have a necklace that was taken."

"A necklace that isn't real," I jumped in, and I got level-three side-eye. Maybe I should have kept my mouth shut but I wasn't holding anything back. Well, except for that conversation I'd heard Darren and his dad have, but I needed to think my way through what it could have meant before I shared it.

"What do you mean it isn't real?" Maribel asked, shooting me and Goldy back-and-forth looks. I was currently making eye contact with pretty much no one because I didn't know whom to look at or what I wanted them to see.

"Goldy?" Pops said with warning in that one word.

"It's nothing." Dipping a chip into the guac, she daintily took a bite, then another, and another, keeping silent while we all were very obviously waiting for her to tell us why she thought the necklace being fake was nothing when it could very well be a whole lot of everything.

"Goldy, if you're not going to help me, then I don't know what more I can do to help you. Is it really nothing or are you still just trying to protect him? What if it was him? What if he's the one who did this and we could have it all wrapped in a bow for the department and get him out of the public?"

"I won't sit here and listen to this. It wasn't him."

"But how are you so sure, Georgiana?" This was from Pops, and he didn't look only baffled, he looked upset and irritated, and a bunch of other emotions were sweeping over his face like a storm rolling in from the west.

"I know. I know he wouldn't do anything like this. He was in love with Jericho, or Sammy, or whatever his name was, and there is no way he would have killed the poor man in the middle of trying to get the whole thing set up for his movie. He just wouldn't. I know him better than that."

"You *knew* him better than that."

"I *know* him better than that, Thomas. You are not going to be able to convince me that he's some horribly evil person after all these years. He's still Darren, and he's still my friend, and there's no way he . . ."

She trailed off because Pops had commandeered my laptop and pulled up a website with Darren's details. The web search went on for at least five pages as Pops kept moving the page forward, and every single hit was a headline or blog or article about Darren Milner and all the trouble he'd gotten into throughout the years. All the scrapes he'd narrowly missed. All the times he'd been put on trial, or accused of something, or brought in for questioning. The crimes ranged from embezzlement to stealing from coin collectors to running chop shops. He'd also been looked at for underground drug running and weapons deals. Every one of the crimes was different, with varying levels of sinisterness. But every single time he'd gotten away without a scrape or a record.

"I'm not sure what to tell you, but this keeps going, in case you were wondering." Pops reached for Goldy's hand, but she tucked it around her waist and looked like she was going to cry.

Part of me wanted to console her, but something in the section for images caught my eye. I was not going to let this one get away from me again.

"What is that picture?" I had a touch laptop and when I pointed, the picture popped up immediately.

"Well, I'll be damned," Felix said, getting up from his spot and bringing Whiskers with him. "Isn't that the logo from the crate we found in the cave?"

"It sure is. Now, what on earth is it for?"

A few clicks and I knew exactly what I was looking at and why it had seemed so familiar, and yet I couldn't nail down what it was for. It was a shipping label with the logo from the cave and Darren's movie shot. I'd seen it in passing hundreds of times on railroad containers and packages and paperwork, but it was such an everyday thing that what exactly it was attached to just hadn't stuck in my brain. Especially since it was a fish jumping above a wave with a hook in its mouth.

Then it hit me. "It was a shipping label from a company I had worked with on the mainland. I didn't remember the name, but this is it with just a few differences. It's strange."

It was familiar and yet not. Shipping, yes, but something was off about this particular one and a little different from the one that had been on the crate and in Darren's film.

I asked Felix about it, and he leaned in. I could smell the light tang of sun and sand and sunscreen on him, and I really wished we were out in the water with that octopus again instead of crammed into my little house with few answers and tempers running high. The logo kept cropping up. The fact that we had seen it in that cave that was now wiped clean, as well as in Darren's mock movie, felt important. Especially when I remembered how stiff he'd been when I asked him to roll the film back, and how he'd never answered my question of whose house it was in before Goldy cut me off that day.

Felix shook his head. I felt the same way. There was something there but I just didn't know what. Yet.

"Okay, look," I said. "I think we've exhausted what we can do tonight. Let's eat the wonderful enchiladas, talk about something that's not murder, and, Goldy, think hard about how far you want us all to go out on a limb for someone you are protecting way more than anyone in this room. Now, I know he meant a lot to you back in the day, and I know I wouldn't want you to tell all my secrets to anyone, but this could be important. We don't need all of his secrets, but if there's something—anything— that might help to clear his name, or point to someone else, it would be a good thing to share. And maybe you should consider whether you actually know him or if you just remember him fondly. I'm not saying he did it, but I do not want my ass hanging out to dry if he did and I tell Ray to look elsewhere when he's on the right track."

She frowned, and a tear leaked out of her eye. I couldn't have told you the last time I saw her cry, but I so appreciated that Pops unbent long enough to take her out onto the back deck, where I heard them murmuring to each other.

"Enchiladas!" Maribel said in a voice that was far brighter than the situation.

"Enchiladas," I repeated. "And then tomorrow you and I are going back out to that cave, Felix, because there has to be something we missed, and I want to know what it is. Or what they're trying to cover up. It all has to be tied together. I just don't know what it is or where to find it."

Chapter 16

I was back in the sea, the waves lapping at my shoulders and the smooth water enveloping me like a cocoon I wasn't sure I wanted to emerge from. There was something about the smell of the ocean and the heat of the sun that made me feel like I was in heaven.

Earlier I'd seen Nick go by in a kayak and we talked briefly before he'd continued paddling on. I'd been looking for my octopus friend and thought maybe Nick cutting through the water had scared him away. But the little cephalopod was quick to find us about ten feet from the mouth of the cave, and this time I welcomed him along for the ride.

I didn't reach out to touch him because I didn't want to get squirted with ink in case he got scared, but he kept whooshing up next to me, sliding out, and whooshing back in. He was more than welcome to stay, as long as he didn't suddenly decide I was an enemy.

Felix swam alongside me with his shoulders bunching and releasing. Out here in the depths, he was a master at the crawl, and there was something so joyous about being here, even if it was for darker reasons than our just taking what amounted to a stroll in the water.

"Do you smell it?" he asked as we got closer to the entrance.

"You can't miss it," I responded, treading water and taking the snorkel out of my mouth. It was chemicals mixed with some kind of stench, and it wasn't pretty, no matter how I tried to breathe only through my mouth.

Felix nodded.

"Did it smell like this yesterday? This is more than just chemicals. This is like chemicals covering something, like death."

"If you don't want to go in, you can wait out here with our little friend. I don't mind, I do need to check it out, though, because you're right, it's not like yesterday. Yesterday was like a Mr. Clean kind of thing. This is far more decay. Maybe yesterday it was so new and fresh, but now the chemicals are wearing off and leaving the original smell exposed."

Anything was possible.

"Do you think we need to pull in the police?" I asked.

"Well, now, that's an interesting question, since technically I am the police."

And that was very true and not always something I thought of. "Okay, so what do we do, and is it okay for me to help you do it?"

"I hereby temporarily deputize you to be my assistant. Let's get out and look around."

He swam toward the shore, and I followed along behind, leaving my new friend at the edge of the water. The octopus kept his eyes on us, moving and flowing with the slight waves kissing the shore.

I had sea socks on so it wasn't too bad walking in the sand, but as soon as I emerged completely from the water, the smell took on a dimension that felt heavy. *Decay* was the right word. The stench was covered by chemicals but was definitely there.

"What are we going to do if we find something dead?" I asked, hoping against hope we wouldn't. Death and the sea were rarely clean or tidy. Especially if it was something that washed up on the shore.

"I'll call it in, and we'll go from there. I don't see anything, though. Do you?"

I looked around, taking in every inch of the stony walls and the sandy beach. Everything looked pristine, just like Felix had said. There were still rake marks in the sand itself, which had to mean something, or why would someone have done it?

I wished I had brought my camera with me, but I hadn't, and my phone was back at the house.

Leave it to Felix to be prepared. "Were you a Boy Scout?" I laughed as he pulled an underwater camera from a pouch strapped to his leg.

"Um, no, we didn't have the resources for that kind of thing, and I had an after-school job from the time I was twelve, so I guess I'm used to being ready for just about anything."

Felix and I had talked long into the night sometimes about our current lives and events happening around us, and what had brought us to where we were within the last few years. But we didn't often go back much further than that. And now I wondered why. I made a deal with myself to change that. He was my boyfriend. I knew his favorite color was green and his music choices ran from deep house to electronica, but there were depths here I hadn't yet plumbed. Maybe it was time I did. The thought made me a little clammy, even in the warmth of the cave. Because if I asked him about his past, then he was going to ask me about mine, and I wasn't sure how much I wanted to go back or even how far. Some things were better left there.

But now was not the time to worry about that, because we were in a cave, trying to figure out if something had died in here recently. But it stayed in the back of my mind for perhaps our next picnic.

Now there were things to find and questions to answer.

I took my time walking along the rim of the cave and inspecting each inch but still found nothing. When Felix and I crossed paths about halfway around the half-moon, he stopped and pulled me in for a kiss. I loved that about him and so much more.

Before we got lost in it, though, I pulled back and smiled up at him with my hand on his chest. "As much as you're tempting me, I have to say the smell in here is starting to clog my nose. And I don't see anything in the area that should be making this smell. What do we do next, boss?"

He looked around and then put his hand on his chest to cover mine. "I'm thinking I let the guys at the station know about a possible disturbance and then we let them figure out if it's something weird. And if they don't take me seriously, then we do some more searching and maybe come back if we find anything new that points to this cave."

"Sound plan." And it was. We got back into the water, and the little octopus was right at my side. I reached out a hand to him before I thought about it and he darted away but came right back and didn't squirt me. Maybe I'd come back simply to see if he would get closer and let me touch him.

That was the last happy thought I had before we came out of the cave and faced a beautiful forty-foot wooden sailboat with its masts bare that appeared to be on fire while being swept along by the current.

What on earth was going on? And did it have anything to do with this whole fiasco or were we in for one more wrinkle in a sail that didn't seem to fit in with the others?

Felix struck out toward the boat, shooting through the water in record time. I was a good swimmer but nowhere near as fast as he was. I trailed along behind, keeping my eye on the forty-foot boat itself to see if there was anyone on it or if it had cut anchor for some unknown reason and was just drifting along with no one to man it.

"Hello! Is anyone aboard?" Felix bellowed as he got closer.

When we were a few feet away from it, it was easier to see that it was not on fire altogether but that there was just a large fire on the deck. Of course it could rage out of control in seconds, depending on the wind, and I still hadn't seen anyone on deck. Nor was anyone coming out topside.

So had something happened and had the boat come from the marina in Avalon Bay? Or had it come from the other direction, or from the mainland in general?

As we drew up alongside the boat, I had a sinking feeling in my stomach. The boat was called the *Darren True* and it was a forty-footer with its sails dropped and smoke rising from the deck.

"Felix, are you sure you should be getting on that?"

He'd grabbed hold of the scupper on the starboard side and was dragging himself up to be able to perch on the railing.

"I don't only dive, Whit, and I am part of the rescue team. Normally, I wouldn't do this by myself, and I'd have protective gear on, but I don't have time for that if there's someone on-board I can get to safety. And if it's bigger than I think it is, I'll dive back into the sea and we'll get to land as soon as possible."

"I trust you. I just don't want anything bad to happen to you."

"You and me both, babe. You and me both." He pulled himself up to be able to look at the decking clearly and called back over his shoulder that it was a fire pit.

You did not have a fire pit on a smallish wooden boat. I would pause before having a fire pit on a yacht, but I'd seen it done. However, a small boat made of wood with cloth sails and ropes for rigging? What on earth was this person thinking? And where were they after leaving a fire burning on deck unattended?

I treaded water about fifteen feet from the side of the boat, waiting to see what Felix would find. I hated not being able to know what was going on but I did not want to get on the boat and be one more person trying to scramble off if something went very wrong.

I didn't want Felix on the boat either, but there was nothing I could do to keep him from danger, except watch for anything going awry.

My legs were getting tired and the thought of having to swim back to shore was not high on my list of things to be excited about. I tried to pull up that wonderful feeling of the ocean surrounding me and cradling me, but being this far out with this much anxiety was not letting that happen.

I was so focused on the boat in front of me, and watching Felix use an extinguisher to put out the flames that I totally missed the dinghy heading my way until it almost ran over me. The slap of oars cutting into the water alerted me when the small vessel was about twenty feet away, and I was just barely able to move to safety. The person manning the boat had curly brown hair put up in a bun on top and wasn't keeping an eye out. I opened my mouth to yell when the craft passed me and I saw it was Elsie who was pulling the oars.

Was this her boat? Had she set a fire to burn the thing down? What was on board that she so desperately wanted to make sure it would never be found?

Since she was coming between me and Felix, I didn't think it would be a good idea to yell to him and have her clued in to the fact she wasn't alone. She used the left oar to paddle herself around to face the boat, and I lost sight of her face, but not the way she shook her fist at the sky or the roar of "Dammit!" as she rowed faster toward the *Darren True*.

All bets were off, then, and I didn't care if she knew where we were. I would be better able to maneuver out of her way if I could anticipate what she was going to do, and, considering the way she was dressed, I highly doubted she was going to jump out of the dinghy and try to catch me in the water.

When she stood up, it was not a casual rowing outfit she was wearing. No shorts and a T-shirt. Not even a pair of jeans and a sweatshirt. No, she was in a full-on gallery-visit kind of getup with a beaded dress and jacket in a plum color that set off her skin tone very nicely. It looked great on her but didn't suit her being out in a boat that could tip or another one that she'd set on fire.

"Felix!" I yelled, and she turned toward the sound of my voice, causing her to lose her footing, and she fell over into the water. Well, shit. Now what was I going to do? I had no life preserver and no life jacket, and the possibility of someone freaking out about drowning and taking you with them when you were trying to save them was very real.

Felix came to the starboard side of the deck just as I started swimming toward the woman, and he dived in toward her too. Maybe between the two of us we could keep her from harming herself or either of us.

But then she popped to the surface about ten feet away from me and started thrashing around in the water. Or actually swimming, if I was watching what I thought I was watching. Her teeth were clamped down around a knife. What the hell?

"Felix, she has a knife. Be careful." I went back to treading water. She stopped midstroke, and Felix hung back a bit so as not to be within reach of her.

"Oh, for God's sake." Or at least that was what I thought she said since she was trying to talk around a knife.

"What?" I yelled, treading backward a little more in case I was wrong.

She let her legs sink, took the knife out of her mouth, and repeated herself. "Oh, for God's sake. I'm not going to hurt anyone."

"Are you certain of that?" I asked, because really you just can't take some people's word, and we were not exactly standing on land, where I could start running if I had to.

"Yes, I'm certain." She sighed and seemed to sink a little.

"Are you okay? Should we get you to the boat or the dinghy? Or do you want to swim in?" Felix, ever the rescuer, was on duty and not going to let a little knife keep him from helping out. He swam in fast, grabbing the knife out of Elsie's hand, then backed off just as quickly.

She spun, obviously angry as she grunted curse words. We all kind of hung in the ocean, waiting to see what would happen next.

"I'll tell you what," Felix said. "Let's get your dinghy tied up to your boat, we'll all get on deck, we'll talk things through, and then I'll give this back to you once you let us know what you're doing."

Pushing her hair back, she spit at him, but it fell back into the sea. That was not what I wanted to swim through, but really the ocean was filled with much worse than human spit.

She hung her head for a moment and heaved a sigh that rippled the water around her. Or at least I hoped that was her sigh, and that we didn't have some other creature circling us and waiting to see who might be the tastiest morsel or the slowest swimmer.

Her head snapped back up and she shook it, tossing around her wet hair. "Let's go aboard. I'm tired of all this secrecy and hiding and trying to do things without getting any results. And I'm tired of always feeling like I'm behind the great eight ball in the sky. So welcome aboard, and let's get down to it so I can get my knife back and you can get the hell out of my way."

That sounded both encouraging and a little frightening. But Felix signaled for me to come along, and I did, hoping this wasn't about to be not only my worst decision but also my last.

Chapter 17

Felix dipped a bucket into the sea for the fifth time and poured it on the deck and the fire ring just to make sure everything was extinguished. I watched as a piece of paper and a glove rose to the surface of the fire ring. Should I grab it or leave it?

Elsie beat me to the decision, grabbing the two things and holding them close to her beaded chest. Were they the things she had been trying to get rid of? What was the significance? Would we be able to pry them away from her if they ended up being some clue in the death of Jericho aka Sammy?

"You're going to want to hand that over now so we don't have to fight over it. I might not be dressed like a police officer at the moment"—he looked down at his swim trunks, which were covered in palm trees and pineapples and frowned—"but I am here as an officer of the law, and we will figure out what it is that you've been doing, as well as why you've been doing it."

Elsie sighed, then handed the things over. I wanted to get a look at them, so I sidled around to Felix's left, always keeping an eye on the woman who looked defeated and didn't seem to know what to do with her hands now that they were empty.

"So where do you want to start, Elsie?" I asked. The glove

was partially singed with the fingertips gone and the ribbed cuff only half there. The piece of paper looked as though it might have writing on it, but until it dried, I couldn't see any real letters or make out anything other than the fact that the ink was blue. "Did you kill Jericho to get to Darren? Are you really that out of your mind to think someone who turned you down fifty years ago and fled the island would suddenly want to marry you because his mother died?" Not to mention that she wasn't the kind of person he'd be interested in anyway, but I thought I'd made my point with what I'd said without taking it further.

She sighed again. And then she harrumphed. A lot of noise but no information.

"Let's go back a little bit further." Felix crossed his arms over his chest and leaned back against the wooden seats lining the deck. "How did you find out Darren's mother had died? I can't imagine they sent you an invitation to the funeral."

"They didn't." Her eyes narrowed, and she pushed her hair off her forehead.

"So how did you know to come to the island on that day, and where did you get the car to crash into the casket?"

"My family still lives here, and since we've been here for a long time, we have a certificate for a real car. I was just here on a visit when my nephew mentioned Therese had died and the funeral was happening at that moment. I knew a car would be faster than one of those ridiculous golf carts, so I drove over. Crashing into the coffin was purely an accident, like I told Captain Pablano. The brakes were giving me some trouble along the way, and I should have stopped sooner and slower instead of trying to screech to a halt."

Her words were right and kind of made sense, but the tone in which she said them felt like she was reciting a story she'd read on a piece of paper. Like she'd rehearsed this before, in case anyone asked.

"And did you honestly believe Darren would be ready to marry you now that his mother is dead?" That question came from me, and she was not pleased with it.

"You don't understand how it was back then. There were many things that could happen, and many ways in which life takes turns you weren't expecting. I had been to an enlightenment session recently and the stars were aligned in my favor. When I heard Therese had died, my coming here, my being available, and my longing for days gone by all came together for me to know for certain this was the man who I was supposed to spend the rest of my life with."

"So things were in alignment, but it was obvious he was with someone else. Unless he contacted you at some point and told you he really wished he hadn't left the island or broken things off with you?"

"Well, no, but I knew there was something between us, and it would have worked if your grandmother hadn't caught his eye and taken him away from me." She pursed her lips and ran a hand down the leg of her dripping-wet dress.

"I'm . . ." Honestly, I wasn't sure what to say. I looked over at Felix, and he shrugged.

"So what were you burning today, Elsie? What is with the glove and the paper? And why did you leave a fire on the deck of your boat when you weren't even here to make sure it didn't go up in flames?"

Felix was going in for the harder stuff, and I appreciated that about him. All those questions were good ones, and ones that needed answers, though mine did too.

Now it would be interesting to see if she would answer any of it.

She clamped her mouth closed and crossed her arms over her chest. For the love of all that was holy, she'd better not decide to clam up now.

"You either talk here, Elsie, or we take you into the station, where you can deal with them in an interview room. There's something going on here. The timing is way too convenient to be coincidental. Did you kill Jericho?" Felix was not kidding around. I promised myself I would buy him his own ice cream later if we actually got some answers. Hell, I'd buy it just because he tried.

"I did not kill Jericho." Her words came out rapid-fire, filled with anger and an undertone of what sounded like grief. Then again maybe I was overanalyzing and watching way too many reruns of murder shows.

"Do you know who did?"

"I do not."

"Did you really show up at the last second after everyone had been moved out of the theater, or did you somehow sneak out and then come around the corner like you had no idea what was going on? Because, again, that timing seemed very convenient."

"It's not convenient," she said, grabbing a pillow off the bench next to her and holding it to her stomach. She leaned over and started keening, a sound I don't think I had ever heard. It was a cross between the rails under a train running hot with brakes and the screech of a raptor.

"What the hell?" I glanced over at Felix, and he looked just as stunned.

"I have no idea." He put the knife down on the seat next to him, then went over to Elsie, taking his steps carefully to see if she'd jump up or run off, because right now this whole thing felt like a weird drama being played out on the big screen.

"What is going on?" he asked her. He didn't touch her but he did sit down next to her.

Good call, because if he'd squatted in front of her, she might have knocked him over when she dived for the knife across the boat.

Instead, I sprang into action, which I rarely did, and beat her to it.

And then she dived off the side of the boat and swam for the dinghy like her life depended on it.

Felix and I had stood staring at each other and then after Elsie as she made a break for the shore. I wasn't going after her again, and I wouldn't have made much progress once she got into the dinghy. She was obviously on a mission. And as much as Felix had said he was a cop and could be doing things as an officer of the law, that was only partially true.

"I guess we sail this back to the bay and beach it? I'm not entirely sure of the protocol here." I picked up the pillow off the floor where she'd flung it and put the knife back on the bench. I wasn't sure what significance it had or why she would have gone for it again, unless she had planned on hurting one of us.

The dinghy was getting closer to the cave where Felix and I had just been, and I was wondering what she thought she'd do there. It had no connection to anywhere else on the island as far as being able to get away was concerned, and we would be able to get someone out there to pull her in. Except we had no cell phones.

I kept an eye on Elsie until she passed into the cove. "Let's find the radio and see if we can get the captain to come get her. I wish we had a dinghy too, so we could go after her, but I just don't know how we can do that, and I really don't want to split up from you right now with her out there."

"I totally get that and was thinking the same thing."

The radio was belowdecks under the stairs. She had a nice setup down below: a small galley kitchen with a table that also turned into a couch as well as a cookstove and sink that could be covered by a big board to make additional counter space. The bathroom was one of those multifunction things where the shower had the toilet in it and the sink was about the size of a big coffee mug. The V-berth where she would sleep if on board was made up with sheets and a comforter. Hanging in the small space between the bed and the ceiling were quite a few pictures of Darren in various settings when he was much younger .

Okay, then. Ray might just have a field day with this once we got in touch with him.

Felix was calling through the radio channels and finally got in touch with someone at the station.

"I have a boat you're probably going to want to bring in. Do you want me to sail it over to the bay or do you want to come out and get it?"

"Sail it in. We just had some kind of vandalism happening over at the Casino and broke up six different fights on Crescent Avenue in different establishments. We're filled to the gills, so thanks and let Whit know that whatever you all have found, I am sure Ray will appreciate it."

The resignation in the dispatcher's voice was hard to hear but present. I really felt bad for him. All of this happening at the same time was a real stretch on their limited resources. I thought briefly about pointing that out to him, but since he already knew, I didn't need to add to it.

"We've got this," Felix said. "You go do what you need to do, and we'll let you know when we're in port."

"Do you want to sail or do you want me to sail?" I asked Felix.

"If I sail, does that mean you're going after Elsie?"

That was the idea, and it made sense. He didn't need to ask it like I was trying to pull one over on him. . . . Of course I'd sail if he really wanted me to. If he *really* wanted me to. But I wasn't against going after Elsie either.

I had a feeling I was going to be sailing, though. "Let me call Nick and see what he's up to."

We had seen him kayaking earlier, so it was possible he was still out on the water and in the mood to sail. He could drag the kayak behind him and go from there. I went topside to look around and decide what to do.

And there he was. He came into view on that slim kayak of his, whistling a tune and jaunting along through the wavelets he was making with his rowing.

"Ahoy there, maties!"

I rolled my eyes because that wasn't something people normally said unless they didn't know any better.

"Nick, we need your help. Can you sail this into the bay for us? We have an errand to run." I tried to make it sound as boring as possible so he'd just agree and we could be on our way. But he was smarter than that. Damn.

"Who are you chasing now? Have you found the killer? Goldy will be so proud. Soon enough you might be in the running for favorite grandchild. Then again, I just have to smile at her, and nothing you do can ever compare."

For the love of . . . "We have things to do. I need you to sail this into the harbor for the captain at the police station. Can you please do that for me?"

"Ooohh, so it is a police thing." He looked way too excited for this, and now I was wondering if I shouldn't have asked in the first place. Felix and I could have moved the boat into the water in front of the mouth of the cave and blocked Elsie from coming out while also being there to confront her.

Damn, why hadn't I thought of that sooner? I should have just waved Nick along and figured it out for myself. I loved my brother, I swear I did, but there were times when I just wasn't sure how we'd grown up in the same house.

"You know what, forget it. We'll move it. I don't want you to have to get out of the kayak. Can you head back toward shore, though, and tell Ray exactly where we are? I think we're going to need some backup."

He paddled off with a salute, and I breathed easier.

"We've got a situation out here, Ray," I heard Felix say into the radio below me. He must have called back or Ray had contacted him after the dispatcher had let him know the situation. I listened because I didn't want to be the one talking, but I also didn't want to miss out on what was being said.

"Listening."

"It looks like Elsie Jacobs was trying to burn something out here on her boat, but then she abandoned it. We came aboard just in case and she almost hit Whit with a dinghy."

"Is Whit okay?"

"When is Whit not okay?" Felix said, laughing, and when he released the button on the radio, Ray was chuckling too. So very nice to be the reason we could all be merry in the middle of something wonky going on.

I hustled down the steps and grabbed the radio receiver, then nudged Felix out of the way. "Elsie was burning something and when we asked about Jericho's death, she doubled over on herself but said she didn't do it. Then she jumped in her dinghy and went into that cave around the south part of the island. We were in there earlier and it smells like decay and cleaning chemicals. I'm not sure why she headed there, since she can't go anywhere else, but we're on her boat and I don't want to sail this back by myself nor do I want Felix to go after the woman who was wielding a knife earlier alone. Can you send someone out?"

"We'll be right there. I'm not even going to ask you to stay put since I assume you're already on your way after Elsie, who happened to go into the cave before you."

"Actually, no, we're not." I was so pleased to be able to say that and take him off guard. "We're going to move the boat a little closer so that if she tries to make a run for it we can be right behind her. She'll be rowing but we're not going in until one of you gets here."

"I don't know whether to thank you for allowing me to do my job or groan because you're in a position to tell me I can do my job."

"We'll be here, watching, for when you come in."

He clicked off and I turned to Felix. "Ten minutes tops?"

"I'm going to go with seven, even if he was in the middle of a seven-course meal five miles away, I still think he'd manage to get here in far less than ten minutes."

Felix had overshot the time as Ray showed up in a motorboat within six minutes. We'd pulled into the cove a little bit more and set the anchor so that we would be in Elsie's way if she chose to make a run for it. I kept looking for my little octopus friend, but he wasn't showing his tentacles. Maybe too much was going on.

Ray waved to us as he moved into the shallower water. We couldn't sail in without risking running aground on the coral or the rocks.

I wanted to dive out of the boat and meet him on the shore to see what was going on. He didn't reappear quickly as I thought he would, with Elsie in tow, and after about three minutes, I started to worry. Well, if I was being really honest with myself, I had started to worry as soon as he cut the engine and was out of sight.

"Do you think he's okay in there?" I asked Felix, trying to peer into the darkened cavern. Nick had paddled to the side of the cave and was watching intently. I should have made him get out and let me go in. There was no way to see anything from here except shadows, and nothing appeared to be moving. There was no sound except for the rushing of the water to shore.

"Ray knows what he's doing, Whit. Let's let him handle this. If he needs us, he'll call out."

"But what if she has another knife? What if we sent him in there after a killer, and he's her next victim?" I bit my lip and hoped I hadn't just made some kind of strange prophecy on the water.

"Damn!" we both heard Ray yell from inside and I couldn't wait any longer. If he was hurt or in trouble, I was not going to be the reason he had to go it alone.

Dropping off the starboard side, I plunged into the water, then popped up to start swimming.

"We're anchored," Felix said right before he dropped down beside me.

If somehow Elsie got back out here and managed to get to the *Darren True,* she'd still have to weigh anchor and get things set in motion before she would be able to go anywhere. And by that time, we'd have more speedboats out this way. I had to believe that.

I had never cut through the water so fast in my life, not even when I once had a very curious garibaldi bearing down on me like he wanted to eat my toes. I put hand over hand and kicked my feet hard to make it as far as possible in as little time as I could.

Felix was next to me and then he shot ahead. I didn't mind one bit, because as long as someone was helping Ray, I didn't care who it was. I hadn't heard anything from the cove since Ray had sworn, and that could be either really good or really, really bad.

When I made it under the arch of the cliff and into the shallower waters, I put the final bit of energy I had into surfacing as close to the shore as possible, then got up and ran. But after taking three steps in the knee-deep water I realized there was really no need to run.

Elsie was not here. Ray was standing on the beach with one hand on his waist and the other massaging his forehead. And he was standing alone. In fact we were the only three people in there, and I had no idea how that was even possible.

Had she disappeared? I had a feeling that might be Ray's first question to us.

Chapter 18

"Where the hell is she?" All three of us asked some version of that question at the same time. I repeated mine louder a second time as Ray and Felix, stunned, looked first at each other and then around the cave.

I was more irritated, better yet, angry, than stunned. This woman had been slippery from day one and now she somehow had managed to get past us when we had been watching the entrance of the cave the entire time. Even if we had blinked, it wasn't like she would have been able to get out of there without someone noticing.

Her dinghy was there, though, right on the beach, sitting empty with the oars broken in half, making them useless for anyone else.

Where had she gone?

I walked the perimeter, wondering how someone could have left without being seen. Dumbfounding, to say the least.

Unless . . .

"Were we both looking at the mouth of the cave the whole time, Felix?"

"Yes, we were," he growled. Okay, so maybe someone else had joined me on the irritation and anger train.

"And did we think to glance into the water?" I stalked over to her dinghy and rooted around under the seat. My heart sank when I came up with the one thing I really wished I hadn't found. A canvas bag. One that was big enough to have held a full set of scuba gear. Diving gear she could have put on, gone deep enough to not disrupt the water above her, and sneaked out right under our watchful eyes.

"I think we've been had." I shook my head and wondered if we'd ever see Elsie again. Although where was she going to hide when we were on the island? We had her boat, she'd broken her oars, and there was no other way for her to escape unless someone up at the airport would let her and her sodden dress on their plane.

I made a mental note to call Nick and make sure he didn't accidentally take yet another criminal back to the mainland in that plane of his.

Unless . . . And this was my second *unless* in two minutes, and it made my stomach roll.

I looked back out to sea and watched the anchor being raised on the *Darren True*. I couldn't see the deck from this spot, but I was pretty positive that if I could, I would have seen Elsie waving to us as she cranked the outboard motor and sailed off with the current.

"I hope you have juice in that boat, Captain, she's getting away."

Ray already had his phone up to his ear and was rubbing his closed eyes. "I need backup. We have a boat leaving the area that I need someone to chase down." He paused. "Yes, Whit is here with me. Yes, she's fine. No, I haven't yelled at her." He looked over at me and frowned. "No, I am not going to hand the phone over to her for you to check."

"Maribel, I'm fine. He's being perfectly pleasant." I heard laughter over the phone and it was very deep.

Ray ended the call, looked me over, and sighed. "That was

not Maribel. The whole station is in on this one, and they're rooting for you, even though they should be just doing their job. This is not a team thing."

"Sarcasm much?"

"Don't push me, Whit. I appreciate any help you can give me, but this is still not your job." He tapped the phone on his thigh. "I don't want you to get hurt running after something that should have nothing to do with you."

"I understand that."

He snorted.

"I do. I don't want to get hurt any more than you want me to get hurt." I still felt the sting of being pushed down that ravine during my first investigation when I'd gotten too close to the killer, and it wasn't a happy time. "But I also want whoever did this on my island caught and taken away. I want to go back to not having to worry about who was killed and why. Do you think I like living in what feels like a murder podcast sometimes?" I put my hand up to stop him from saying anything. "The answer is no. But people talk to me, and I see things differently than you do, and if I can help, then I would like to."

Felix put his arm around my shoulder and kissed my hair.

"Maybe give him some room, Whit. I know you want to help, and of course he's always open to citizen tips, or if you'd seen something. But you're bringing him stuff, and he's still trying to prove his worth here on the island. That can't be easy if every time he has a big issue you come in and are able to get the murderer before he can."

I knew what Felix was saying and I even agreed with it, but it still felt a little like a set-down, and I was not a big fan of those.

I removed his arm from around my shoulders and stepped away from him. "Really?"

"Yes, really. You know what I'm saying is true. So don't fight with me."

Now there was definitely going to be a fight, but it wouldn't happen here in front of everyone. Oh, no, I would hit him with my words when he least expected it and I'd relish every moment until I could do just that.

He seemed to read my mind at the last minute because he closed his eyes and groaned.

"Thanks, Felix. I appreciate the backup but that's not exactly the kind I was asking for. I told her she could help this time, and I'm sure if Whit finds out anything while snooping around that she'll be the first to tell me or someone on the force instead of running after leads herself."

I was quick to agree with my mouth, but in my mind that was probably not going to happen, and we all knew it.

"Of course. Of course. I wouldn't want to do anyone else's job and you're very capable of whatever it is you think you're doing out here. I'm sure you would have seen Elsie at some point before she burned the note and the glove, and then caught her before she sailed away to wherever she was going."

I heard the motor of the harbor patrol boat outside the cave.

Glancing over at Ray, I caught his sigh and really did feel bad for the guy. If I was trying to do my job and someone came in and stole my thunder, then I wouldn't be the happiest of campers either. I almost laughed when I realized that was exactly what Goldy had done at the shop, and to say I wasn't happy at first was an understatement. Although now that I'd seen her do her magic, I knew it would be ridiculous not to let her help. Although that had to be a lot different from having someone come in and solve your case when you were the captain of the police force and the murder solver was a shopkeeper who also sometimes drove a glass-bottom boat. Just saying . . .

It wasn't quite lunchtime when I arrived at Dame of the Sea. I'd heard from Captain Pablano that the *Darren True* had been boarded and seized with little to no issues. Elsie wasn't exactly forthcoming with the info, but at least that was one more thing I didn't have to worry about. And if she was the killer, then that was two things off my plate.

I'd inserted my key into the front door when my phone rang. Goldy. I'd expected a call from her earlier, to be honest, and was surprised she hadn't been harassing me most of the day. I'd texted her to let her know about Elsie or at least what I knew about Elsie. She texted back that I should have believed her in the first place instead of needing someone to prove her right for me to take her seriously.

I'd been thankful at that point that she wasn't in the store so that she couldn't hear my scoffing or scold me for rolling my eyes. I leaned against the wall with the key still in the lock, determined to at least enjoy the sunshine if I had to have this talk.

"What can I do for you, Goldy?"

"You can solve this case is what you can do. Why do you have the shop open when you should be looking into what Elsie was burning and also at what she was hiding? And where did she go? Did harbor patrol get her?"

"I've already talked with Captain Pablano and he said that he's interrogating her right now." He had actually said questioning, but I thought the harsher word might appease Goldy. I, of course, was wrong.

"You could have been the one interrogating her and probably gotten a lot further than he will. Don't you understand what kind of rules they have to play by? You don't have any."

"Or, conversely, I am the ruler of the dirty pool handbook per some of our residents."

"Then act like it, dammit."

"I'm doing my best. You don't have to swear at me. I do get what you're saying, but if she'd told me something, Ray couldn't do anything about it unless she was willing to tell him too. This is a better thing if you'd just look at it from the law's perspective."

"I don't want to look at it from the law's perspective. I want to look at her through a set of bars."

"We don't even know what she did. I didn't see her in the theater and she didn't arrive until after Darren's dad."

"And she knew things she shouldn't."

"Or she knew things because someone on the island called her and told her what was going on. Or even texted her."

"I doubt it."

"And I'm not going to fight with you about it because neither of us knows, and it would be pointless. Now, what are you up to today?"

Changing the subject, or at least trying to, rarely worked with Goldy, but this time she actually let it slide.

"Darren is gathering Jericho's things to send them back to the mainland."

"Is he allowed to do that?" I had a hard time believing Ray wouldn't want to keep the dead man's possessions, even if it was just to get a better idea of who he was and, by extension, who might have wanted to kill him.

"He's allowed to do whatever he wants. Especially if Ray already has the right suspect in custody."

I was sure Elsie had done something, but I just wasn't sure I believed she killed Jericho. Yeah, she was hung up on something from years ago, but that didn't necessarily lead to murder. Especially when she seemed to think she'd win Darren back no matter what his circumstances or preferences.

It was all so confusing, and I really wished I could get a bead on what had happened in each incident and then take it from there to figure out the why and then, and the whodunit. I wasn't really any further along on the journey than I'd been just yesterday, and that felt a little like I was behind instead of really helping at all.

So I needed to do some sleuthing and then start putting things together. I had to work at the store for a while, since it would be ridiculous to once again miss out on having Dame of the Sea open.

"I don't know what you want me to do. I have to work sometimes and Ray is on it."

"And he's looking at Darren again. We just got a call."

"We?"

"Yes, Darren and I."

I let that hang in the air for a few seconds. "I thought you were out at the conservancy with Pops."

Not to be outdone, she let that hang for a full minute where mine was about twenty seconds in reality. Should I apologize? Did I just stick my foot in my mouth? Did I care?

I did care, so I wasn't sure what to say. She answered before I had to come up with how to make this right.

"Here's the thing, Whit. Let's get down to the brass tacks."

I would have expected that from Pops, not her.

"Why are we going for brass tacks? It's been stripped down to the basics. I'm not getting anywhere because something new keeps popping up."

"We're going for brass tacks because something is happening on the island, and we need to be on the watch for what's going on. What happened with Elsie earlier?"

"I have no idea. Ray hasn't decided to tell me what he has or has not figured out from her yet. And if you say I should be calling him to find out, I will hang up with you so you can be the one to call him and get him to talk to you."

She scoffed. I held my tongue because that was all I was going to say about that.

"Whit . . ."

"Goldy . . ."

She sighed, and I got a beep on my phone letting me know another call was coming in. Pulling my phone away from my ear, I saw that the police department was calling me. Maribel? One of the guys? One of the detectives? Maybe Elsie was using her one call from jail to call me. I mean, at this point I wasn't going to dismiss anything anymore.

"Goldy, hold on." I didn't wait for her to stop talking before I switched to the other call.

"Hello?"

"Whit, Maribel here. Keep your head down and watch out for this group of guys that seem to be causing some serious issues throughout the town."

"Ray let me know about that this morning."

"Interesting. He didn't say anything to me. But here's the thing. It's getting worse and I don't know why they're out causing chaos."

"Who the hell knows why anything freaking happens anymore?" Exasperation, thy name was my current mood. What was all of this, and why wasn't any of it making any sense? It was driving me over the cliff but also keeping me in a weird place where I couldn't do anything but think about this.

We were nearing Labor Day, and I just wanted things to slow down so I could finish enjoying my summer before we started the new rush of tourists.

"Ryan just brought one in a few minutes ago, and I caught him trying to look at my computer. Then I found him in the file room trying to get a few of the drawers open. I had to push him back into the waiting room by myself. I tried to call someone to get him but everyone is being sent out to pick up more and we're running out of hands."

"So arrest them and put them in rooms."

"I don't have the authority to do that."

"They don't know that. I think you should grab Felix and make him earn his keep."

"I don't want to irritate him."

"When you get that degree, you're going to have to irritate a bunch of people, so you might as well get used to the feeling now."

She laughed, but it was nervous.

"Maribel, you got this."

"I do. Of course I do."

"So go do it."

"I'm going to go do it."

"See you. Bye." I hung up, wondering how on earth she was going to be able to move into a position of authority. Or was I making too much out of this because I wanted her to fail so she wouldn't leave me?

I didn't need to think about that at the moment.

When I jumped back to my other call, Goldy had hung up. I wasn't surprised, but I was concerned that would come back and bite me in the ass.

No matter what, I was opening the store and hoping to do brisk business in the four hours until I closed.

I locked the door behind me because I needed to set my things down in the back room and I didn't want anyone coming in and surprising me or making trouble. I was taking Maribel's warning very seriously.

Heading for the back room, I checked over inventory and made a short list in my brain of what I wanted to bring back out to restock the shelves. I used a second key to open the back-room door but hesitated for just a few seconds in the doorway.

Something felt off. Maybe it was the wind whistling behind the tube of wrapping paper coming right at my head.

Chapter 19

I will never know exactly why I rocked back a step when I hadn't even registered what was happening, but I thanked my gut anyway and promised it a chocolate peanut butter cone later for its service.

My hand flew up and I caught the cardboard tube an inch from my forehead. Yanking it away from whoever wielded it wasn't easy, but I did it anyway, stoked by my anger about these last few days.

"What in the hell are you doing?!?" Definitely needed the interrobang on that one because I was livid.

A woman with dark hair and a vaguely familiar face stared at me, then shifted her glance around the room like a caged animal. And she had every right to do that. Because after the last few days I'd had I couldn't promise I was going to consider letting her free until she told me whatever I wanted to know. How in the hell had she gotten in here? That would most likely be my first question after I found out who she was.

"I . . . I . . . I . . ." Her eyes went wide as she started to shake, and I honestly did not care.

"Who are you and how did you get in here?" That was me

channeling every villain voice I'd ever heard booming from a cartoon movie.

"Narina. I'm Narina." Her lips quivered around the words. Part of me was shocked to have her here and the other part still wondered how she had entered.

"Ah, Narina, who dated my brother briefly. Narina, who worked at the day spa and called Merry to let her know she was done and running. Narina, who tried to talk my brother into flying her to California with a stolen necklace. That Narina?"

Every word made her cringe, and I started to feel like a big old meanie. Damn my conscience!

"Yes, that Narina. I did try to return the necklace to that old man but a woman wearing gloves backhanded me into the wall, so I dropped the necklace and ran for it." She touched her cheekbone where it bloomed with the beginnings of an ugly bruise.

"Who hit you?"

"I don't know her name. She came into the salon the other day, but I wasn't her stylist. You could ask Annaliese or Becca."

I could but I didn't think I'd have to. Gloves, woman, slightly off her rocker. I was betting on Elsie. "Did she have curly brown hair? About seventy years old?"

"Yeah. She took the necklace when no one was looking but me."

Son of a sea biscuit! "Are you related to Jericho?"

"Is that the name he's using these days?" Her eyes were not nearly as wide. And since I was getting so much information, I wasn't ready to turn her in for breaking and entering just yet.

"It was the name he was using before he died."

"That sucked. People were trying to say it was an accident, but I knew better. He might not be the most honest guy in the world, and he'd hurt plenty of people, but no one deserves to die for trying to make a living."

"And what exactly did he make a living doing?" I sat on the edge of my desk, waiting for her to answer.

She twisted her hands together. Her gaze darted to the back door and then the one leading out into the shop. I was perfectly positioned to keep her from running into the store, and from here I could see the back door was locked. She wasn't going anywhere.

"Listen, if you can give me some solid information to work with on Jericho's death, then I'm not against saying I talked to you, you said you dropped the necklace and I believe you, and they need to look elsewhere. And definitely at the woman who hit you. But I need information, Narina, and I need it now."

Her shoulders slumped. The dejected look on her face would have broken my heart in any other set of circumstances, but not this time. "He was a swindler. He was a commodities broker. He was an insurance guy. He was a lot of things, but mainly he was interested in the operation his lover's family has had going for years and wanted to be a part of their huge and very lucrative business of shipping things that don't always make it to their destination, which they then sell on the black market."

Well, I'll be damned. Perhaps Darren hadn't killed his partner, but he was far shadier than Goldy was going to be able to handle.

"Why didn't you leave when the cops released you?"

"Because I have nowhere to go and if Darren thinks I've told on him, there could be hell to pay. I just wanted a chance to rest for a few minutes and gather my thoughts."

That did make sense but I wasn't letting her off the hook. "Have you always been involved in these kinds of shady businesses? Do you have records or proof you'll be able to share with the cops?"

She looked at the floor and heaved a sigh. "I really don't want to do that, since most things I have also implicate me, but I guess if it will help the cops figure out who killed my cousin, then I don't have a choice. He was one of my best friends and I was leaving the island to do research of my own."

"Research on what?"

She didn't answer and I couldn't force her to tell me, but I made her promise to tell Ray everything. She wasn't happy about it, but it was my price for not pressing charges.

Of course Ray showed up at the back door right at that moment. Damn. I hadn't even had a chance to call him yet. It was like he had a radar for possible trouble involving me, and showed up without any need to contact him.

As she was leaving, I remembered one last question.

"Why my back storeroom?"

"Everyone has always told me you never are in here when there's a murder on the island, so I figured I was safe. You might want to change the back door lock, though. It wasn't easy to jimmy open and I'm sorry, but I think I broke it."

I waved her out, took a look at the lock that seemed fastened but was in fact broken, and figured I would handle it after I closed. I had only two hours left with the store open and I was not going to prove everyone right who thought I was closed all the time.

I'd use the time to make notes about what Narina had said and how everything could potentially be tied in together.

First, though, I had customers coming in and needed to pay attention to what I was supposed to be doing. The two men wandered around the shop and seemed to have no plan or even a real desire to be in here. They'd go from one end of the store to the other, then start weaving back and forth through the aisles. Every time they met in the store, they'd eye each other up and down, grunt and then continue. I had a feeling they weren't here to shop, but were they here to steal anything from me? Because I didn't have a lot to steal unless they thought they could find a brisk underground black market for unpainted rocks and a few hand-crocheted blankets.

"Can I help you find anything?" I asked, raising my voice. I projected it as I'd been taught when I was younger to be heard over the ocean and the waves.

"No, thanks," one of them yelled back, and then I heard whispering and decided to see if I could move a little closer to hear what they were saying.

I took my time crouching down and pretending to check on something on the bottom shelf. Then I crept over, nearly on my knees, to hear what they were saying. And if that wasn't weird, I didn't want to know what was. I only hoped no one would decide to come in right now and see me cleaning the floor with the knees of my shorts.

And I hoped these guys wouldn't stop talking before I positioned myself to hear them.

"Look, Jer, she's here alone and this is the perfect time to get her. If we don't, the boss is not going to be a happy camper, and I don't want an unhappy camper on my hands. I don't want to be a camper at all but that was the only thing left on the island. It's like everyone and their mother is here to pick up the slack, but we have to be first or Teddy is not going to be happy. He might burn down that really cool tepee he's staying in, so let's not do that, okay?"

I was so very lost in this whole thing. What the hell were they talking about, and who the hell was Teddy? Why was everyone and their mother here? What did that have to do with picking up the slack? What slack? And was he saying that there were no hotel rooms available because so many people were here for something that no one seemed to know about except all these tourists?

To say I wanted to pop up and start demanding answers was an understatement, but there were two of them and one of me. I wasn't sure I could take them on or if they would then end up "taking" me, as the one had said they needed to.

I gulped and looked through a hole in the merchandise to the other side, where they were standing. I gasped when I found myself staring into a pair of blue eyes that were both very pretty and scary as freaking hell.

I shot straight to my feet and looked for an exit. Where should I go and how should I get there? I could duck into the back room, but then everything out front was up for grabs. And if I tried to make a run for the front door, I didn't think that would work either. So I was stuck. And because there were two of them, they could cage me in from both sides of the aisle I was in, leaving me with nowhere to go.

I was going to get hurt. I could feel it in my bones. I really did not want to get hurt. So I straightened my shoulders and stood my ground. In my mind I dared one of them to try to hurt me, because I would open that can of whoop-ass that I'd been saving for just such an occasion as this. They were going to get the blowback of every single thing that hadn't gone right in the last few months since I'd moved here and then promptly found my first dead body.

Curling my hands into fists, I planted my feet on the floor and moved into the position like the one that yoga teacher had instructed me in long ago on a girls' night out with Maribel. I kept my knees loose and my mind open to see the possibilities of what could be swirling in the air around me but also listened to what was happening so that hopefully I could anticipate anything coming my way and counter it without too much effort or exertion. All because it would be part of the flow of the event.

It was exhausting just thinking like that.

Which was why when the guy on the left took a step toward me, I pretty much screamed and made a run for the door. I went to knock the other guy over, but he was far bigger and planted much more like a tree than my shallow weed roots earlier. He went nowhere and didn't move except to wrap his meaty hands around my biceps.

I went for it, kicking and trying to wiggle out of his grasp, swinging my lower arms as best I could. Yet I made no contact. I stopped long enough to see him give a quizzical look over my shoulder to the guy who I assumed was standing behind me.

"You done yet?" the one behind me asked.

I tried to land another kick, but the guy in front of me sidestepped my poor aim and pretty much just let me dangle in front of him while I wore myself out.

"Now?" he asked.

Finally there was only one answer. "Yes, I'm done. And I would like to leave a note for my family and friends to make sure they have everything they need. I haven't made a will, but I'll try to get it all written down adequately. Neither of you happen to be a notary, do you? That would be awesome, so I could make sure it gets notarized. A lot to think about. If you could just put me down, I'll get some paper and start those letters, and then you can do whatever you have to do."

"Good Lord, why do they always have to be talkers?" the one in front of me asked, and then set me down. "Please just be quiet and let us tell you what we need. We're not taking you anywhere, or going to hurt you, or whatever your little television brain has cooked up. We have simple questions and are trying to get some answers, but we'd like them before anyone else comes around snooping."

"Wait," I said. "What?" I shook out my arms, and the one who'd held me flinched like I was going to take a swing at him. I had no need to at this point, but he had better be thankful I hadn't had to show him how it was done. "Who are you?"

"That's for us to know and you never to find out after we take care of one Darren Milner, aka the Great Swindling Swine."

Chapter 20

"What do you know about Darren?" I asked the two guys. I was not going anywhere, major phew! And we could just have this nice and friendly conversation about murder and mayhem right here as we figured out what in the name of Neptune was going on.

"We're the ones asking questions, not you." The big guy leaned in.

"And what is your name?" I supported myself against a shelving unit because my knees were starting to hurt.

He scoffed. "Like I'm going to tell you that."

"Stever, why can't we just tell her our names so she might be willing to help us more?"

Stever rolled his eyes at his partner. "Thanks for that anyway."

The other one looked embarrassed, but I patted him on the arm and told him it was okay, which got me another scoff mixed with a snort.

"Look, I don't have to tell you anything, and I'm not even sure what you're looking for, and whether I know anything about it. So we're kind of at an impasse, from what I can see." I stood my ground when Stever moved toward me. This was my store, my information, my freaking island, and I was not going to be bossed around by some thug who'd come over for something I didn't have.

"Here's the deal," I continued. "I don't know you, and I don't know what you want. You are more than welcome to try to manhandle it out of me, but in the end I think this would work out so much better if you kept your threats to yourself, and we tried to see if I even know what you want or if you need to go ask someone else, and be far more polite with them than you were with me."

The corner of Stever's mouth kicked up for just a second as our gazes met.

I admitted I was cheeky, and I appreciated that he thought so too. However, that didn't mean I was going to give in to whatever they wanted whenever they wanted simply because he wasn't a complete jerk. Why did they think their muscle would make a difference here?

I moved around Stever, and this time he let me as I went back to the counter and waited for them to approach from the other side.

"What is it you need to know?" I asked as soon as they made it to within ten feet of me. Stever stood with his hands clasped, and the other guy crossed his arms over his not-as-impressive chest while trying to look intimidating.

"Did you not hear the part about us asking the questions, lady?" the smaller one challenged with belligerence and started bouncing on his toes.

"You coming for me?" I asked in my best New York accent, which wasn't very New York. But it did the job. It stopped everyone in their tracks until Stever smacked the back of the other guy's head and made him take a seat on my dusty-pink needlepoint chairs I had picked up to have somewhere to lounge when things weren't hopping in here.

The other guy finally sat when Stever put his hand on the

guy's shoulder and shoved down with constant pressure. He finally gave in and sat, and I chose to remain behind the counter.

"Now, what is it you want?" I watched the crowd passing by on the street and wondered if there truly was going to be an invasion of rough people looking for something I had no idea about. We didn't have a ton of hotels and houses for rent, but there would be enough to house quite a few people even with two weddings and an anniversary family reunion here this week.

"We need to get our hands on Darren. He's been elusive and we were tracking him until last week, when he totally disappeared. We saw him in the paper this morning and thought it might be best if we came over and got some answers instead of waiting for him to come back to California."

"Why do you think I know anything about this? I have nothing to do with him. My name has never been linked to his and it seems ludicrous that you would think I, out of anyone, would have the most sway at all."

Stever fumbled his phone out of his pocket and swiped the screen. When he turned it toward me, it was a picture of me smiling and helping Darren to his feet as well as leading him along the street. It was recent, of course, since I'd only met him a handful of days ago. I remembered smiling in my effort to assist him up, not because we were friends. But to someone who didn't know us, it did look like we might have been friends, especially when I read the story that went with the picture.

"I can assure you I just met Darren and don't know a whole lot about him."

Stever scoffed again. "Just like you don't know Alex and haven't been with him for ages."

"Um . . . who is Alex and what are you talking about?"

"I'm talking about this guy who is married to you and who've you've been with for years. You know him and we know him and he knows you."

"I assure you I don't know who or what you're talking about. I'm not married. Never have been."

More scoffing, and I was starting to feel like I might want to ask this guy if he needed a bottle of water. But we weren't such good friends, and if he didn't stop trying to threaten me, I was pretty sure we never would be.

"Let's stop playing games. You have info we want, and we want it now. You give it to us, and we go away with no one the wiser and no one hurt. Simple as that."

"Are you trying for the wise-guy thing? Because I'm going to have to tell you that you don't quite have it nailed. You sound like California trying to get to Boston and NYC by way of Long Island."

Stever laughed, but I think I finally pushed the other guy over the edge. His eyes darkened and he wasn't laughing anymore. "I'm not going to tell you again. Tell us where he is and we'll make this all go away." He dropped his voice. "Or don't tell us and we'll make this all go away."

That was far more threatening and made me believe he was willing to make everything here go up in flames, myself included, whereas the first one had been more whimsical. It was amazing how things could change with a simple tone. And now I was scared.

"I'm really not telling any lies. I have no idea what you're talking about. I was looking into a murder on the island of a guy named Jericho, but he also goes by Sammy, I guess. And it might involve the Milners, but I'm not quite sure how. They're all at their house. Then there's Elsie, but she was last at the police station and might be out in the boat again if the fire didn't damage it." I shrugged and spread my hands out in front of me as if to show I had nothing left to hide, and they might want to take one of those instead of rooting around for something else.

"Nothing about Alex?"

"No, I swear nothing about anyone named Alex. I don't

have the first clue what you're talking about, and I have no involvement beyond trying to figure out who killed Jericho so that no one else gets hurt, hopefully." I looked them both over as they drooped their shoulders and seemed to shrug at each other. "Who is this Alex that you're looking for?"

"Best damn smuggler who ever lived, and into some other shady stuff too, but nothing you need to know about. It would be better if you keep your head down and your nose clean. We're not going to trust you all the way, but for now we'll leave you alone. We have more important things to do. So if we see anyone else we know, we'll be sure to let them know the info is wrong and you're not the one we're looking for."

"I'd appreciate that. Can I get either of you a water?" Now we were friends enough for me to offer. But what exactly were they looking for? And when were they going to find it? More important, who else was looking for it?

Everything kept leading back to Darren in my mind, and that meant I needed to talk to him again. Preferably without Goldy this time. I felt that he did a lot of posturing when she was around. Probably because he wanted her to continue to think of him as this nice guy when I was sure he hadn't made it through the last fifty years without some scrapes and bruises to his reputation. Most seemed to be legitimate, even if the law couldn't convict him.

Goldy had told me that she was waiting with Darren as they went through Jericho's things, so I might not have the chance to do this without her. But maybe if she heard that I'd just been threatened over him, it would help her get over her youthful expectations of what Darren used to be as opposed to what he was now. And maybe she could try to figure out who Alex was and why there was now another player in the game.

It didn't take long to get to Darren's dad's house, just as it really didn't take long to get anywhere around here. But after closing the store, I had taken the meandering path in an effort to sort out what I wanted to say and how I wanted to say it before I got to Darren and Goldy. I needed to know if he knew either of the guys, and why there might be so many others on the island, and what on earth was going on to bring about this kind of interest. Of course a summer holiday was coming up and it was normal to have an influx of people, but this was different, and they seemed to be taking up the whole island, like a bunch of vultures hanging out on the wires above a dying animal. And I wasn't having it.

Once I finally got to the front door, I listened for anything happening on the other side and didn't hear anything. I rang the bell, then waited to see if anyone was in there.

I was ringing it again and again when I heard voices. I couldn't make out what was being said. At least this time it didn't sound like people yelling at each other. I was tired of that.

I banged on the front door and waited for someone to open it. I was not going anywhere until I got a chance to talk to him and find out what he knew. I also needed to know what he'd done and if it really was true that he had gotten into trouble all those times for a real reason as opposed to always being in the wrong place at the right time.

I knocked again and Goldy came to the door, not happy, and sweating. "Do you have some new evidence to clear Darren?"

I pushed past her into the house before I answered or she might not have let me in. "I wasn't given much except some damning info from Narina about Darren and his family. Not that you'd listen to me about that anyway."

She stood her ground, and I knew I was right. "She's a liar and a thief, Whit. I'm not taking her story over Darren's truth."

Of course not. "I'm not going to fight you about that at the moment but I need to see Darren. We've had a new wrinkle in things, and I need to know what he might have done on the mainland to have people all coming over to get a piece of him now that they know where he is."

"Whit, you are not going to ask him that." The shock in her voice was enough to make me burst out laughing, but it never happened. Mainly because I was pissed and angry and wishing she'd stop defending this guy so totally and give me at least a little credit.

"Goldy, I have no time and no inclination for this shit anymore." I didn't normally swear near her but this felt needed, dammit. "Something is going on with all of this and there is something much more here than whether or not a guy fell out of the rafters accidentally or was pushed. I will get to the bottom of this before someone else tries to scare the crap out of me in my own store and threaten to kidnap me unless I tell them what they want to know."

I felt her grab my arm as I started up the stairs. I let her hold on for a second without tearing away and finishing the climb.

"Someone threatened you?"

"Yes, they came into the store and they didn't look like my average tourist. It turns out they're filling up the hotels around here because something is going on and the word is out that I know something about it. Or at least someone named Alex who maybe used to work in my storefront before it was the Dame of the Sea? It's the only other thing I can think of. But they were going to take me somewhere and try to get answers out of me, except I had no idea what they were talking about."

"Someone threatened you?" The storm brewing in her eyes should have been scary, but I had no energy left.

"We need to move past that, Goldy. I'm no longer being threatened. But I would like to talk to Darren to see what else I should be on the lookout for and whether he understands why everyone is here."

"Yes, I think I'd like to know that too." She kept hold of my arm as she bypassed me on the stairs and then let go to climb in front of me. So much for storming in and demanding answers.

Now I'd be behind Goldy, who would probably want to coddle him first.

I hung back so that I didn't have to be a witness to the coddling, but she reached back and grabbed my arm to pull me with her.

When we arrived in the room, I assumed it was the guest bedroom and that Darren was going through Jericho's things, but there also seemed to be some evidence bags mixed in with the stuff, as if the police had taken things and given them back, which made a kind of sense. Until two things happened at once— I saw the logo again and Goldy started yelling loud enough to wake up all the dead pets at the cemetery behind the house.

Chapter 21

It took me at least fifteen seconds and about twenty words to understand that Goldy was ripping into Darren with the force of a gale wind, all because he'd put me in danger. She went down the list of all the things she'd believed him on that I had questioned. She went over the things that had happened when they were younger. There were a couple of juicy nuggets in there, but nothing that we really needed to be addressing right now.

"Goldy, it's all good."

She was in the middle of telling about the time when apparently Goldy had Pops make a map for Darren and wasn't sure if she should continue the charade of dating him. Pops was someone she really wanted for the rest of her life, but she didn't want to leave Darren hanging. So then Darren had decided that night to leave, after getting the map, and she hadn't even been sure what the map was for, and he'd left without saying goodbye, and then she hadn't heard from him for years, and who the hell treats their friends like that, she wanted to know.

Phew!

For Darren's part, he looked like a trapped animal who might choose at any moment to bite off his own arm to escape the trap of Goldy standing in front of the guest room door and blocking the exit. Unless he was willing to jump out the second-story window, which at this point I didn't think was too far out of the realm of possibility.

Time to step in and stop her before she busted something in her straining throat or Darren's exposed head.

"Goldy, Goldy, Goldy." I took her hands in mine and rubbed the insides of her wrists with my thumbs, just like she used to do when I'd get really upset about something, be it a bad grade, someone not being nice to me, or not getting to say good-bye to my parents once more as they left in the middle of the night. I'd wake up to an empty house that was only filled by Goldy, whistling as she made special pancakes to take away the sting of being left without a word yet again.

"Goldy." I said it one more time, and she stopped long enough to face me and cup her hands around my cheeks.

"What?"

"There's no need to go through all this. I'm here, I'm fine, and I'm sure Darren is going to tell us everything he knows so we can get this all sorted out. Isn't that right, Darren?"

"Uh, yes, of course it is." He looked a little shaken. I would be too if that was the first time I dealt with a truly irritated Goldy. It wasn't a pretty experience, no matter how hard you tried to make it better. So here we were, and here we would stay until Darren answered her questions or managed to mow her down on his way out the door. I was betting on that first one, since it was Goldy and she was not happy.

"So tell me, Darren, what did Jericho do? For a living, that is . . ." Goldy asked. Going in for the kill right at the beginning. Nicely done.

"I think he was a banker?" Darren sounded like a child as he stuck that question mark on the end of his response. How did you not know what a partner did after weeks and weeks together? That seemed strange even to me.

"He was a banker or he stole things?" I asked. Goldy shot

me a look, but she was not going to be the only one trying to get information, especially when I was the one who had been threatened and nearly held hostage in my own store for something I had nothing to do with.

I stalked around the room, wondering what I could find that might help answer the question because Darren stood there with his hand over his eyes and was taking deep breaths.

And that was when I spotted it. A crate with the logo on it, or rather it was a picture of the logo on a crate, and attached was a letter. Before he could open his eyes or drag his hand down his face, I decided to pocket the thing and look into it later. He didn't want to answer? I'd get those answers myself, then.

And right next to it—no kidding—was a map that looked like something Pops had drawn. I didn't know what I was getting myself into or even what I was taking, but I did know that at this point I was extremely tired of people telling me half-truths or not telling me anything at all and just expecting me to follow along because that was what they wanted done. And I was tired of fighting Goldy or having her flip back and forth between people because her loyalty was strong but maybe not always her judgment.

I'd look at this all once I got out of here and moved into what came next. I wasn't taking this anywhere near Ray either, since that only ever got me in trouble. Then I'd have to explain where I got things instead of bringing a fully realized idea with facts to back them up to him and not being shut down because he didn't think I knew what I was talking about.

But how to get Goldy out of here now that I had what I was looking for?

"Goldy, we have to go get things ready and you have dinner with Pops, don't you?" I asked it sweetly in hopes she'd get the message and move it along.

But though she had come in like a Valkyrie earlier, now she

had been appeased by Darren saying he didn't know what was going on.

"I think that's enough for now, Whitney. He's innocent and didn't know what was going on. This poor man has lost everything. We need to give him some time and space to process everything he wasn't aware of." She stroked his arm and I wanted to scream.

Well, it had been nice to have her stick up for me at the beginning at least. I had that and I'd have to hold on to it while I waited for the rest to unfold.

So I left her there, hoping she'd be okay if anyone came by. But I was not able to really save her anymore—if she wanted to believe Darren, she could.

But I could see what Pops had to say and what he thought about all this. I wanted to know how it might all come together to give us something for Ray either to exonerate Darren or put him away. At this point I didn't feel that I leaned too much either way. As long as he left and took all his issues with him, I'd be fine.

I found Pops in his workshop in the back of the house. He was the ultimate handyman and a tinkerer if I ever saw one. We'd spent days upon days making all kinds of things, some useful and some entirely whimsical. Nothing was too small or too trivial for Pops to at least try. I still had pretty much any and every project we had ever made together, and I treasured all of them.

Now I had to see where this treasure map went to and who should have kept it a well-guarded secret instead of letting it be photocopied into a map and then left behind.

I'd left Goldy at Darren's family's house, knowing I might get the third degree from Pops when I arrived without her. I also knew that sometimes things were easier to do with fewer people and less input. So here I was, and we'd see what he had to say.

I found him in the shed and took a moment to smile at the

way he puttered around. He moved back and forth between the treasure chests and the small toys we sometimes put into them, if the whole point of the treasure hunt was the hunt instead of the prize.

I didn't want to seem awkward, so I called out to him after about thirty seconds and he turned around with a smile. It was a little tired around the edges, but it was still a smile, so I took it.

"Hey there, Pops. How's it going? What are you up to?" I thought it might be better not to jump straight into trying to figure out what I had in my hand or mentioning Darren immediately if I wanted this to go well. Although if it did make it that Darren was a bad guy and should go away from Goldy ASAP, then Pops might be all too ready to make that happen.

"What's up? Where's your Goldy?"

"I left my Goldy where I found her, but I do have something I wanted you to look at. Do you have a minute?" I held the map under my arm, folded in half instead of rolled into a tube. I didn't know what I might hear about it, but it was giving me more butterflies in my stomach than I had expected.

"She's plenty old enough to take care of herself. I learned that the hard way and relearned it this week. I'm sure there is something good about this Darren person or she wouldn't be so protective of him. Your grandmother has always been good with knowing what's what, and I shouldn't be doubting her."

I clamped my arm down over the map and wondered if he'd still feel that way if I told him where I'd left her and who this map was from. No time for either, though, because I wanted to figure out what I was looking at before I said anything to anyone else.

"So I found this map and I was wondering if you remember making it. It looks like a replica or something, but I don't think I've ever seen this one before, and I know I've never sold one with these directions. So where does it go?"

Pops stopped what he was doing and bowed his head for a moment before turning toward me and taking the map.

"It was for your grandmother, but she said she had to give it to someone who needed it more. I thought she was going to bury something out there for me, but she said she never did, and I didn't ask for clarification, since the next day she agreed to be my wife, and that was all I cared about."

"Wait, that sounds like she didn't answer you at the moment you proposed. . . ." I let the sentence trail off when he shook his head. How had I not known that? How had I never heard that Goldy did not immediately jump at the chance to be with my grandfather forever? And how long after they started dating did he ask her to marry him?

"When she said yes, I never heard about the map again, but I never made another out that way for two reasons. One, I didn't like where it ended up, and, two, I didn't want someone to accidentally dig up something they weren't supposed to on a whim."

I bit my lower lip and shuffled my options through my mind. There really was only one I was willing to go with. "Will you tell me where this starts out and where it finishes up? I'm not sure but I feel like this is important and it might need to be dug up ASAP before someone else gets it and we're out of a clue. This could have nothing to do with Jericho's death, but it could also possibly have everything to do with his death."

Pops turned toward me with his eyes narrowed. "Where did you get this? It's a copy."

"I got it out of Jericho's luggage or very close to it. I have a feeling there's more going on here than we're aware. And I'm not going to be able to get Goldy out or prove anything to her until I have solid proof. So where does this start and where does it end?"

He sighed and took a pencil out from behind his ear. "It starts right here and funny enough it ends at the pet cemetery right down the road. Give me a minute to get myself together and I'll come with you. I don't want you out there all alone with the kind of jerks that appear to be on the island right now. I'm not willing to take a risk with you."

"I get that," I responded. "But I feel the same about you, and I'm a little more spry than you are these days. What if I take Felix with me?"

"How about you take me and Felix with you and we have Ray on speed dial just in case."

I gave in because I didn't want to fight with him, and even with the starting spot, it was hard to tell what was where since it was the only map I had ever seen without his signature North Star drawn on it.

The map was raw and had very little detail compared with the ones we had available now, but so many of them led to standard places, and we'd had time to perfect them over the years. People loved them and sometimes asked for the same one over and over again to make sure they got the experience they wanted. But this one was new and yet old, and I wanted to see where it led.

Pops and I headed out in his golf cart, leaving mine at the house, since he didn't want to be conspicuous, and mine was definitely conspicuous.

It was rare that I got to travel around the island with my Pops. He tended to be the one in the background and let Goldy ride in the front seat all the time. It wasn't that he was afraid to be seen, it was just that he didn't necessarily need to be seen to know he was doing the work. I took after Goldy more than him, but there were definitely parts of me that were all him through and through.

"So how are things?" I asked as we tooled along the road from their house and down to the main road that ran along the beach.

"Fine, fine. I'm putting some new cabinets in for Goldy and making sure she has all the things she needs for the three different projects she says she'd like to get started for the gift shop. She wanted shelving and also the pieces for making a few new items."

I was afraid to ask what all that entailed since she hadn't mentioned anything to me about changes, though I should have been ready and waiting for her to try to do something like that. When wasn't she trying to change everything and make it all hers? Not that I minded, but this seemed even bigger than the unpainted rocks she had introduced a few months ago. Maybe we should be talking about what she wanted to put in the store instead of trying to save an old boyfriend who might not be able to be saved.

"So did you make this map with the destination at Goldy's request?" I had to ask, because it would only make sense if Goldy had asked for something and then never let him know what. She was like that sometimes.

"She had asked for it as a present for someone else, and of course I made it. I was sweet on her even then, but she was dating Darren and I wasn't going to try to poach on someone else."

"What if she'd wanted to be poached?" And wasn't that a funny word, when I always associated it with eggs? I tried not to laugh but it was a close thing.

"Honestly, Whit, if she'd wanted to date me earlier, then she'd have to have let me know. I wasn't that good at reading any kind of signals back then. I'm not a hell of a lot better now, but it is what it is and I'm sure she probably let me know she was interested at exactly the right time, so it all worked out okay."

Oh, to not overthink any little thing. Maybe when this was over, I'd sit with Pops a little more and see if I couldn't learn his Zen-ness via osmosis instead of trying and failing every day to get myself to a place where I flowed.

We pulled up at the pet cemetery along Crestline Boulevard, and Pops gave me back the map. "If you look here, this is the spot where the walking starts. We could have walked the whole thing, but I get the feeling you need answers soon and not a leisurely stroll down our back roads."

I kissed him on the cheek and grinned. "You are absolutely right. Now, help me find what was buried so I know what we're dealing with."

Pops pulled a shovel out of the back of his golf cart, because of course he had one, and we walked a few feet with me calling out paces and places like I used to when I was little. But when we got to the last step, Pops hesitated. "Are you sure we want to stop here and turn right? That's going to lead into a place that isn't very safe for anything, much less burials." We both stood near the edge, and I saw there were a ton of brambles that had probably been there for a whole lot of years as well as a culvert that I was pretty sure had been here for at least the last several decades.

Pops didn't move and kept looking from the culvert to a spot off to his right. "Now, you're sure the steps don't lead over here? Because I'm pretty sure I had made it to go over here. It's the only way I would have drawn a map, because anything else doesn't make sense. This looks like my work, except for those last few steps and the X. See how it doesn't have the flourish that I usually put on it? What the heck is up with this map?"

I had no answers except to start digging and find out.

"Do you have another shovel and should we split up? You can go look at where you think you put the X the first time, and I'll do this bramble-hunting and see what was left over here. We can keep in touch, since we're not that far away and let each other know what we find. Deal?"

I really hoped he agreed to it because, the alternative would be to let him dig up both, which could take all day. He was young at heart, but he also wasn't getting any younger in the body.

"That works for me. But make sure you keep me up to date, and I have my cell phone with me if you need me sooner."

I saluted him and we went our separate ways. After grabbing

the other shovel from the back of the golf cart, I followed the last few steps to the place that normally would have been marked with an "X marks the spot" for the kids to get the full experience of buried treasure.

But this was different, and I had no idea what to expect, much less what to hope for. I dreaded anything that was gross or would make this case even worse than it already was. Of course, I should have thought that through before I let it be whispered out into the world, because now it was going to happen. I could feel it in my bones.

Chapter 22

What I should have been doing was listening with my ears instead of doing things with my bones, because maybe then I would have heard Darren being led by Goldy up the path from the parking lot. She did not look or sound happy, but there wasn't much I could do about that. I didn't try to walk away from the cart, but I did tuck that map into my back pocket and wait to see what Goldy had to say before I offered anything.

"What are you doing here?" she asked. Darren stood behind her and to her left. He looked exhausted, as if he just wanted to lie down for a short nap, but Goldy would never let anyone have one when she was on a mission.

I felt for him, but at the moment I didn't care. I wanted them gone, unless he was ready to answer some questions. Then he could stay as long as he wanted.

"I was talking with Pops and he mentioned a map that had never been used, so we came out to check out what's here."

She squinted at me and said, "Can I see the map?"

I really didn't want to show it to her, but how else was I going to know if it had belonged to Darren, and if Jericho had made a copy of it or what its origins were? I had to take a chance and hope this worked.

As soon as I handed it over to Goldy, Darren went sheet-white and stumbled back. I was quick to grab his wrist and keep him from falling backward into the brambles.

"I take it this was your map, then. Good to know," I said as Goldy turned it around and around and finally hit on the direction I was going in.

"This is not right. Something is off on here. I don't remember this, and the paper is all wrong."

I kept an eye on Darren to see if he'd dart. But his shoulders slumped, and it looked more like he was finally admitting he was caught, or defeated, and either way he needed to give it up so we could lay this whole thing to rest, including his partner whom I was beginning to think he really had killed.

But why? Without a motive, I didn't get it, although it could just have been that Jericho was asking too many questions. Except I didn't have to guess. I could ask once I got Darren to admit what he'd hidden out here and why he looked like he was going to be sick at someone actually finding it.

"What is it, Darren? What are we going to find and where are we going to find it? Why did Jericho have this in his luggage?"

"Wait, Jericho had that in his luggage? That's where you found it?" he asked, gripping the edge of his collar and fisting his hand in the fabric.

"Yes? I was there and you were going through his things. I saw the map, so I took it to see if Pops knew where it went."

Goldy was obviously not pleased when she turned her back on me and consoled Darren for my rudeness, but that didn't last long when Darren tried to shake her off and come after me.

"Why did you take this? It wasn't yours to even touch much less actually take out of my house. Who else have you shown?"

With each question he got closer and seemed to get taller. He hulked over me at the end until Goldy got between us with a push, a shove, and I'd bet she stomped on his instep with her heels. "Back up."

"But, Goldy—"

"Back up now. She did what she did, and while I'm not happy that she removed something from your father's house— emphasis on *your father's*—it also bears thinking about. Is this your copy?"

When he reached for it, she kept it out of his reach. "Surely, you can tell simply from looking at it if this is your copy. The one I gave you would have been different paper, but maybe you got rid of that one?"

He sighed and shook his head. "No, this would be a copy that someone made after the fact. I still have the original, and it's slightly different."

"Like the X is somewhere over there?" I gestured over to where Pops was digging but didn't point out that he was here and ready to do business.

"This is bullshit, Darren." Goldy finally turned to him and seemed to think it was about time to come to terms with how things actually were versus how she'd like to see them. And from what I could tell, it wasn't going to be pretty for Darren.

"I had a map made for you all those years ago and it did not come to this spot. It went over there, and I have no idea what you buried but I never tried to find it. So what's here and how did someone get this map and make a copy of it? It would be like *Romancing the Stone* or something if you have a big, huge jewel buried. But why would you have done that all those years ago?"

Darren's expression was pained, with a crinkle in his forehead and his mouth turned down in a frown. "I can't talk about this, Goldy. I'm so sorry. I want to tell you everything, but if the word is out that this map exists, then there could be so much more trouble than you can even imagine." He took his phone out of his pocket and called someone. After a few rings he hung up and tried again. "Come on, Dad, pick up."

And again.

"I have to go see what's going on. He can't be left to fend for himself, and you might have just seriously brought the shit down on his head."

I was not going to feel sorry for that.

"How about if I go with you, and we have Goldy and Pops stay here to make sure nothing is taken and we'll go from there. Should we call the cops?" I had to ask, because I didn't want to be the one to make that decision, but I also didn't know if whatever he thought was going on really warranted them coming out or if he was blowing it out of proportion just to get rid of Goldy and me.

"I'll come with you." I wasn't going to insist but he had started to walk off without acknowledging me, and that was not going to happen this time.

"Whitney, I need—"

I stopped him in his tracks and felt a lot like Goldy when I grabbed his arm. "Look, I'm not playing around here, Darren. I was threatened with kidnapping this afternoon and supposedly everyone is after you for one reason that I can't seem to get anyone to tell me. So let's stop playing games. Maybe you aren't all those things Pops saw on the internet about you, but there is definitely something here, and I can't let it pass. If it leads to whoever killed Jericho, then even better."

His shoulders dropped and his eyes got glassy. "Jericho. I should have never come out to this cursed island."

"Well, you're here now and we need to find out who killed your partner and why. And if there is anything at all you can tell me that might help, then I'm here for it. Seriously. This has to end soon."

He shook his head.

"Are the guys on the island thieves or cops?"

Darren shook his head again. "I have no idea. I don't know why any of this is happening, just like I didn't understand what was happening with my family all those years ago before I left. I remember a lot of screaming when I was younger. Both my brother and I left on the same day, and I never knew why he left, but I've never heard from him personally since then. I'm not sure why on that either. It's all so jumbled in my head. Whit. I don't know."

"Let's go to your house and see if we can get our hands on the original and find out what the difference is and maybe how it happened."

He nodded and we took two golf carts. I was willing to give him some leeway on what was going on, but I did not trust him to drive me around or to not leave me stranded without a cart at his house if something not so good went down.

When we arrived, we found the front door open. Again Darren sprinted up the stairs like he had earlier today when I'd found them on the floor. My God, had that really been only this morning? It felt like forever and at least five days.

Regardless of my inability to guess with time, this was similar, and I considered walking straight in but then decided at the last minute to creep around the side and see if I could again eavesdrop without being seen. It wasn't the most polite of things to do, but then again neither was stealing or killing people, so I had a long way to go before me and the killer were even in faux pas.

"Dad, what's going on?" I saw and heard Darren but was having a hard time seeing Stu. I could hear him, though, which was just going to have to be enough for the moment.

"Son, there's a lot going on, and I tried to save you from so much of it, but now it's found us here."

"What does that mean?"

I so wished I could see Stu's face to get at least some kind of reading on what he was feeling. He sounded so flat, there was no way to tell if he was resigned or angry or sad or anything else. I quickly dialed 911 and told them to hurry.

"Dad, is something wrong?"

"Well, it might just be the scissors sticking out of my back that I can't seem to reach."

He turned around and I gasped as I hustled into the house, no longer trying to stay out of sight. The scissors didn't look deep and there wasn't a lot of blood but that had to hurt. "I already called nine-one-one and they'll be here soon. Before you go, though, Stu, what do we need to know? Someone killed Jericho, and now I've been threatened, and Darren feels unsafe, so what do we need to know? What is going on around here, and how does it lead to you being stabbed in the back?"

Stu shook his head and leaned forward in the chair since he didn't want to have the scissors go in any further, but he wouldn't let either of us pull them out just in case the blood gushed out after the pressure of the steel was released.

"I thought this would all be over when your mom died, Darren. That's why I encouraged you to come out for the funeral after she was gone. I thought it would all die down and maybe for once we could finally have a normal family, but now we have the death, and the weird people running around causing issues, and the map out and about, and I just don't know what to do anymore. Your mom was one of the biggest jewel and art and goods smugglers in the world right here in our little town in Catalina. She did all kinds of things she shouldn't have and I tried to turn a blind eye because she was providing for us, and she loved what she did. She roped me in by handling the shipping, but I'd asked her to stop and then she died, and now I have to deal with all the fallout. Dammit!"

Well, that was a whole lot to take in, and I wasn't sure where to start. I knew I wanted to call Maribel and talk with her, but that might have to wait if this map was a real treasure map of some kind and people had wanted to get their hands on it, like in *Romancing the Stone*. It was a movie that I had thought was funny when Goldy let me watch it in my teens on a rainy afternoon but not if it were actually real now. Especially if someone had already died for it.

My stomach dropped at the implications and what Goldy and Pops might be facing and the fact that I hadn't yet called Ray. Even if I had, where should I send him first? Part of me wanted to confront the two men about the conversation I'd overheard where they were fighting about what Stu owed Darren, but I had more important things to do, like save my own family. I heard the ambulance coming up the road, so I turned back to the two guys in the room. "I'm going to go back to Goldy and Pops. Stay here with your dad, Darren, and I'll let you know what we find, if anything. I'm sorry this is the kind of homecoming you had."

"It's not different than usual," he said as I left out the back door. I had to get back to my own family and make sure nothing happened to them.

I jumped into the cart and felt the longer flowers on the street thwack against my calf as I pulled away from the curb. The pet cemetery was not far at all, but I wasn't going to take the time to walk, because I needed to get there now.

Pulling into the parking lot, I watched the cops pull up in front of the Milner house with lights going and sirens on. Thank goodness I'd gotten out of there when I had, so I wasn't waylaid to answer a bunch of questions Darren already had the answers to, and probably better ones than I had.

After parking, I ran to the first site at the culvert and found no one and nothing. It looked as if something had been dug up, and I really hoped that just meant Goldy had unearthed a chest and then taken it to where Pops was digging up his own little piece of land.

When I took the path to the right, though, I listened hard because there seemed to be a lot of people running around in the whispering grass at this very second. A few lowered voices were communicating with one another and there were far more people in this place than there probably had ever been before. Were these the other people Stever and company had warned me about earlier? Were they all looking for some kind of jewel or haul of something that Therese had left behind? I still didn't know what this map was for, but I was really hoping I could get to my grandparents before anyone else did and without being seen or confronted.

I stayed close to the bushes the island had put in to give animals—the living ones—a place to go do their business if there for burying one of their brothers or sisters. I had never had to bury anything here because I'd never really had any animal that belonged to me until Whiskers. I adored my girl and hopefully it would be lots and lots of years before I ever had to set foot back in this place.

But first I needed to get to my grandparents. I almost ran into someone at the fourth grave marker I'd seen, for "Spotty," but I narrowly avoided them by sinking down behind a huge statue that reminded me of Clifford the Big Red Dog. I really hoped Pops and Goldy were staying quiet and smart enough to not try to stop anyone who was wandering about.

But it appeared that maybe those were the only two sets of people I had to worry about, because I came across no one else as I found Goldy and Pops leaning against a tree and kissing like a pair of teenagers.

"All made up?" I asked. "Good, now, quick, let's get this figured out before anyone comes by, because I have a feeling this thing is about to explode."

"Literally?" Goldy asked.

"No, but we can't take that chance. Now, what did you find?"

Goldy brought over a treasure chest much like the ones Pops still made for the shop. It was older and more weathered and had brass fittings.

"Does it need a key?" I asked, wanting to wrench the thing open myself. But I waited. Depending on what was in here, it might be evidence and I didn't want to be the one to get in trouble for messing anything up.

"That's not one of my chests," Pops said. "Goldy?"

"I've never seen it before. I just gave the map to him, I didn't have anything to do with what he buried. But it shouldn't be too hard to open." She glanced at Pops, who grinned and took out a small kit that he opened on a rock.

"Lockpicking? I'm shocked." And I really was, but Pops and Goldy looked like little kids who'd just snuck an extra snack before the teacher realized. I wasn't going to be the one to spoil their fun after the crap we'd been dealing with over the last couple of days. Plus I wanted to know what was in that chest and I wasn't against whatever it took to make that happen.

Except that once Pops pried open the lid, the inside was completely empty, just a velvet-covered bottom and that was it.

"That can't be," Goldy said, rubbing her hand along the bottom of the chest. "There has to be something in here or he wouldn't have buried it, right?"

Who the hell knew anymore?

Pops took the chest from her and knocked on the velvet-covered piece of wood. "Hollow. There's something in there."

While they dealt with that, I went back to the hole in the ground. Why here, and what was here, and how the heck long had it been here?

The bigger question, though, might be how I was going to explain to Ray why I had chosen to open things and touch things and move things without calling him. Although, to be fair, I would definitely not have expected him to follow a treasure map from decades ago in the hopes that something might come of it. I was the one who should do that kind of thing and just hand him the results.

"Holy shit!" Goldy yelled.

Well, that couldn't be good. . . .

Chapter 23

It was as if the hills were alive with people. Goldy shouted and they all came running out from the trees, including Felix. He ran faster than anyone else, so he was able to hold off the others, who seemed to think this was some kind of show and I should be offering popcorn. Some were not kidding around, though, but they were facing off against a good portion of the police force. Where the hell had everyone come from? Probably Goldy. I'd thank her later, after I got over being shocked and not sure what to do next.

As soon as people saw uniforms, they sank back into the trees. I heard a bunch of golf carts start back up. What in the freaking hell was going on? But I had to let that go for a moment, because Goldy looked like she had seen a ghost and was off to the side by herself.

I sank to the ground beside her and saw what was in her hands.

"Is that shell necklace also special?" It looked like a puka shell necklace, one my mom had given me from Hawaii and one that a lot of people from back in the day liked to wear.

But why was she crying?

Taking her hands in mine, I had some idea when I saw that

the necklace had been removed from the bottom of the box, but a skull remained nestled inside. I had my phone in my hand already. I didn't care if Ray was already here, he was going to get a call. And he could answer while he was walking toward me for all I cared.

I heard a phone ringing about twenty feet away and waited for him to answer. When he did, I simply said, "Just come to the west corner. We have an issue that may or may not have anything to do with the rest of these people in the woods, but I can tell you it looks like we have another dead body, and I'm thinking this one is from quite some time ago. And it is definitely not a dog."

There was nothing I could do after Ray and his cohorts descended on Goldy and me at the pet cemetery. I hated to make more work for him, but it seemed like everything was related. I just didn't know how or why. But I wished I did.

I took Goldy and Pops home and left them to take a breather after all that had happened. That necklace had been something special to Darren's older brother, who he'd been told had left the island at the same time as he had. But the skull in the makeshift grave made it a distinct possibility that was a lie. One that created far more questions and offered no answers at all. Damn.

On my way back to the house, I sat for just a few minutes because I needed a breather too. How had this gotten so incredibly out of hand and how did it all come together to make any kind of sense? I focused on the murder board in front of me and could see no patterns or clues, despite all the effort Maribel had put into making sure it was completely organized. But what was the flow and how had it come to be? I wished I could see it! Damn.

That logo kept catching my eye, though, and while it probably played almost no part in this, there was nothing else that I could really do, so I concentrated on the one thing that might not kill me at least.

I pulled out the computer and started looking around. And while I was there, I thought maybe I should look a little further into Elsie. She might have been the injured party from many years ago, but she also seemed to pop up whenever she was least expected and had the most invested in a lot of things. Plus, I remembered Narina saying Elsie had stolen the necklace when no one was looking and that she had been backhanded. So how far in was she?

Bopping around the internet with my earbuds in so I could listen to one of my favorite podcasts, I wound up on a website called Truly Delightful Designs, and the picture of the creator was none other than our dear Elsie. Now, what the heck did that mean, and why, when I went through her gallery of images, was one of the first ones the freaking logo that I couldn't seem to get any real answers on except that it was used for shipping? Kind of . . .

Maribel wandered out of her room and shook her head at me with her brow wrinkled and my cat in her arms.

Our eyes met and she shook her head at me again. Taking my earbuds out, I shut down the podcast I'd been listening to and waited for whatever she thought she had to say.

She wasn't forthcoming, though, and I had to ask. "What's up?"

"So many things but no one seems to remember that I'm here, so I guess nothing."

"Wait . . . no . . . that's not true. I know you're here."

"Have we talked recently? Other than me always calling you to see if you know the latest piece of info and then hanging up so you can go chase things down?"

It had been only a few days since the murder, but trying to tell her that, or use it as an excuse, would not do me any favors.

I gulped because, uh-oh, that was the way things had been working lately and it was not nice at all. I was going to have to start groveling. I was not a fan, but this was Maribel. She was my very best friend, and I was not going to leave her feeling that way. So I closed the laptop, turned away from the murder board, and followed her and Whiskers into the kitchen.

I watched as she made tea and pulled out a muffin from the bakery box on the counter. Should I be the one to start the conversation or should I let her talk first?

You know what? It didn't really matter in the least because my friendship and my friend were far more important than any kind of etiquette when it came to this kind of shit.

"Talk to me. What's happening?" I leaned back against the counter and waited. Maribel was one of those people whom you did not push after offering her the branch of conversation, but this might be one of those times when I pushed anyway and she could be pissed at me. Although it looked like she was already pissed at me, so it wasn't like it was going to get much worse than that.

"I'm pretty sure I could name at least five things I did wrong, but I don't want to build on a list that you probably already have, so let me know what I did and I'll see if I can make it better." I was going to have to keep pushing.

Whiskers swiped at me from Maribel's shoulder as Maribel walked around me to get her creamer out of the fridge. More silence. I was dying a little inside. I could start naming things but I didn't want to give her more ammunition than she probably already had.

She turned toward me, opened her mouth, and then closed it and turned away.

"Please don't do this, Maribel. Whatever I did wrong, whatever I didn't do right, just let me know and let me see if I can fix it. You know I would never intentionally hurt you. What did I do?"

"How about pretty much leaving me out of things except when they happened at the house and you couldn't keep me away? I'm just the person who calls to let you know what to do to keep safe. The one who gets her ass handed to her by her boss for stepping out of line. But then I don't hear anything until someone at the station files a report or happens to mention it near me. Then suddenly I'm not completely in the dark, not completely blindfolded with canvas but more like a tissue over my eyes because I have to act like I know, even though I totally don't."

That had to be incredibly frustrating, especially for someone who was trying really hard to be part of the force and our team too. Though we didn't really have a team, at least not according to Captain Ray. But, according to Maribel, we did, and she was feeling left out and not appreciated, and that was most definitely not okay.

How to fix it, though?

I waited for Maribel to put her muffin down and turn toward me. I didn't want to talk to her back. I wanted to see her face when I apologized to see if she believed it or was just putting me off. I couldn't handle that.

Finally the silence got to be enough that she set everything down and turned to me.

"I'm sorry," I said. "I'm sorry because I've just been trying to get things done and talking with anyone who is near me instead of keeping everyone in the loop. There's a lot going on, and I haven't stayed on top of it with you."

Maribel sniffled and smiled at the same time. "This is silly. You shouldn't have to apologize for trying to help out and not making sure that each of us knows everything. I'm just feeling left out, and I don't like that."

"Totally understandable, plus we should be running things by you, since you have the degree and stuff or almost have the degree. We're not doing this right, and I'm so sorry."

"Well, now I feel stupid."

"Crap! How did I do that already? Usually it takes me a little longer to say the wrong thing. Really you should never feel stupid at all, because you aren't, and I didn't mean to make you feel that way. I would never want you to feel that way." I sighed and rubbed my forehead, because what else could I do?

Because she continued to look at me as if waiting for more, I gave it to her.

"Maribel, the very last thing I want in the world is for you to ever feel left out. You're my go-to when I don't get how things are connected. And this murder board is phenomenal. I know it was wrong not to keep in touch with you, but I want to do it right."

Maribel laughed for real that time. "Listening to you is like following one of those mazes on the back of the place mat at a restaurant. I know you're going to get there and I'm in for it but I'm not always sure where the end is. Was that the end?"

"Yes, that was the end." I sank into the couch and laid my head back against the top. For once Whiskers came over without my having to grab her, and I gave her a hug before she'd want to run away. Although, to be fair, she stayed right where she was. She purred in my ear and rubbed her head under my chin as I contemplated what I'd done and how to undo it.

"So what can I do to help bring you up to speed?"

"It's like I'm the secretary and get the notes to type up after the meeting."

"I can see that, but that was never my intention. I always thought of you as Velma or Daphne, and I'm like Scooby, always looking for those snacks to get me to want to do anything."

She sat on the couch next to me and bumped my shoulder with hers. "You know that's not true. I'm here, and you're here, and you try really hard. I was just having a moment. It's not like you have to call me every single time you make a move. Who would do that? I don't need to know your every step."

My antennae went up and my brain kicked into hyperdrive. "Wait, say that again."

"I don't need to know your every step?"

"Yes, Maribel! Yes! Every step! Darren wears one of those watches that maps every single step, so it could tell us where he's been the last couple of days and what he's been doing every time he disappears and then reappears conveniently."

"Do you want me to look into that?" Maribel asked. "As long as you don't think I'm being a whiny baby."

I laughed and leaned into her side. "Never would I think that. You're my best friend, and that takes precedence over everything and always will. I'm not going to avoid this, and we can talk about it later, but I keep wondering what you're going to do after you graduate and leave me behind for a bigger and I'm sure better job. They'll totally be more awesome for having you, but I can't tell you how much I'd miss you."

"Wait, is that why you've been shutting me out a little? Because you're afraid I'm going to leave and you're making it easier for yourself by being the first to step away?"

"I see that psych class you took did wonders for you."

Maribel rested her head against mine and sighed.

"We're a pair."

"Yep."

"And I'm not going anywhere."

"What? But when you're done, are you going to want to sit at the front desk and keep doing what you're doing just with an extra piece of paper with your name on it?"

"I have some idea that we'll talk about it after this is all over. And I promise I won't go anywhere. I love it here too much to leave, so I'll make it work."

"I really did not expect you to make everything better. I thought that was going to be my job today."

"Nah, you did it yesterday so it's my turn today. Kind of like taking out the trash, which, by the way, today is your day." She patted my leg and got up from the couch. I sat for another few seconds thanking whoever was listening that this was my life. It was late and my bed was calling me.

First thing tomorrow, I had to find out who had killed who and what the hell it was about this logo and a cave that had been disinfected that all tied into something that killed Jericho without a single noise from him.

Chapter 24

Once again I was in the water, but this time it wasn't for leisure, although I could certainly still enjoy it. I was out bobbing in the ocean with Felix again in his fun movie shorts with all his favorite comic book characters on them.

And while I hadn't wanted to, we donned our scuba gear instead of the snorkels. Depending on what we might find, if anything, we would need to be able to dive to greater depths than I or anyone could handle with just a snorkel.

I wasn't sure how much Captain Pablano knew about our exploration back into the cave to see what we could find, but I left that up to the diver next to me who happened to be with the department and would be able to make a case for why I was out here if he had to.

We treaded water for a few minutes after entering the sea from the shore. It wasn't really deep here, but it would help to limber up in the water itself before taking off and expecting myself to deep-dive as necessary.

"We're going to the cave again?" I asked before putting the mouthpiece in. It never hurt to make sure everyone was on the same page, just as I had been finally able to do with Maribel yesterday, and I was incredibly thankful for that.

He nodded, put in the mouthpiece, put down his goggles, and set out for the cave. I followed behind and sank to just below the surface as we went around the bend. It allowed me to stay out of sight but also to make sure everything was set up right before I had to use it in earnest.

Just as I came around the corner on the approach to the cave, I kept an eye out for that boat Elsie had been in or anything else that might be in my way.

Instead, I came up with my friend the octopus, who crawled a little closer this time and kept pace with me. I wasn't sure if he'd be okay since I was in a different outfit, but he seemed to be fine. I still didn't want to get inked, so I made sure to keep my distance and let him be the one who closed the space or not.

As we made our way into the cave, I was very pleased that we had brought flashlights with us this time. When the sun was out and the light reflected in through the water, we could see in the dim setting, but now it was pretty much dark and I did not want to get caught with no lights at all. Too many things could happen in the dark that I was not willing to take chances about. Especially before six in the morning.

And thank goodness, because when Felix came out of the water with the lantern in his hand, he flashed it over the walls of the cave, and, wouldn't you know, right in front of him was one of the guys I'd seen in my shop, the one who thought they might need to kidnap me. Well, shit . . .

He must have been waiting for Felix, because he swung before Felix was able to do anything more than take a step forward. Felix went down in a heap while the guy started wading into the water to get me. Not this time. He was the meaner one of the two, and I wasn't going to give him a chance to get to me.

I turned to move back out to sea and the octopus was right there. I did not want to hit it by accident, so I hesitated, and felt a hand grip the back of my hair. This was not going to go well. Shit times two.

Although apparently it didn't hurt to have octopus friends, because the grip on my head released and the guy screamed as his entire face was soaked in dark black ink from my little buddy. I didn't stick around to see if he was in pain. I rushed to the shore, grabbed Felix, and started swimming. I'd either make it or not, but I was not leaving the love of my life in there to fend for himself.

I looked back and saw the guy writhing on the beach. Good for him, and hopefully he'd still be there once I got to shore and called Ray to come handle this. There would be no way for him to skip past me.

Except that I turned again to swim on my back as I dragged Felix with me and the guy was gone. What in the actual hell was going on in this cave?

Felix snapped to and fortunately did not fight me. He sank into the water, slicked his hair back, and looked around when he resurfaced.

"Well, that didn't go quite how we had hoped it would, huh?"

"Nope, but with some help from our friend here, it went better than it could have in the end. I know he was down, and I know he couldn't have left, so he has to be somewhere in here, Felix. He has to be."

But how to find him? We approached the shore again and cautiously stepped out of the water.

I didn't see anything at first. I looked around as much as I could without my own lantern, but there was nothing. Except . . . he had wiped his hand through the ink and there were a couple of blotches on the sand, and then another couple of blotches on the sand. A few on the wall caught my eye from when he had walked along, trailing his hand on the rocks. And what was he looking for? I had no idea, but the streak ended abruptly and a slow-moving breeze whisked over my face for a full minute before I realized where it was coming from. A fissure. There was a fissure in the rock.

"How much do you believe in Scooby-Doo?" I asked Felix, and grinned. I was going to be one of the happiest people in the world if my hunch was right. Not because I had done something good but because I'd found something very cool. . . .

And there it was. I knocked, Felix knocked, we ran our hands over the surface of the rock, swirling our fingertips, looking for something to be different, some kind of latch or grip or anything that would explain how a guy was here one minute and then gone the next without getting in the water.

I banged my fist on the wall at one point because COME ON! And there it was, the fruit of my frustration came out to play when the rock slid sideways into itself like a pocket door, and I almost fell back at the scene before me.

Who knew there was essentially an Aladdin's cave under the island and how the hell did this get here? But more important . . .

"Who the hell owns this?" Felix said, echoing my very thoughts as he took the lead and walked on into the cavern of wonders.

"What is all this? It's like a dragon's hoard!" I said as I entered behind him, because really everything in here sparkled and glowed. I was very afraid we might find a dragon or something. Obviously that would be pretty outlandish, but so was walking into a sliding rock door and coming up on a literal trove of riches laid out like in all those movies I loved to watch. Was this what those two guys who were looking for Alex had thought I could lead them to?

There were paintings and vases and carpets rolled up leaning against the smooth rock walls. There were display cases with jeweled necklaces, daggers with rubies in the handle, and blades that looked like they could slice through anything in less time than it took to think about it.

Where in the whole of Catalina were we, and how long had this place been down here? More important, who owned it and where were they? My mind automatically went to Therese and her nefarious activities, but I couldn't be absolutely positive without proof.

I saw a few more traces of dark ink throughout the cavern and followed it no matter how much I wanted to stop and admire all the beautiful things.

And that trail led to a staircase that wound up in a spiral that looked a little dizzying but definitely doable. We removed our flippers because trying to go up a set of stairs with those big floppy things on was not a good idea. And I was not going to miss out on finding out what was above because of flippers.

Hell, I would have done it even if I had to climb a rope. I'd come too far not to see this through to the end, dammit.

Who would know whom this belonged to, though? Real estate? Could I find info about it at the archives with Reese at the newspaper? She'd absolutely die to be in here, and I was still trying to figure out how to get her a free pass to at least look when Felix joined me at the bottom of the stairs.

"We going up?" he asked.

"I think we pretty much have to. I know we should go back and probably call Ray to let him know what we've found, but at this point I want to see it through to the end before I make any calls. Because once the call goes through, we're cut off, or at least I am, and I want to know who this belongs to." In my head I was trying to figure out, geographically, where this would come out, topside, but I couldn't pinpoint exactly where the staircase would exit to.

"Plus, there's ink on the handrail, and I feel like we really should know what we're bringing the captain into before we call."

Felix kissed me at the bottom of those stairs and my heart fluttered. He pulled back before I was ready.

"My intrepid investigator, lead the way and let's see what kind of tomfoolery we're dealing with here."

For the first time this week I laughed, more like a snicker, but it wasn't a feeling of crying either, and that was not a bad thing.

Felix walked up behind me as we mounted the spiral staircase. The trek was not easy and there were a couple of times I wanted to sit down and pull off the wet suit to finish the climb. Thank goodness we'd left our flippers down below.

When we reached the top of the staircase, there was a kind of landing and a door.

But the door was locked, and no matter what we did or how long we did it for, there was no budging that thing.

Felix and I looked at each other and shrugged. "So what now?" I asked. "Do we go topside and see if we can figure out where this is on the ground? Maybe see which house it's attached to? For some reason I can't seem to figure out which house this would be under, and all the people up there don't strike me as anyone having the mentality of a dragon. I'm pretty sure a lot of this is not here legally."

I'd read an article about an item stolen from a museum last month and if I'd had my phone with me, I could have verified that the item was on a pedestal right here in this room.

But I didn't, so I couldn't. Instead, Felix and I descended the staircase, grabbed our flippers, and walked back through the cave of wonders to the beach.

"Now what? I hate to leave this here unattended, but we don't really have a choice. If we talk with Ray as soon as we get out of here, then no one should have enough time to get rid of all the loot." I was really torn.

"We have to know, though, and we won't if we stay here. No one is going to come looking for us here with all the other stuff that's going on in and around the island."

"That's convenient, isn't it?" I asked as we put the flippers back on at the water's edge and walked backward into the water.

My friend the octopus was there waiting for us and looked very pleased with himself. I was pleased with him too and gently held my hand out to see if he'd let me pet him. He swam right up under it and bumped into my palm a few times before shooting away and then coming back. He needed a name, and I'd have to visit here more often.

But first we had to catch what I thought might be a thief and then maybe a thief that was stealing from the thief? And possibly a murderer?

Who knew, but something was going down, and it was going down above, so we needed to get there to make sure we didn't miss anything.

When we stepped out of the ocean, I waved to my little friend and pulled off my dive suit and flippers. I had left a small bag of things in the golf cart, so I quickly threw on my clothes and tapped my foot impatiently while Felix did the same.

"Come on! Come on!"

"You sound like Goldy," he said, laughing. We started walking in the direction we thought would lead us to the entrance from above, and I called Maribel to keep her in the loop while Felix was stuck on the phone with Ray. Good for him. I wasn't going to be the one who did it this time.

It wasn't two minutes later that Maribel was by my side and winded.

"Did you run here?" I asked. "There's no way you did."

"I ran to you from my golf cart, does that count?"

"Of course it does, and I'm happy to have you here. Now what comes next? Anyone have any idea where this opening up top might be? I was thinking in a house at first but I'm not seeing anything up here that would fit, unless we're totally off base?"

"I don't know. We need to get in here, though, before anything else happens." Maribel pulled out her tools, and I wondered what else she could do that I didn't know right at that moment.

Maybe we'd be able to look it up under property details or maybe someone had registered for a permit to build this years and years ago. Although who would have done that and how long ago?

These were all things I was considering when we heard rustling in the trees. I motioned for everyone to be quiet and hide ASAP.

And I was very glad we did because there came Stu and his son through the woods. Stu had a blotch of dark ink on the sleeve of his shirt, and Darren was chastising him for being clumsy.

What was going on?

"I told you I wanted to be done with all this. I'm not going to keep doing these things. Your mom died and took all this bullshit with her, and I'm not going to bring it back. I don't care what you want, and you're not using my property for it. I never wanted that in the first place, and she sullied everything I own and everything that belongs to me, even my kids. I'm not putting up with this shit anymore. If you want to follow in her footsteps, do it in another city."

"Dad, you don't mean that. Look, we're perfectly positioned. Just bring Jackson back and it can be the three of us, like it's been the three of you for all these years."

Except I remembered seeing the puka shell necklace and wondered if Darren really didn't know his brother was dead, not just out traveling the world without a working phone.

"It's over, Darren. I'm not doing this anymore, and your brother hasn't been here since the day you left. I'm not sure why you believed your mother over the years, but they got into a fight and she nailed him with a statue and then left him for me to clean up. I used your map because I didn't know what else to do and figured, if anything, we could blame it on the mapmaker. We would have come up with something. But we didn't have to until now. Because here you are, and now things are going to come up, and I'm going to be miles away when that happens. Not here trying to work out what you want from a blackmailer or as the blackmailer."

While this was all very interesting and I couldn't wait to tell Ray, I did notice that someone else appeared to be hiding in the bushes, and I wanted to know what exactly she wanted and how she fit into the puzzle.

"Why don't you tell him about how things had gotten out of hand, and you didn't know how to get her to stop, and she was moving to bigger targets." Elsie moved out from her hiding place and took Darren's hand into hers, then held it up to her cheek. "I tried to get things to work out with us so we could take over from your parents. I know you'd be far more into it than your dad was, what with your history of all those failed attempts. But you've never seen my name in the paper because I slip under the radar. I could help you do that too. I'm pretty sly. I almost had Whitney out of the picture too if she hadn't charmed those men I'd sent after her fake husband, Alex. I'll deal with her later."

My mind was whirling and I was trying to take all this in. So Elsie was also a thief and a blackmailer and thought she and Darren should be together and run this smuggling empire from this tiny island as Darren's mom had, but his dad didn't want to. Umm. Okay.

"Are you going to let him know how you watched your wife crumble onto the floor with a heart attack and then you just left her there to die? You didn't call for an ambulance before you were sure she couldn't be resuscitated. Believe me, I don't blame you, but I thought she was the cold one and turns out you have the real ice in your veins. Burying your first son and telling no one. Hurting your other son, taking things from people all these years and enjoying them even while knowing it's wrong, then letting your wife die when you know you could have helped her. Very cold."

Darren stared at his father with his mouth open and probably so many thoughts running through his head, it felt like being in an appliance store with every TV set on a different channel. That's how I felt, and it wasn't even my family.

"You . . ." Darren cleared his throat. "You let my mom die?"

Stu faced his son and simply nodded. Darren launched himself at the other man, but Elsie still held his hand and yanked him back.

"Darling, we don't have to be violent, do we? Your father did us a favor and I'm sure Therese is wherever she's supposed to be after all she did in her lifetime. This will be our time now. I can't wait to get started."

Hiding in the bushes gave me a chance to think my way through everything I was hearing. I wished I could talk with Felix and Maribel to see if they were interpreting this conversation the same way, but that would have to wait.

So Stu had watched his wife die and had buried his son all those years ago after Therese had killed him with a statue. Darren's whole life was a lie. But how did Jericho fit in?

Everyone had gone so silent, I hoped no one could hear me breathing. I waited for the next cannonball to be lobbed. There were still a lot of things that hadn't been brought up.

And then Stu did it for me. "And when do you think you'd like to share that you took the necklace after slapping that girl? She was scared and didn't know what to do. She offered to give me the necklace back and I would have been fine leaving it there. But you assaulted her and then stole the necklace while everyone else watched her run away."

"I didn't steal it. It belongs to us now. It will be the beginning of us making our own fortunes."

Darren appeared to be frozen in place. I kept waiting for him to hit something or yell or . . . I had no idea. But it certainly wasn't just stand there and let this all roll through like a storm off the coast.

"Don't think you're taking anything that belongs to me," Stu said. "I've paid for every single thing year after year and I won't stand for being robbed. Your blackmail is over now, Elsie. I want nothing more to do with you, and if you'd see beyond your own needs for one freaking minute, I think you might notice you're not Darren's type; you never were and you never will be."

"Darren will love me," she yelled.

Darren finally unfroze and shook Elsie off. He bent over and when he came back up, he had a gun in his hand. "So which one of you killed Jericho?"

Chapter 25

I couldn't help myself, I gasped. I did not want to see anyone die today. There had been enough death to last me for as long as possible. But I couldn't wait to hear who was going to admit to the dirty deed.

My bets, after everything I'd pieced together, were on Stu. And I'd texted as much to Ray just a few seconds ago. He needed to hurry if he was going to be able to lock these people down for the rest of their lives.

Stu had shown himself to be cold-blooded as well as logical to get what he wanted. Plus, the information about Jericho I'd gotten from Narina had already made me think it had to be the dad. Believe me, I had wanted it to be Elsie, but she'd done enough bad things to be put away for a while regardless. As long as Ray got here soon.

Darren shifted the gun back and forth between Stu and Elsie. "You didn't sell her the house, she blackmailed you out of it. And, Elsie, if you think that necklace will get you anything more than a single scoop from Garry, then you are very much out of your mind. It's worthless. I sold the real one all those years ago when I escaped you. There is no way on this green earth I would ever get together with you. None. None whatsoever. Even if I was straight, I'd say no."

Her demeanor changed immediately. Her every muscle stiffened and her hands, balled into fists, started to shake.

"Told you, Elsie," Stu said with a chuckle. "All this for nothing. Every step, every steal, every time you thought Darren would be impressed . . . they were all for nothing, and I hope you choke on that."

"I wouldn't wish choking on anyone, dear old Dad, since you haven't been exactly a beacon of hope. How could you let Mom die at your feet? Why didn't you tell anyone Jackson was dead? Why did you use my map to hide him?"

"These are all things we can talk about later, son. Right now we have to get that room below cleaned out, and then we can sail off with no one the wiser. Elsie can keep the house, and you and I will go on adventures like we never got to before. I never even really traveled, even though that's what we told you I did for a living. Instead, I stole and shipped and stole and shipped again. That logo is a symbol of my distaste for everything we did."

"Boo-hoo," Elsie said, and had Darren turning back to aim the gun at her.

"I'm going to ask again. Who killed Jericho?"

"I did," Stu answered. "He asked me to meet him at the theater in the Casino, where he started pressuring me to let him into the business, thinking you were an integral part and he wanted in. When I told him no, he threatened to go to the police and point the finger at you. I didn't mean to do anything more than shove him out of the way to come find you but gravity had other plans, and I can't say I'm sorry about that."

"Well, now, that was going to be a question I wanted answered too. Thanks for filling in the blanks." Ray strolled out of the trees surrounding our little group, as if he had not a care in the world. With the cave directly below us and the steel hatch that granted access to it at our feet, we were just about standing on a goldmine of information, and he seemed to know it. He glanced at the gun and the three people at this little soiree and nodded. "Interesting seeing you all here together. I have people downstairs in the cave, Stu, so you might want to step back in case they open that hatch right under your feet. Wouldn't want you to go to jail with any more injuries, you understand."

The three now seemed frozen, until Elsie made a break for it. She didn't get too far, though, when Deputy Franklin caught her and dragged her back into the clearing. He gave me a thumbs-up in the bushes, and I wondered how he could see me.

"Now, we can do this a couple of ways. You can all come in and give statements—truthful statements, mind you—about what has happened and how we got here. I'd recommend that one, since the other way is a little less comfortable. But for the citizens of Catalina Island, especially those like Whit, I'm willing to turn a little heat on to get you talking."

Elsie was bad-mouthing Ray, and he just smiled through every word.

Darren stood to the side and tried to disappear into the woods, but Deputy Mannon was right there to block his exit.

And Stu? Well, Stu looked like this had been the moment he had been running to all his life. He'd glowed when he'd talked about sailing around and doing all the things he'd never been able to do. But that dream was dead in the water now, and I can't say I felt any sympathy for him.

They all deserved whatever they got from the courts.

Mannon held his hand out for Darren's gun. He handed it over, then was immediately frisked for anything else he had on his body. Mannon grunted at one point and then yelled for Ray. For his part, Darren looked like he might throw up. Why?

There was a small conference with Mannon and Ray, and then Ray turned back toward all of us.

"We're moving this to the station. There's too much to do

here and I'd rather have you all in interview rooms." He stared toward my hiding place. "Whit and company, if you want to be in on any of this, just follow us over to the station. I'm sure you know how to get there."

Someone nudged me from behind, and I turned to find Felix smiling. "Nice job there, Whit. You let Ray be the one to take the credit but you knew long before he did."

"Like I said, I don't need to be the one who does everything, but I'll be damned if I'm not going to help."

After getting out of the bushes, I decided I needed a shower far more than I needed to sit in on an interrogation of any of those three. I'd get whatever I needed from the newspaper unless Ray wanted to share. I was hanging up my figurative deerstalker and heading to the beach as soon as I was sure I was free of brambles and twigs.

Someone banged on the door as I was stepping out of the shower. I assumed it was Maribel, but just in case I asked.

"It's me, silly!" Yep, Maribel. "Hurry up. Felix is coming back and we're going back to the pet cemetery to see what Darren hid before he left."

I was pretty sure I had never dressed faster, and that could be obvious by the fact that my shirt was on inside out and backward. Whatever.

Six of us who went to Crestline Boulevard this time: Goldy, Pops, Nick, Maribel, Felix, and me. Even if we weren't really a team, at least we normally worked well together.

Pops kept digging once we all arrived and eventually found a box about two feet down. Bending over, he grabbed the edges to get it out of the hole, and Felix was there to hold the back of his belt loop to make sure he didn't fall in.

That guy was a keeper. They both were, in their own ways.

Pops presented the box to Goldy and we all gave her room to decide how she wanted to do this. Personally, I wanted the lid ripped off and all the contents scattered wherever. Then again, we probably should have brought it to Ray before opening it, in case it was important to the investigation.

But there was no time for that now. Goldy opened the lid and then pulled out a piece of paper. On the back there were hearts and swirls and decorations galore. Which made me very curious to know what was on the front.

Goldy read a few lines, her eyes rapidly shifting back and forth across the text. And then she cried. Pops held her. He handed the letter over to me and I read about the love Darren had for her. How he never would have been able to be strong enough to live out his life without her. How she meant the world to him and when she got this box she should contact him through the Navy so he didn't feel so alone.

But she never did, and that was breaking her heart.

"Pops, why don't you take her home? I'll let you know anything I hear." I patted Goldy's shoulder. She turned and buried her head in my chest. "It's okay."

"It might be later, but not right now. I'm so sorry for everything I put you through over the last few days. I value you and love you more than you'll ever know. Darren was the first person who ever truly believed I was good. . . ." She sniffed and I kissed her on the cheek.

"You and Pops were the first people to believe that of me, so I know how special it is." I squeezed her in a hug, then let her go. "Now, why don't you go home with Pops? Get some dessert or something, take one of those hour-long baths, or find a good book and escape into it. We'll be at the store tomorrow to discuss all your new ideas for the store."

She hugged me tight again and then went along and kissed Nick, Maribel, and Felix on the cheek. "Let me know what you hear, though, okay?"

"Of course," I hollered as she and Pops disappeared around the corner. "But not until tomorrow," I said quietly.

"That was wild." Maribel jumped up and down next to me, then shook her booty in a little dance. Felix and I looked on and laughed.

"It was wild and now we have so many things to do, like keep your octopus safe, and I believe I'll be helping clear out that cave if I can talk Ray into it."

"Lucky. I'll be fending off Goldy and her great ideas while trying to sell seashells on the seashore."

"Until next time," he said.

But there wasn't going to be a next time.

Ensconced in my wonderfully comfortable couch with Whiskers stretched out along the back, I closed my eyes and thought of what I wanted to do next. How could I open up to Felix more. And I still needed to yell at him for the set-down, but today wasn't the day for that.

Flipping on the TV, I picked out a murder show from the nineties and prepared to go to sleep, just for a little while. But before I drifted off my phone rang.

"Mmmm, hello?"

"Whit, you'll never guess what just happened."

I sat straight up, dislodging Whiskers in the process, who batted at my head.

"Maribel? What happened?"

"Ray just said that you were the mastermind of the whole operation to catch the eighteen people we have to process, and he'd like you to get a medal from the state of California for all your hard work to assist the police. How cool is that?"

"Uh, pretty cool. Pretty much an about-face but still pretty cool." I looked around to make sure I hadn't actually fallen asleep and I was having a dream. Whiskers was kind enough to smack me in the face with her paw, and it hurt, so obviously I was awake for real.

"Wait, did you say eighteen people? Who are the other fifteen?"

"Actually it's another sixteen."

"Which one of the three did they let go?" I couldn't think of any of them that deserved any kind of leniency.

"Darren. Seriously, it was wild. We have people double-teaming in the lobby and the breakroom for all these interviews and half the people who had infiltrated the island were Special Forces. Guess why!"

And something snapped in my head. The knowledge Darren had about certain things but his absolute cluelessness of others. The many charges brought against him that never went anywhere. The fact that he'd gone into the military instead of starting over in Los Angeles or any other city with the money he should have received from the sale of that necklace.

"Darren is with Special Forces, isn't he? He's been undercover for a whole lot of years. He was here trying to figure out who the smugglers were, and when he realized it had something to do with his dad, he didn't know what to do. That would be why he had a gun, and Mannon must have found his badge or something when he patted him down."

"Ding, ding, ding, the lady wins a purse." Maribel laughed and I laughed with her. Talk about convoluted. "But don't tell Ray I told you. Act surprised, okay?"

"Of course, Maribel. I always do."

"Let's keep it that way. Good night, sleuth girl. Sweet dreams."

"Yeah, you too, when you get home in the morning." I hit the end call button and looked out my front window. It was late and the streets were quiet. I loved it here, especially the breeze coming in off the ocean.

I took the postcard out of my pocket and laid it on the coffee table. I needed to stop carrying this. I needed to stop letting the past rule things in my life that it had no business being a part of.

And I knew just how to get started.

"Hey, Felix, I owe you an ice cream. Meet me at the Daily Scoop in twenty and we'll celebrate."

He agreed and I kissed Whiskers's nose as I went into my bedroom to get dressed. I might be sleuth girl on some occasions and good at it, but what I really wanted to succeed at was being my best self and free of drama.

Until next time . . .

Visit our website at
KensingtonBooks.com
to sign up for our newsletters, read
more from your favorite authors, see
books by series, view reading group
guides, and more!

Become a Part of Our
Between the Chapters Book Club
Community and Join the Conversation

Submit your book review for a chance to win exclusive
Between the Chapters swag you can't get anywhere else!
https://www.kensingtonbooks.com/pages/review/